Rick touched her shoulder

Kate lifted her eyes to his, afraid he might see how much she wanted him to stay. He looked as intent as he'd been the first time she'd met him. With a tinge of softness.

She closed her eyes then she leaned over and kissed him.

Not a peck like she was thanking him.

But a full-fledged kiss.

He moved in and allowed his mouth to soften beneath hers. She opened slightly, tasting him. He tasted like spearmint gum and warm male, so she tilted her head and opened her mouth a bit more. He took advantage, deepening the kiss, sliding his hand to her jawline. His hands were big and calloused.

Something dangerous slithered inside Kate, a flash of warning. She pulled away, breaking their connection before she did something she might regret.

Dear Reader,

Sometimes a character pulls at you and begs to be written. Such was the case with Kate. Of course, Kate would never beg…just demanded to have her story written. As I wrote, I discovered she was far more than a snappy comeback or a brazen move. This girl had baggage—it was designer and bursting to be unpacked.

Kate's childhood wasn't easy, and it made her tough, hard and so much more vulnerable than the average girl. She needed someone to guide her, so I gave her Rick, a guy who's already walked a tough path himself. He's perfect for holding her hand, pushing her forward and folding her into his arms as she faces her past. Like many people, Kate has to empty her heart of pain and anger, so she can fill it up with love.

Time to go back to Texas with Kate. Of course, the same old gang is waiting in Oak Stand—Nellie, Bubba and crazy Betty Monk among others. I even threw in a mangy stray named Banjo. Let me know what you think. Write me at P.O. Box 5418, Bossier City, LA 71171 or through my website, www.liztalleybooks.com.

Happy reading!

Liz Talley

A Little Texas
Liz Talley

HARLEQUIN®

TORONTO • NEW YORK • LONDON
AMSTERDAM • PARIS • SYDNEY • HAMBURG
STOCKHOLM • ATHENS • TOKYO • MILAN • MADRID
PRAGUE • WARSAW • BUDAPEST • AUCKLAND

Recycling programs
for this product may
not exist in your area.

ISBN-13: 978-0-373-71680-7

A LITTLE TEXAS

Copyright © 2011 by Amy R. Talley

ABOUT THE AUTHOR

From devouring the Harlequin Superromance books on the shelf of her aunt's used bookstore to swiping her grandmother's medical romances, Liz Talley has always loved a good romance novel. So it was no surprise to anyone when she started writing a book one day while her infant napped. She soon found writing more exciting than scrubbing hardened cereal off the love seat. Underneath her baby-food-stained clothes a dream stirred. Liz followed that dream and, after a foray into historical romance and a Golden Heart final, she started her contemporary romance on the same day she met her editor. Coincidence? She prefers to call it fate.

Currently Liz lives in north Louisiana with her high school sweetheart, two beautiful children and a menagerie of animals. Liz loves strawberries, fishing and retail therapy, and is always game for a spa day. When not writing contemporary romances for Harlequin Superromance, she can be found working in the flower bed, doing laundry or driving carpool.

Books by Liz Talley

HARLEQUIN SUPERROMANCE
1639—VEGAS TWO-STEP
1675—THE WAY TO TEXAS

Where would I be without friends?
This one is for a few good ones:
for Dianna for suggesting I write;
for Rachel, the most generous person I know
(who else would take me to Commander's
on her dad's dime?);
for Connie, who keeps me on track
and should own stock in Starbucks;
and Sandy, who I'm convinced
really can run the world better.
There's a bit of each of you in this book.

CHAPTER ONE

"YOU DID WHAT?" KATE NEWMAN asked, tossing aside the letter from the IRS and shuffling through the papers piled on her desk. Maybe she would find something to negate what she'd read. Something that would magically make the whole tax mess disappear. "Tell me this is some kind of joke. Please."

No sound came from the chair across from her. She stopped and looked up. "Jeremy?"

Her friend and business partner sat defeated, shoulders slumped, head drooping like a withered sunflower. Even his ever jittering leg was still.

She picked up the letter again. Only one question left to ask. "How?"

A tear dripped onto his silk shirt before he lifted his head and met her gaze with the saddest puppy-dog eyes she'd ever seen. Jeremy enjoyed being a drama queen, but this time the theatrics were absent. He shook his head. "It's Victor."

"Victor?" she repeated, dumbly. "What does he have to do with the salon? With paying our taxes?"

The small office at the rear of their salon seemed to rock as the reality of the situation sank in. IRS. Taxes not paid. Future in peril. Kate grabbed the edge of the desk and focused on her business partner.

He swallowed before replying in a near whisper, "He's got cancer. It's in his bones now."

"Cancer?"

"He's dying."

Her legs collapsed and she fell into her swivel chair. "Oh, my God. What kind?"

More tears slid down Jeremy's tanned cheeks. He closed his eyes, but not before she saw the torturous pain present within their honey depths. "He was diagnosed with testicular cancer two years ago. He underwent treatment, and the doctors said he was in the clear. We didn't think it was a big deal. We never even told anyone. But six months ago, the cancer came back. And you know when he lost his job, he lost his insurance."

Kate couldn't think of a thing to say. Her feelings were swirling inside her, tangling into a knot of sorrow and outrage. How could this happen? How could Jeremy's life partner be sick and her business at risk? The world had tipped upside down and now Kate was hanging on by her fingernails.

"I didn't know what to do. He was so sick…*is* so sick, and there was all that money sitting there in the bank. I thought I could pay it back in time. Kate, he's my life." Jeremy's last words emerged as a strangled plea before he broke into gut-wrenching sobs. "Please forgive me, Kate. I needed the money for his chemo. To stop the cancer. It didn't work."

She closed her eyes and leaned her head against the leather chair. She wanted to cry, to express some emotion, or punch Jeremy in the mouth. But all she felt was emptiness. Then fear crowded her heart, choking her with the sour taste of failure. How could she have let this happen? Why had she assumed Jeremy was taking care of their taxes?

"I don't know what to say, Jeremy. I'm seriously contemplating murder."

His shoulders shook harder.

Shit. As angry as she was with him, she knew she'd have done the same thing.

The sunlight pouring in the window seemed way too cheerful for such a day. It pissed her off, so she jerked the blinds shut. "Why didn't you tell me? Let me help you before it came to this?"

His sobs subsided into an occasional sniffle. She knew he hurt badly. His partner meant everything to him. The two men had been together for four years—they'd met at the launch of Fantabulous, Jeremy and Kate's high-energy salon located on the outskirts of Las Vegas. Jeremy and Victor had hit it off immediately, acting like an old married couple almost from the beginning. They were the happiest couple she knew.

"I couldn't. Victor is so private and didn't want anyone to know. He was adamant about it. You're my friend, but he's my partner. I promised, and until now, I kept the promise."

His eyes were plaintive. He could offer no other explanation and Kate couldn't blame him. She'd felt much the same way her whole life. Private. Elusive. Never one to offer up a motive.

"I don't expect you to forgive me, Kate, but there was nowhere else I could go for the money. I even called my parents." Jeremy's long fingers spread in a plea.

"They wouldn't help you," she said, shifting the colorful glass paperweight her friend had given her for Christmas. She wanted to yell at this particular friend, get it through his gel-spiked head, that somehow she would have helped, but it was too late.

"No. Didn't even return my call."

"So what are we going to do? Can't we stop this? Put the IRS off somehow?" Kate knew she sounded desperate. She felt frantic, sick. Vomit perched in the back of her throat. Although Vegas had taken a huge hit economically, they'd been making it, but money wasn't flowing the way it had when they'd first opened.

"I talked to my friend Wendell. He's a bankruptcy lawyer. He said if we could scratch up ten thousand, we might hold them off then see where we stand. He also said we might cut a deal with the IRS and pay a lesser amount on the back taxes."

"Ten thousand?" she echoed. She only had about three thousand in savings and she'd been dipping in to cover extra expenses for the past few months. She didn't own anything she could use for collateral, and they'd put a second mortgage on the salon for an expansion right before the economy tanked. She looked down at the three-hundred-dollar boots she'd bought before the holidays and thought she might be ill on them. She felt stupid. Dumb. She should have been better at saving her money.

Jeremy dropped his head into his hands.

"That feels like a fortune. I don't have it right now. No one does in this economy. The banks won't give us free suckers anymore, much less a loan," Kate said.

"I don't have the cash, either," he said. "I mean, obviously."

She pushed her hands through her hair and looked at the IRS letter. It ridiculed her with its tyrannical words. She wanted to rip it up, pretend it was a silly nightmare. Lose her business? *Ha. Ha. Joke's on you, Kate, baby.*

But no laughter came. Only the heavy silence of defeat.

Like a bolt of lightning, desperation struck. Once again she was a girl lying in the small bed inside her grandmother's tinfoil trailer, praying she'd have enough to make the payment on her class ring. Praying she'd have enough to buy a secondhand prom dress. Praying no one would find out exactly how poor Katie Newman was.

Her unfortunate beginning had made her hungry, determined to never feel so insignificant again.

She had to get out of the salon.

She snatched her Prada handbag from the desk drawer.

"Where you going?" Jeremy's head popped up. He swiveled to watch her stalk out of the small office.

"Anywhere but here," she said, trying to keep the panic from her voice. She felt as if someone had her around the throat, closing off her oxygen. She could hardly take in the temperate air that hit her when she flung open the back door.

"Kate! Wait! We have to tell Wendell something."

"Tell him to go to hell. I'll rot before they take the salon," Kate managed to say through clenched teeth. And she meant it. She didn't care what Jeremy had done. She wasn't going to lose her business. She'd go Scarlett O'Hara on them if she had to. The image of her clutching a fistful of deposit slips in the bank lobby crying out, "As God is my witness, I shall never go hungry again!" popped into her mind. She saw herself sinking onto the bank's cheap Oriental rug, tears streaming down her face.

She yanked open the door of her cute-as-a-button powder-blue VW Bug, plopped her purse on the seat and slid her sunglasses into place. "Screw 'em. I ain't giving in. Even if I have to sew a dress from my stupid-ass curtains, I'll get that money."

She wasn't making sense. She didn't care that she

wasn't making sense. She needed money. She needed it fast.

And there was only one way for her to make money fast in Vegas.

Blackjack.

THREE HOURS LATER, KATE SLID onto a leather stool in the casino lounge. For all the clanging and clinking going on outside the bar, it was eerily quiet in here. Curved lamps threw soft light on the polished dark walnut tables scattered around the room. Kate had chosen the nearly empty bar over a cozy table. She needed to be close to the liquor.

Blackjack had not been her friend. In fact, blackjack had taken her last hundred dollars and bitch slapped her.

"What'll it be?" said the bartender. He wore an old-fashioned white apron that suited the Old World ambience of the place. Soft music piping from the speakers settled over the few patrons.

Kate pursed her lips. "Grey Goose, twist of lime, three cubes of ice."

"Nice. I like a woman who drinks like a man." The voice came from her left. She glanced over at the guy.

"I wasn't aware vodka was a man's drink," she responded with a lift of one eyebrow, a move she'd perfected in junior high school.

"Touché," he said, sliding a predatory smile her way. He looked good. Toothy grin, disheveled brown hair, five o'clock stubble designed to make him doubly irresistible. Any other time and Kate might bite.

But not tonight.

She gave him a flashbulb smile and turned ever so slightly to her right. *Stay away, buddy.*

But he was like any other man—couldn't read a woman's body language.

She felt him scoot closer.

The bartender set the glass in front of her. Without hesitating, she picked it up and downed the vodka in one swallow. It felt good sliding down her throat, burning a path to her stomach.

"And you drink like a man, too," her unwanted companion said.

Kate turned toward him, not bothering to toss him a smile this time. "How do you know I'm not a man? We're in Vegas."

His eyes raked her body. "I can see you're not a man."

Kate narrowed her eyes. "Good vision, huh? Well, don't trust your eyes. Don't trust anybody, for that matter."

She didn't say anything else, just turned from him and studied the way the light illuminated the bottles lining the mirrored bar. It made their contents glow, made them seductive.

Bars of "Sweet Caroline" erupted from her purse and she rifled through it until she found her cell phone. A quick glance at the screen and she knew her friend Billie had finally got around to returning her earlier call. Finally. She could seriously use a sympathetic shoulder. And not of the rumpled, sexy, "can I buy you a drink" variety.

She punched the answer button on her iPhone. "Where the hell have you been?"

"Oh, my God, I'm like *so* having an emergency here." Billie's normally sarcastic tone sounded like neurotic chicken. A whispery neurotic chicken.

"What's going on?"

"He freakin' proposed!"

"Nick?" Kate asked, picking up the fresh drink in front of her.

"No, the Easter Bunny," Billie huffed into the phone. "I'm in the bathroom. Oh, God. I don't know what to say…I think I'm hyperventilating."

Kate pulled the phone from her ear and stared at it. Where was her calm, self-assured friend? The one she needed now that her business was doomed? "Okay, first thing, head between your knees."

"The toilet area's not real clean. I'm gonna stand."

Kate wanted to scream that she'd lost everything today and didn't need to hear about Nick and his damned proposal. But she didn't. Instead she said, "Okay."

"Kate, he has a ring and everything. He actually got down on one knee." Billie's voice now sounded shell-shocked. "I didn't know what to do."

Kate picked up the vodka and tossed it back. It felt as good going down as the first one. "So you said…"

"I said I had to go pee," Billie whispered.

Kate couldn't help it. She laughed.

"Don't you dare laugh, Kate Newman!" Billie snapped. "This is not funny."

Kate sobered. Well, kinda sobered. The vodka was working its magic. "You're right. It's not funny. It's sweet."

"You can't be serious," Billie whispered. "He's talking marriage. *Marriage,* Kate!"

Kate heard something muffled in the background, then Billie's quick intake of breath. Then she heard Billie call, presumably to Nick, that she'd be right out.

"Okay, stop chewing your hair."

"What?"

"Do you love him?" Kate asked.

"Yes. I totally love him," Billie whispered.

"Then say yes."

"Are you joking?" Billie said. "Did you just tell me to say yes? You don't believe in marriage."

It was true, she didn't—well, at least not for herself. Love was fairy-tale bullshit. She shouldn't be giving relationship advice to a dead cockroach, much less a living, breathing friend. "I don't. But you do."

The line remained silent.

"Can you imagine waking up with him every morning even when he's old and wrinkly and…impotent? Can you imagine watching your grandchildren together? Filing joint taxes? Painting a nursery?" Kate couldn't seem to stop the scenarios tumbling from her lips. "How about picking out china patterns or cleaning up your kids' vomit—"

"Okay. I get it. Yes," Billie said.

"Then hang up, open the door and take that ring."

Kate punched the end button and tossed the phone on the bar. If Billie was so stupid as to reject a man who loved her despite her seriously weird attributes, then she deserved to stay locked in Nick's bathroom. With pee on the floor.

When she looked up, the bartender and her previously pushy friend stared at her as if she'd lost her mind. Well, she had. And her business along with it. And now Billie wasn't even available to her. Kate was on her own.

Like always.

Before she'd hit the ATM machine several hours earlier, she'd contemplated borrowing the money she needed from Billie. As a successful glass artist with international acclaim, her friend had steady cash flow even in a bad economy. But Kate never asked for help. And to do so now, with a friend, felt not cool. With a possible wedding on the horizon for Billie, ten thousand would be hard to spare. Besides, if she were going to borrow money, it would be from her absolute best friend who lived in Texas and was loaded to the gills with old oil money. But Kate had never asked Nellie to help her before, not even when Kate had dropped out of college her freshman year to go to beauty school and spent three months eating bologna and ramen noodles.

She couldn't bring herself to do it. Kate had always relied on herself to make it through whatever problem arose, and this was no different.

But what *would* she do? There was no way the salon could generate extra income in the coming months. It was post-Christmas and debt squashed unnecessary services for regular customers. Many spas had closed their doors and many friends had gone from esthetician to cocktail waitress in the past few months.

The bartender finally moseyed toward her. He eyed her a moment before asking, "You want another?"

Kate waved her hand over the empty tumbler. "No thanks. If I have any more, I might go home with Pushy over there."

"In that case, I'd like to buy her another drink," the bed-rumpled hunk deadpanned.

Kate laughed. What else could she do? Her life was falling apart and someone wanted to pick her up. Just not in the way she needed.

She turned to the guy. He stared back, amusement in his brown eyes. She almost rethought her position on taking him up on his not stated, but obviously intended offer. "Listen, you don't want to deal with me tonight. It's been a hell of a day, and I just lost eight hundred dollars at the blackjack table. Unless you've got ten thousand dollars in your pocket, there isn't much else I want out of those pants."

The bartender laughed. "She's got you there, partner."

The hunk joined in on the laughter. "Not only sexy, but a smart-ass mouth. Damn, if I don't want to take you home right now."

"How much are you worth?" Kate asked, raising her eyebrows.

"Not nearly enough." He slid his own empty glass toward the bartender. "But I figure I can at least afford to buy you another drink."

Kate smiled. "Well, I'm gonna pass. It's almost midnight and that's when my car turns into a pumpkin."

She rummaged through her bag, found her matching Prada wallet, flipped it open and tossed her credit card onto the counter. As she snapped her wallet closed a small, yellowed piece of paper caught her eye. She'd carried it with her for years and years.

She pulled it from the pocket in which it had been nestled. Written in her grandmother's shaky handwriting before she'd died was a name. It hadn't mattered that Kate already knew the truth about him. That nearly everybody in her hometown had known the truth about the man. Her grandmother insisted on putting it in writing. Like that mattered.

Justus Mitchell.

The name of her biological father.

The man who refused to claim her.

The man she hated.

She fingered the timeworn edges of the paper. Justus Mitchell had once been the richest man in East Texas. His lands had stretched as far as the eye could see and his oil money went as deep as the earth that sheltered the precious commodity. The man was rich, powerful and politically connected. In his heyday, he'd owned everyone from cocktail waitresses to governors. He still held influence, or had the last time she'd checked. But even the powerful were vulnerable to hidden truths. Look what illegitimate children and mistresses had done to politicians.

Kate had morals. She had character. But she wasn't beyond blackmail in order to save her salon. And a lowdown snake like Justus had mounds of money sitting in the bank.

So…if she needed money, he might as well provide what he'd refused to give her so many years ago.

Child support.

He owed her. She'd feel no guilt because Justus wasn't a victim.

And neither was she.

CHAPTER TWO

RICK MENDEZ SWALLOWED the words he wanted to say as he watched Justus Mitchell roll his way. He shouldn't be here. There was no need. Rick could handle the center without the old man's meddling.

Rick watched as Justus navigated the maze of the recreation room. The sloped shoulders, withered legs and blue-veined hands betrayed the power of the man halting his wheelchair before a table set with dominoes. He could no longer walk, but he still commanded any room he entered.

"So how are things progressing, Enrique?"

Rick set the bill for the sprinkler system on the Ping-Pong table and moved toward the older man. Only Justus called him Enrique. "No problems yet."

"You know, I've launched many ventures over the years, but none of them have been as important as this one. This one is for Ryan." His chin jutted forward emphatically, as if Rick could forget how intricately involved Justus's son had been in the initial idea of Phoenix, the Hispanic gang rehabilitation center. Ryan had given it the name, believing that, like Rick, others could rise from the ashes and become new again.

Rick looked at the old white man staring at him with violet-blue eyes. They were Ryan's eyes…yet different. At that moment, Rick missed Ryan as keenly as he ever had.

"I haven't forgotten, but I'm not doing this because of Ryan. This center isn't a memorial. It's vital. And working with gang members isn't going to be easy. Theirs is a different world." Rick unconsciously rubbed a hand across the tattoos on his chest before catching himself. "There will be resistance in the gang community, resistance that might not be pleasant."

"We can deal with thugs. You of all people should know that."

Rick raised an eyebrow. Justus shifted his gaze away, a small measure of retreat. Old Man Mitchell knew better than to remind him of who he'd been. "You'll have to trust me. I can do this."

"I want to be involved."

Rick tamped down his anger. "You are involved."

Justus snorted. "I'm only the bank."

"*Si,*" he said, just to remind Justus of how different they still were. "That has been your role since the beginning, and it is a most worthy role. You can't relate to the men who will come here. I can. I know the path they've walked. I know the pain and regret."

Justus didn't flinch. "I know regret, too."

Rick nodded. "I know, but that doesn't change the fact that the men who come here will have almost nothing in common with you. Other than wanting to shake free from the life they now lead."

"Fine. I didn't come here to oversee you."

Rick felt a moment's relief, then a prickling arose on his neck. Justus wanted something.

"I have a request. It's quite, ahem, delicate."

Rick crossed his arms. He didn't need this now. Justus had employed Rick when he'd first come to live at Cottonwood and since then he'd done many things for the man before him. Nothing illegal, but some of those tasks made him feel uncomfortable in his skin. Of course that had been before Ryan died. Before Justus's stroke. Before he had changed. Before Rick had tired of being Justus Mitchell's lackey. Yet, Rick owed Justus more than he liked to admit.

And he owed the man's late son.

If it hadn't been for Ryan, Rick would not be the man he was today. Ryan's death had bound him to the Mitchells with invisible ties that would never be severed.

"What?"

Justus's eyes closed for a moment, before opening and piercing him with their intensity. "I have a daughter."

"You have a daughter?"

"Si," he said to be annoying. Satisfaction flashed across his face before he continued, "No one knows about her. Well, rather, they don't talk about her."

"Why?"

The old man rolled a bit closer, banging into the foosball table and causing the little soccer men to spin. The low pendant light cast a gray pall on his pasty skin. "Her mother was a waitress over in Oak Stand. I'd been with her five or six times, but there could have been others. She didn't seem the choosy type. The child could have been mine, or not. I never bothered to find out."

"Then why worry about her now?" Rick eased himself onto the corner of the new pool table. The green felt was stiff beneath his fingers—very different from the one at the deli in the barrio where he'd won money off leathery broken men. He'd been a ten-year-old hustler with the instincts of a shark.

"Because of this." Justus's eyes shifted to the tray on the motorized wheelchair. The debilitating stroke had caused him to lose mobility in his right arm. His left arm was weak, but he could use it.

Rick picked up the folded paper. The heaviness of the paper spoke much about the sender of the letter. This woman meant business.

He unfolded it and read silently while the old man watched him. The note was brief and to the point. The woman wanted money to keep quiet.

"Well?" Rick said, refolding the paper. "You want me to kill her?"

Justus laughed at his jest. It was a running joke between them. Justus didn't need a Hispanic jack-of-all-trades to take out his competition. The old man could crush whomever got in his way. Money was his weapon, always had been, and Rick knew the power of that particular sword.

"No, I want you to bring her to me."

Rick stiffened. He didn't have time to play nursemaid to some upstart claim to the Mitchell fortune. He had a center to open. The rehabilitation center was the promise Justus had made him the year after Ryan died, and starting next week, Rick would be attempting the near impossible—bringing gang members from the streets of Dallas to the countryside of East Texas for a chance to change their live's direction. It was a bold undertaking, but Rick wanted to give others what had been given to him. A second chance.

"I can't. I'm no longer employed by you. My focus is on the center."

"I can't trust anyone else." The old man rolled even closer. So close Rick could smell his Aramis cologne, see the deep grooves around his shocking blue eyes. "Please."

"I have to focus on Phoenix."

"You must do this for me, Enrique. This is all I shall ask. One last favor and I will sign the land over to the foundation. Think about it. The center would be secure."

Rick felt his heart pound. Mitchell did not part with much in life. The center was funded through Ryan's foundation. They'd received some federal money, but much of it came through the foundation. Justus was now offering something more. "All for finding this woman and bringing her to you?"

The old man smiled. White veneers flashed, a gold crown winked. "Finding the girl won't be hard. She used a post office box. Probably thought I hadn't kept tabs on her, but, of course, I always have."

Rick glanced at the folded note in his hand. It had not been signed. Just a post office box number given. The girl lived in Las Vegas. "Of course you would. You always know your enemies."

Something flashed again in Justus's eyes. It was an emotion Rick had seen before in those blue depths, and he knew it well. Regret stared at him in his mirror each and every morning.

"She's not an enemy. There is much of me in this girl. She's determined."

"And underhanded," Rick said. "How can you admire a girl who would threaten to ruin you unless you give her money?"

"It's not so different than what I would have done once. She's got her back against a wall. Otherwise, I wouldn't have heard from her. Besides, there's not much left to ruin, is there? Other than the money, of course." The smile Justus gave reminded Rick of a clown in a fun house. He supposed the atrophy on the man's right side was to blame, but still, he couldn't help the prickles that crept along his skin.

The only sound in the room was the hum of the

restored soda machine in the corner. Rick wasn't sure he wanted to tangle with this woman, but the allure of owning the hilly land surrounding the center won over the doubt embedded in his gut.

He'd started trusting Justus Mitchell long ago and hadn't regretted it yet. The man had been ruthless, conniving and dangerous, but the day Ryan died had changed everything about Justus.

Nothing defeated a man like the death of his son. And nothing gave a man purpose like finishing the job his dead son had started. Justus had lost Ryan but found Jesus, and he'd declared himself transformed. From that day on, he had tried to perpetuate Ryan's legacy of seeing value in helping others.

"Fine. I'll go to Vegas, but it has to be tomorrow. The center opens next week and I've got five guys coming. That's more important than this girl."

Justus frowned but didn't disagree. "Good. I'll arrange for the flight. She's expecting me to send the money with no questions, but she'll have to give me more than some contrived claim. When you show up, we'll see how serious she is about this venture. The girl will dance to my tune if she wants something from me."

"Don't we all?" Rick said.

A laugh blasted past Justus's lips. "You learned long ago, didn't you? I'm a hard man, there's little doubt of that, Enrique, but I have a heart somewhere in here. I think." The old man moved his left hand jerkily toward his shrunken chest.

Rick nodded. "What's her name?"

"Kate Newman."

"She's gonna be trouble," Rick said, slipping off the pool table.

"All women are."

KATE BALANCED ON HER TOES in order to check the box at the post office. Why they'd given her one in the highest row she couldn't guess. At barely five feet, it was obvious she'd have a hard time obtaining the mail. Must have been retaliation from the clerk, whose invitation to the movies she'd turned down. Some guys couldn't handle even the gentlest of brush-offs. Jeez. She'd been nice about it. Or as nice as she could be.

She tottered on her toes, her hand barely brushing the inside of the empty box. Damn. Nothing.

"Can I help you, *chavala?*" The low-accented question came from over her shoulder.

She dropped back onto her three-inch heels. "Nope."

She turned around and met eyes as dark as sin.

The man stood with one arm against the tiled wall. His posture affected ease, but she could tell there was nothing easy about him. Energy radiated from him like a wave of heat off the Vegas desert.

"You sure?"

Kate bristled. "Yeah, I'm sure."

His gaze slid down her body, but she was used to men looking her over. She waited while he took in her high-heeled boots, textured black tights, ruffled blue taffeta skirt, skin-tight lycra turtleneck, hoop earrings and short raven hair. "Get your fill?"

A quick smile crossed his lips. "Not quite."

A strange heat gathered inside her at his words. They were spoken quietly, with a hint of a Spanish accent. "Well, too bad."

She spun and stalked toward the glass doors at the front of the post office. She could feel him following her. Alarm curled around her gut.

She faced him. "Listen, buddy. That wasn't an invitation. Back off."

The man stopped, crossed his arms and grinned. "Oh, man. You're a live one."

Kate swallowed. He acted as though he knew her. "Whatever."

She turned around. He followed her. Alarm shrieked in her head. This dude, though seriously sexy, was off his rocker. What kind of lowlife stalked women in a post office? She tried to ignore him, but it was hard. He seemed right on her heels. In fact, she could smell his spicy warmth. It was dark and delicious. Forbidden.

She pushed through the doors and emerged into the blinding Nevada sunlight. Her car was parked under a withered palm tree, right beside an economy rental car. The man still trailed her. She didn't know what to do. It was broad daylight—surely he wouldn't try to abduct her. There were people crawling over the whole complex. It would be lunacy. Stupid. And the man didn't look stupid.

She slowed and watched as he passed her. He pressed a button on his key ring and the rental honked a greeting. Relief washed over her.

She unlocked her own car and tossed her purse onto the passenger seat.

"Kate."

She froze, one leg in the car, one still on the pavement. The guy knew her name. Her heart pounded and the first thing that popped into her mind was that the IRS had found her.

Which was ridiculous. Wendell had said she and Jeremy would have a month before any action should take place. And the IRS didn't have field agents, did they?

So how did this guy know her?

She looked at him. He rested a forearm on the top of the silver rental and pierced her with his dark eyes. She eased into the depths of the VW, not sure what to do next.

"How do you know my name?"

He smiled. White teeth flashed in the brightness of the afternoon. "There's much I know about you, Miss Newman. But the most important thing I know is that if you want to carry through with your threat against Justus Mitchell, you'll have to get through me first."

Not much shook Kate, but his words made her shiver in the temperate Vegas air. "Wh-what?"

"I read the letter. I know what you want."

"Who are you?" Her legs quaked as adrenaline surged through her. Time to decide—fight or flight?

"Let's just say I'm a good friend of Mr. Mitchell."

Jeez, Louise. Who did her father employ? Henchmen? She looked around. A security officer sat in his little clown car about thirty yards away. She climbed from the car, slamming the door behind her. She knew how to stand up to men like this.

"Well, good friend of Mr. Mitchell, I guess you already know my father is a low-down, no-good bastard who spreads his seed all over Texas and leaves it to sprout with no help. He never acknowledged me or helped my family. I figure he owes me."

She advanced on the man. She could tell he hadn't expected much of a fight from her. What did he think she'd do? Squeak like a mouse, hop in her car and speed away? She'd sent the letter. She wanted the money. The bastard owed her that much. Likely more, but she wouldn't be greedy.

He watched her as she stalked around his car.

She stopped in front of him and planted her fists on

her hips. "So, does that get the attention of his majesty? Or do I have to write Mrs. Vera a little note signed 'Kate Mitchell, your husband's illegitimate daughter'? Or maybe I can take out an ad in the *Houston Chronicle*? Bet that'd get the governor's attention."

The man blinked. Then he smiled. "You *are* his daughter."

She narrowed her eyes and waited.

"Justus wants you to come to Texas."

"No. I don't take orders from him. I'll go to a lab and have blood drawn. I know he's my biological father. I've known it for years. My mother and grandmother were not liars."

The man crossed his arms and released a sigh. Though he was slightly under six feet, he towered over her. His shoulders were sinewy and tight, his body trim and coiled. He reminded her of a soldier. Perhaps he was one. "Mr. Mitchell's instructions were firm. You want the money. You come to him."

There was no way she could go to Texas. She needed to be at the salon raking in all she could, and if she canceled her appointments, she'd likely lose her clients. That was something she couldn't do. She needed steady customers—her future depended on it. It was one of the reasons she hadn't gone to Texas in the first place. That and the killer airfare.

"I can't. I have responsibilities."

"The salon?"

A thread of unease snaked up her spine. Did her father know about her financial troubles? Surely not. "Yes, if you must know. I can't pack up a suitcase and head to Texas to satisfy some old man's whim. I—"

"But you expect him to satisfy yours? Meet your demands with no proof? It's more than reasonable to expect to meet you face-to-face. That was his offer. Take it or leave him be."

Kate chewed on his words. "If he wanted to meet me face-to-face, why send you? Why not come himself?"

The man swallowed what she assumed to be aggravation. "You evidently didn't do your research well. Mr. Mitchell is ill and confined to a wheelchair."

Now, that was something she'd never expected. The powerful Justus Mitchell confined to a chair, crippled and sick? Something stabbed her insides. She was certain it was guilt. After all, she stood there ready to blackmail an ailing man and his reputed angel of a wife with dirty laundry from years past.

But Justus Mitchell wasn't a victim.

Kate didn't consider herself a victim, either. But she'd also grown up without the necessities of life while her father and his wife ate Chateaubriand and drank Perrier. She'd lived in castoffs from the Oak Stand Pentecostal Church while their precious Ryan had galloped upon a pristine lawn in a smocked John-John suit. She'd crawled into a used single-wide trailer each night praying it wouldn't storm while the Mitchells tucked into plush beds in one of the seven bedrooms at the family estate, Cottonwood. And worse still was that everyone knew she was his daughter…and felt sorry for her.

Kate deserved the money.

But she'd rather face a firing squad than go to Texas.

"Here's a plane ticket for tomorrow morning. Either you get on the plane or Mr. Mitchell will fix it so you never see a dime from him. Your choice." He shoved an envelope into her hand.

"You're threatening me?" Kate felt her toes sweat in her boots. They always did when she felt scared. Damn it.

"Turnabout is fair play, Kate."

With those words, the man opened his car door and climbed inside. Kate barely had time to step back before he pulled out of the narrow parking space. She couldn't tell if he watched her in his rearview mirror, standing bereft in the parking lot holding the envelope. He'd put on dark sunglasses that made him look even more menacing.

"I didn't even get your name," Kate muttered to the taillights of the car. "Rude ass."

There was nothing left to do but climb into the comfort of the VW. She blinked back desperate tears. Justus played hardball.

But what had she expected? The man hadn't risen to the top of Texas by letting people run roughshod over him. Of course he'd be as tough as the West Texas landscape that held his oil wells.

So now she had no choice. She'd have to go to him if she wanted to get the money for Fantabulous. She only hoped she could pull it off. Everything depended on her playing the game well.

CHAPTER THREE

RICK DROVE OUT OF THE PARKING lot as his cell phone jittered beside him. He glanced at Kate in the rearview mirror. She stared after him looking not the least bit happy, her lips forming words he couldn't hear. He could only imagine the curses being shot his way.

Who could blame her? The tables had been turned on her little blackmail game. And strangely enough, it hadn't amused him to get beneath her skin. He knew how it felt to be jacked around. But she'd brought it on herself.

The phone vibrated again. And again. He glanced down at the persistent humming. Justus's number flashed on the BlackBerry's screen.

He didn't want to talk to the old man right now. He needed to process Kate Newman.

She was a smart-mouthed, sexy piece of work. He liked her style—the edgy look she wore like an attitude. She'd responded to him. He hadn't missed that. And she didn't seem afraid of him like other women were. There was little doubt she was Justus's biological daughter—not because her manner was as brash as his, but because she had his eyes.

Ryan's eyes.

Justus had stamped his mark on his two children.

Kate's eyes were like an exotic sea glittering at sunset. They dominated her delicate face, even overshadowed her tempting lips. He imagined men tripped over each other for a shot at her. She had a daring vibe, an appeal that would make people draw near to see what she'd do or say next.

Something stirred inside him. He wanted to tell Kate to stay in Vegas and not worry about Justus. There was a pall hanging over Cottonwood. It would suck her in and suffocate her.

Mind your own business, he told himself.

But logic couldn't stop the feelings rising inside him. The one that said "protect her" and the other he didn't even want to acknowledge. The one that whispered "bed her." Those responses were asinine. Kate didn't need protecting—he hadn't seen so much as a hint of fear or regret in those Mitchell-blue eyes. And as to the other, well, he wasn't that man anymore.

The phone sounded again.

He stopped arguing with himself and pulled into an empty lot, pressing the answer button. "Rick."

"Where the hell have you been?"

"Yes, I'm having a nice day. And you, Justus?"

"Skip the bullshit. You're in Vegas. You've seen her."

Rick grimaced. "Yes, I've seen her."

"And?"

"And I think she'll come to Texas, but I can't be certain. She's not what I expected." Even as the words left his mouth, he knew he shouldn't have said anything about Kate. He should let the man draw his own conclusions about his biological daughter. *Don't involve yourself. Keep your distance. The less said, the better.*

"What do you mean?"

"She's…salty. She won't be pushed around easily."

"So she *is* my daughter."

Rick's gaze roamed the lot surrounding his car. It was empty. Yellowed weeds poked through zigzag cracks. Boards covered the windows of a vacuum cleaner repair shop and a series of blue graffiti marked the boards. Staking territory. The number thirteen was displayed prominently, as was the letter M. He'd parked on Sureño turf, the street gang that had once been his sworn enemy. "You keep saying she's your daughter, so why go through all this? Just give her some money. You owe her at least that."

But Rick knew why Justus wanted Kate to come to Texas. He'd lost Ryan three years ago, then he'd had the stroke that nearly killed him. His wife, Vera, clung to the past, drowning herself in grief. Things were bad at Cottonwood. Justus needed deliverance. He thought he could get that in Kate.

"I need to see her. For proof."

Just look at her eyes. The words sprang to his lips but he didn't give voice to them. "I'll be back tomorrow, with or without her."

The old man sighed. For a brief moment the silence sat heavy on the line. "Okay. Tomorrow."

The line went dead. No platitudes about having a safe trip back. No polite farewell. Justus had never used niceties on Rick.

He shifted the car into gear and eased toward the road. From the corner of his eye he caught sight of two young guys crossing the back of the empty lot. Young Hispanic men. Flat-billed caps, thigh-length jerseys, baggy jeans, blue bandanas in pocket. Tattoos covered their forearms. Gang members.

The guys laughed, punching each other on the arm, but their laughter died when they saw him. He could feel them stiffen, grow aware.

He drove from the lot, leaving only sympathy behind. Sadness for a childhood lost. He wasn't sure if it was for the two bangers or for himself.

His mind cut to the center. The true test was about to begin. Next week, he'd find out if he'd bitten off more than he could chew. Reality was he didn't know squat about rehabilitating gang members. He only knew how to be one.

Maybe knowing the life would be enough.

THE NEXT MORNING KATE PUSHED her sunglasses to the top of her head as she entered McCarran International Airport. She glanced through the sliding doors to where Jeremy sat in her car. She gave him a wave and he saluted before pulling away from passenger drop-off.

She wanted to run after him, tell him *he* screwed up, *he* should have to fix everything. But she didn't. Because Jeremy didn't care about Fantabulous as much as she did. And because his partner had taken a turn for the worst and was under hospice care. And because that morning, the IRS letter had mocked her from its position on her fridge. She swore it even gave a snicker when she opened the door to grab a bottle of water and a yogurt. Two weeks ago, life had been much easier.

Now she had a mere three weeks to get ten thousand dollars to Wendell.

Or lose her salon.

That made her throat tighten. She tried her best to ignore the gut-clenching thoughts tumbling in her head as she stepped into a security line that seemed to be moving as slowly as the Vegas economy. One step every two minutes. At this rate, she'd likely miss her flight.

She scoured the crowd for the man who'd confronted her in the post office parking lot the day before. She didn't know if she would see him again. It didn't take a genius to figure out that he'd tracked her down through the post office box. If she really didn't want her father finding her, then she should have devised a more anonymous method of contact.

She should have known this whole blackmail thing was a stupid idea. Blackmailing a man who took pleasure in crushing anyone who got in his way—who did that? She knew the answer. Only someone who was desperate. And now look where it had landed her. She'd set something into motion. Could she handle what was about to happen?

A woman tapped her on the shoulder, pulling her from her thoughts, and pointed toward the moving line.

Finally, Kate made it through the checkpoint, reassembled everything in her purse and carry-on, and headed for the gate. The ticket was in her hand. It was one-way, and that made her nervous.

"Kate."

Her name sounded like a caress on his lips. She turned to face the man who'd shadowed her dreams the night before. He looked calm, as though he'd actually slept. The bags under her eyes sagged lower. "I'd say hello, but you never introduced yourself."

His lips twitched. "Enrique Mendez, but everyone calls me Rick."

He offered his hand. She ignored it. "Do you work for Justus, or just stalk random women at post offices for fun?"

Amusement flashed in his dark eyes before his face went blank. "Not necessarily."

The man was totally vague, but at least she knew his name. "Are you local or are you from Texas?"

His eyes scanned the crowded airport. He took her elbow and started walking toward the gate. "I'm from Texas. I'm flying back with you."

Kate tugged her arm from his grasp. "I can walk by myself."

He didn't react. Simply kept moving toward Gate D-13. She followed, but put space in between them. She studied him from behind as he moved purposefully toward the Delta Air Lines desk. He wore his dark hair clipped close, military-style and had on a black Nike athletic jacket, jeans and hiking boots. The boots didn't fit the look, but she imagined he didn't care. They were probably comfortable. Rick was one of those guys.

He stood in line behind two other people. She didn't bother. She already had a seat on the plane. Instead, she plopped into one of the bucket seats next to a dapper Asian guy reading on a Kindle, parked her stuffed-to-the-max suitcase next to her and watched Rick.

The man who'd made her so uneasy at the post office smiled at the attendant. The dour-looking older lady was forty pounds overweight with a horrible dye job, but she melted like a Popsicle in July at Rick's coaxing.

She wondered what he was trying to get from her. She also wondered why she hadn't been treated to such a smile.

The woman nodded, fluttered her lashes a little and took his boarding pass. She studied the screen before her, tapped a few buttons on the keyboard, and looked up with a triumphant smile. She pulled something from a machine beside the computer and handed it to Rick.

The ass had obviously been upgraded.

The woman grabbed the intercom and asked all passengers seated in business class to please begin boarding.

Rick didn't even glance Kate's way as he stepped into the line.

Great.

By the time Kate had stowed her carry-on, popped a Xanax and sank into her seat, she decided she didn't like Rick Mendez one bit. He was chatting with an attractive flight attendant, his legs stretched out in front of him, while Kate had the sharp elbows of the guy to her left to look forward to. Not good.

She blew away the pieces of hair hanging in her eyes and settled into the not-so-comfortable seat. She had forgotten her iPod, so she'd spent her last bit of cash on a book at Walgreens. She hoped the legal thriller could take her mind off the jitteriness she felt at sitting inside the metal bird of death. If that didn't do the trick, the medication would likely kick in to soften takeoff.

She didn't like to fly. She did it when she had to, but only when it was absolutely necessary. Given a chance, she'd have elected to put the top down on her VW convertible, flood the car with her new Pink album and set out for Texas. Nothing better than the wind in her hair, but it was the end of January and she didn't think icicles forming on her nose would be a good look.

She took another peek at business class, but the flight attendant jerked the partition closed, throwing a knowing look at the people sitting in coach. Kate sighed. *Yeah, yeah, sister. We all want to be in there.*

"'Scuse me," Sharp Elbows said as he nearly pierced one of her lungs.

"No problem," she muttered, shifting aside and praying no one would take the seat to her right.

Her prayers went unanswered when a granny toddled toward her, counting off the seat numbers. Sure enough, she was 23E. The woman wore a floating caftan, had poofy hair and carried a purse so big it threatened to topple her forward onto Pokey Elbows's lap as she passed him. She grinned at Kate, showing her silver-framed partial and yellowed teeth smudged with fuchsia lipstick. No doubt she had jeweled sunshades and a brag book of grandchildren lurking in her purse.

"Honey, I'm over there next to you."

Kate lifted herself so the woman could slide into her seat. The ginormous purse smacked her on the thigh.

"Sorry, honey. I'll get settled…right…here." The elderly lady huffed and puffed as she adjusted her seat and tucked tissues in the pouch in front of her.

Kate really hated Rick Mendez. He was getting free liquor. While she was tucked in tight between Lemony Snicket and Mrs. Roper. Kate yawned. The Xanax was kicking in, leaving her feeling sleepy and foggy. She only used the medication for flights. Okay, and when she couldn't stop the merciless anxiety that sometimes swamped her and kept her pacing the floors at all hours of the night. Jeremy had forced her into getting some when she'd let it slip that she suffered from periodic anxiety.

Jeremy.

He wasn't so bad, even if he *had* risked her future without asking. She still loved her flamboyantly gay friend. Besides, she was as unsinkable as Molly Brown. She wasn't going to throw their friendship away over his moment of insanity. After her ill-fated blackjack game, she'd phoned him, listened as he threw himself a pity party, then told him her plan.

Part of the blame fell on her. She'd gotten lax in double-checking the books. Lord knew her accountant had harped on it enough. But she'd never thought Jeremy would endanger their business or friendship. Never.

Which went to prove what she'd known all along. She had to rely on herself. No one else.

"Ma'am?"

A smartly dressed flight attendant with a fake smile and a platinum bob jarred Kate from her musings.

"Huh? I mean, what?"

"You can follow me. I've cleared you for business class."

Kate couldn't stop the smile that sprang to her lips, the first one she'd hatched in weeks. Hell, yeah. "Absolutely."

She turned the smile on her former seatmates. "Well, I'm outta here."

"I don't blame you, honey. I wish I'd had the time to show you pictures of my Pomeranians. You know I show them all over the country. Little Boy Blue just won the Hanover."

Kate nodded at the prattling granny. "Sorry I didn't get to see them. Have a good flight."

Then Kate followed the lithe attendant toward the Holy Grail of the plane. If the plane went down, at least she would die in first class.

It was small consolation.

But it was consolation.

"YOU LOOK GROGGY." RICK didn't mean for his words to sound accusatory. Hell, he didn't really know Kate. And shouldn't care. But he knew she was on something. Her eyes showed it.

"I'm fine. Just took a little pill to help me fly," she said sinking into the seat next to him. "Wait. That didn't sound right. What I meant is I get kinda nervous when I fly, so I took a Xanax."

He eyed her. *Xanax?* "Should you be taking that?"

She raised her perfectly sculpted eyebrows. "I only take it when I feel anxious."

"You want a drink?"

"It's nine o'clock in the morning." Her voice sounded sleepy, reminding him of rumpled bedsheets and lazy morning sex. Not good. This was Justus's daughter. No sense in fantasizing about her.

"I meant a Coke or something."

Kate laughed. It was a smoky laugh. He felt himself grow semierect. Shit. What was wrong with him?

"Now I know you're from Texas. You called a soda a *Coke*."

He blinked at her. She was an odd one. Or maybe the medication was making her loopy. And talkative. He could have sworn she hated his guts.

She fell silent and fumbled for her lap belt. Rooting around, her hand bumped his thigh, which only served to heighten the flash of desire he felt for her. He reached down and grabbed the belt before she could slip her hand beneath his ass and pull it out.

"Sorry," he commented, reaching over and snapping the belt into the end she held against her stomach. He got a whiff of her perfume as he pulled away. Something expensive. And sexy. It made him want to dip his head closer and smell her hair or the silkiness of her collarbone where the perfume had no doubt been applied.

"Thanks," she muttered before opening a book.

He spent several minutes studying her out of the corner of his eye as she read. She'd shown up in tight jeans and an even tighter yellow shirt that wrapped her torso and cupped her small breasts. Yesterday, her hair had been spiky, tinted blue. Today, it was a mass of raven curls, making her look younger and softer. Dangly earrings brushed her shoulders. Her legs, encased in brown high-heeled boots, were crossed at her ankles.

Finally the engines roared to life, causing the huge 737 to thrum with power. He glanced at Kate's book. The cover showcased shadowy figures behind a blood splattered dagger. Horror? Thriller? He couldn't decide, but he'd never seen anyone so engrossed in a book. She hadn't moved.

Then he looked at her face.

Her eyes were closed. Not reading. Her nostrils flared lightly as she took calm measured breaths. Her knuckles weren't white from the suspense in the book.

He pried her fingers from the book, closing it and tossing it toward her crinkled-looking bag. Her eyes flew open.

"What are you—"

"Shh," he said, wrapping one of her cold hands in his. Her small hand felt delicate. It also seemed clammy. He threaded his fingers through hers and gave her hand a squeeze.

She opened her mouth to speak but closed it when he gave her a nod.

"Thanks," she whispered as the plane began its taxi down the long expanse of runway.

Rick thought about winding an arm about her, but that would be stepping over a boundary he shouldn't cross. He shouldn't care about this woman who'd stooped to blackmail her own father. He shouldn't enjoy the feel of her hand in his so much.

But he did.

Even as his rational mind threw up a roadblock, he squeezed her hand again as the wheels left the ground. She glanced at him.

Her blue eyes were twin pools of vulnerability.

"No problem," he said.

She pressed her lips together and nodded.

The plane hit a pocket of air and tilted ever so slightly. Kate took deep breaths as they climbed higher and higher. He rubbed small circles on her wrist with his thumb, offering what little comfort he could, but enjoying the hell out of her tender skin.

They hit one final air pocket before leveling out. Kate let loose her breath. "Okay. Okay. We made it."

"Yep, we made it." He released her hand.

Kate looked at him. "No problem."

But he couldn't respond because he knew there was a problem. And her name was Kate. And she was Justus's daughter. And she had Ryan's eyes. And she stirred some tucked away feeling of protection.

It didn't help that she wore tight-ass jeans and low-cut sexy shirts. That she pranced around in teetering heels, smelling of spicy earthiness. That she knew how to handle a man.

He had to resist her, so he didn't say a word. Because he knew.

Big problem.

CHAPTER FOUR

ARRIVING IN OAK STAND, Texas, felt like being tossed into a game of pickup at a state prison. At the end of the day, someone would likely get shanked. The bucolic Texas countryside framed ten square miles of hypocrites and busybodies all wrapped up in a Norman Rockwell-style package with a gingham bow. Kate felt the prying eyes and raised eyebrows as she climbed from Jack Darby's massive pickup.

Yep. The bitch was back.

She stretched, glad the two-hour ride from the Dallas airport was over. She'd been cooped up far too long and needed to move her legs.

"You sure you want to walk to Tucker House? I don't mind dropping you by after I make this deposit," her friend's husband said, doffing his baseball cap and tucking it into his back pocket. Jack looked around as if he too felt the curiosity of the townsfolk. They'd parked in front of the Oak Stand Bank and Trust, the hometown bank with a friendly smile. Service you can bank on.

"I need the walk," Kate said, refusing to remove her sunglasses. She didn't need the protection from the graying sky—she needed it from the prying eyes.

Jack's brow crinkled as he eyed her high-heeled boots. "You sure?"

"I started walking in these when I was five."

"You had big feet, huh?" Jack chuckled.

"Yeah, that's it. And all the kids called me Bozo," Kate drawled, grabbing her purple Balenciaga handbag and slamming the truck door. "I know the way."

Nellie's husband threw her a salute much as Jeremy had earlier that day. Kate never minded a man saluting her. Even a smart-ass like Jack. The man lived to get under her skin, even though she knew he held a grudging affection for her. "See you back at the house, Katie."

"Kate," she said as she yanked the belt of her Burberry raincoat tighter and looked around.

Oak Stand looked about the same as it had the last time she'd visited except The Curlique Salon had gotten a new sign out front and the town square's grass was faded yellow. That was pretty much it for change.

Tucker House wasn't far. She could see the huge white structure across the square, right behind the statue of Rufus Tucker, founder of Oak Stand and great-great-grandfather to Nellie. She could cross through the park on the flagstone-paved path easily enough, but she decided to take the long way around to decompress a bit. Prepare herself. Everything had happened so quickly, she felt cut loose. Floating above herself.

It didn't help that the plane ride seemed a misty memory. The Xanax she'd taken had calmed her too much. She could barely remember the journey. But she remembered Rick, the way he smelled, the way he felt next to her.

She looked down at her bare hand. She'd forgotten her gloves at home, but she hadn't forgotten his touch. The way his thumb had stroked the skin on her wrist as the plane had climbed into the sky. Then once again as the plane prepared to land. Kate had had guys do lots of things to her hands—hold them, squeeze them, kiss them, suck her fingers—but she'd never had a man comfort them.

She tucked her hand into her coat pocket. She didn't have time to think about Rick Mendez and the weird tingling his touch had awakened in her. She'd bought herself some time, but she needed a plan.

When Jack had pulled up to baggage claim at the airport and tossed Kate's carry-on into the cab of his truck, she thought Rick might protest, but he held back, nodding to Jack as he passed him. Rick had told her Justus was expecting her, but she wanted to meet her biological father on her own terms. If this were some sort of a game Justus was playing, she needed home field advantage. Nellie, not Oak Stand, had always been that for her.

She approached the steps of Tucker House feeling as if she'd stepped back through time. As always, the porch was freshly painted and Margo met her at the door.

"Well, I do declare, Miss Katiebug Newman, as I live and die."

"Hey, Margo. And it's Kate, by the way."

The diminutive woman grinned. "I know. Just like to ruffle your feathers is all."

Kate rolled her eyes. Margo had worked for Nellie's grandmother when Nellie was a child, cleaning house and ironing all those Peter Pan collars Nellie had had to wear. Margo had taken a break to help raise her own grandchild, but returned to Tucker House when Nellie had started the senior care center a few years ago. It was good to see Margo holding the door open again.

"Come on in. Nellie's out back with Mae trying to dig up some bulb she wants to plant at her place."

Kate stepped into the heat of Tucker House. The walk had made her plenty warm, and several older ladies and gentlemen peered unabashedly at her as she shrugged out of her coat and hung it on a peg by the beveled glass door.

"You're Myrtle Newman's granddaughter," a spry silver-headed lady said, rising from the couch. The woman wore lavender yoga pants and a sweatshirt that said Hot Yoga Mama.

Kate felt herself stiffen even as she smiled. "Yes."

"Myrtle made a good pie," the lady said, her eyes twinkling in a friendly manner. "I tried to make her chocolate pie one year. Just wasn't the same. I'm Ester."

"Oh, yes, Ester. You taught Sunday school." Kate tried to smile, but it felt stuck. Something about Oak Stand made her feel claustrophobic. As though she was knotted up and couldn't move or breathe.

"Yep. Taught it for twenty-eight years before I got too tired to deal with kids kicking my shins. But you never kicked me, Katie."

"Kate."

"Kate. Of course," Ester beamed at her.

Kate needed to get out of here. Other ladies were creeping closer. "Well, I need to find Nellie."

Kate bolted before anyone could ask her anything else about her late grandmother, her past, her future or her dietary habits. She could never live in Oak Stand. Too many nosy people. Margo laughed at her as she scurried through the kitchen and out the back door.

Kate let the screen door bang against the house as she exited. Nellie dropped the shovel and turned. "Kate!"

"Finally, someone gets my name right," Kate grumbled as she trotted down the stairs toward the only person who felt like family.

Nellie looked terrific. Her blond-streaked hair was

in a lopsided ponytail and dirt smudged one cheek. She wore tight jeans tucked into polka-dotted rubber boots and a hooded sweatshirt that hung midthigh. A chubby baby in a pink knitted parka and matching cap clung to her knees. The smile Nellie gave her made the cloudy day seem brighter.

Kate gave her friend a hard hug before dropping to one knee. "Hi, Mae flower, it's Auntie Kate."

Mae blinked green eyes at Kate, then hid her face between Nellie's knees.

Nellie patted her daughter's head. "She's going through a stage. She won't look at people. No one. Not even Margo."

Kate rose. "That's okay. I'm not good with kids anyway."

Nellie sighed and shook her head. "Kate, how would you know? You're probably brilliant with kids. She loves the boots you sent her. Don't you, Mae?"

They both looked down at the baby, who still clutched Nellie like a street peddler would clutch a shiny penny.

"Here's the bucket you wanted," a voice came from behind Kate. A voice with a soft Hispanic accent.

Kate spun around. "What the hell are you doing here? I told you I'd meet with Justus when I'm ready and not before."

Rick shrugged, a slow smile spreading across his face. "I didn't know you were here. I stopped by to talk to Nellie."

Kate faced her friend. "You know this creep?"

"Kate!" Nellie said, scooping up Mae and taking the pail from Rick. "Rick's not a creep. He's a friend. And why are you meeting Justus Mitchell? What is all this about? You never come to Oak Stand."

Kate opened her mouth then closed it. She turned to Rick. "What are you doing here?"

"He came about Phoenix." Nellie said, dropping an absentminded kiss on her daughter's forehead. Mae peeked out at Rick and gave him a drooling smile. Kate guessed Mae looked at good-looking, sneaky guys. Traitor.

She pulled her eyes from the baby. No matter what Rick said, he'd come to Tucker House because she was here. She'd irritated him when she'd turned the tables on him at the airport. He'd seemed to handle her leaving with Jack calmly, but she'd be willing to bet he didn't like it one bit.

"Phoenix is a gang rehabilitation center," he explained. "A place to help gang members make a break from the life and get an education and job training. The rehab center is right outside Oak Stand. Nellie's on the foundation board and I'm the director." Rick's eyes met hers. They were powerful, those dark eyes. Full of mystery and determination. They were obsidian chips of intent. Strong intent. And they made her toes sweat.

"Oh," Kate said.

Nellie looked confused. Kate felt something sink in her stomach. She hadn't told Nellie about trying to blackmail Justus. She hadn't told her friend much of anything except she was coming to town and needed a place to stay. Perhaps Rick had already told Nellie what Kate had done. Or what Justus wanted from her. But she didn't think so. He didn't seem the type to spread anyone's business around town.

"How do you know Rick?" Nellie asked her. "And what's this have to do with Justus?"

Rick smiled at Mae and chucked her on the chin. Kate averted her eyes and watched some small gray birds hop between barren branches before dive-bombing a bird feeder. She didn't say anything. Finally, she met Nellie's gaze and gave her the signal they'd developed when they'd been girls. Two blinks meant "later."

"Okay," Nellie said, shifting Mae to her other hip and dropping some strange-looking potato things in the bucket Rick had brought her. "Let me wash my hands and get those papers."

Nellie shoved Mae into Kate's arms and stalked up the stairs. The baby immediately began kicking and crying, and one of her little boots caught Kate in the upper thigh. This was her punishment for lying to Nellie.

Rick glanced at the squirming child. "Want me to take her?"

She set Mae down. "No, she can walk."

Mae immediately dropped to the ground and wailed. Kate could have sworn it was on purpose, but surely fifteen-month-old babies couldn't be so devious.

He bent down. "Mae, come see what I have in my pocket."

"Bet you say that to all the girls," Kate drawled.

He shot her a look before focusing on Mae. The baby sat up and studied him. Her cries stopped as abruptly as they'd started.

"Here," Rick said, pulling a package from his pocket. Kate blinked. It was a package of crackers from the airplane.

"Crackers? I hope that's not what you actually give all the girls."

Mae reached out a grubby little hand and grunted.

"Babies love crackers," Rick said, opening the package and handing one to Mae. Sure enough, the baby took it and crammed it in her mouth. "And if I have something in my pocket for you, it won't be crackers."

She frowned at the double entendre, but she *had* started it.

Kate stooped so she could see the baby's mouth. She didn't know how to do the Heimlich maneuver on an infant. "Does she even have teeth?"

"Yeah, she has teeth. Not all of them but enough to gum a cracker." He lifted the baby and gave her the sweetest of smiles.

Something plinked in Kate's chest. She wasn't sure what it was because she'd never felt anything like it before.

Nellie returned holding an envelope. She shoved it toward Rick and gathered Mae in her arms. "Everything is signed and notarized. I'll come by Phoenix sometime soon. I can't wait to see the guys there. You've worked so hard, Rick. It's going to be fantastic."

"Let's hope so." Rick tucked the missive under his arm before turning to Kate. "I'll pick you up at Nellie's at 9:00 tomorrow morning. Justus will expect you before lunch. Bye, ladies."

He headed around the corner of the house.

Nellie shook her head. "What the hell is going on, Kate?"

Rick turned before she could bustle Nellie up the stairs. His eyes flashed something almost naughty, but he didn't say a word. Just nodded and then he was gone.

Kate closed her eyes and blurted, "Oh, nothing. I just have to go meet dear old dad about a blackmailing scheme."

Her friend didn't say a thing, so Kate cracked one eye open. Poor Nellie looked like she'd swallowed a bug.

Her mouth opened then closed. Finally, she managed to choke out, "What?"

"What can I say except what you already know? I'm a bastard child." Kate shrugged, trying to pretend she blackmailed reluctant biological fathers every day.

"You're admitting Justus Mitchell is your father?" Nellie asked, shaking her head.

"Shh!" Kate clamped a hand over her friend's mouth. Mae contemplated her with blank green eyes. Gooey cracker mush dripped from her mouth and landed on Kate's arm. "Don't."

Nellie pulled Kate's hand from her mouth. "Holy shit!"

Kate looked at Mae. "She didn't mean that, Mae flower. She meant holy shuckins."

Nellie swiped at the baby's chin while Kate scraped off the mess. She was glad she hadn't worn her Burberry outside.

"Would you be serious about this?" Nellie huffed.

"I am."

Mae squirmed in her mother's arms. Nellie set her down and studied Kate. "Kate, how is this… I mean, why haven't you ever said anything? And blackmail? I don't understand."

"Look, I'll tell you about it when we get to the ranch. Now's not the time."

"Kate—"

"Please. Let it ride, Nell." She stalked up the steps without looking at her friend again. She'd tell Nellie that night. After dinner. After Mae had toddled off to bed. After Jack had dozed off in the recliner. But not now. Not when her nerves felt shredded and her stomach felt like it harbored rocks. Really heavy rocks.

She'd screwed up when she'd devised this plan.

She should have let the salon go. It was just a business. People lost businesses every day. She could start over, get a job in L.A. She'd done it before.

But it was too late. What she'd put in motion had to be ridden out. She'd poked the devil with a stick, and messing with the devil was dangerous, especially when he had huge stockpiles of supplies and a sexy henchman who made her pulse flutter. And that was the scariest thing about facing the battle that would come in the morning. Something about the devil's henchman made her want to sleep with the enemy. And that couldn't be good.

War really was hell.

RICK PULLED HIS CAR INTO the drive of Cottonwood Ranch, Justus's colossal spread. The drive leading up to the enormous white house was long and straight. No meandering for a man like Justus. Direct and to the point.

Rick knew Justus would be irate with him for not bringing Kate directly to the ranch, but he'd rather deal with Justus's anger than deal with being thrown into prison for binding and gagging Kate Newman then shoving her into the backseat of his car.

The thought of controlling Kate appealed to him. He envisioned her under his power, and desire stirred inside him. That was seriously whacked, so he checked that feeling as he parked on the checkerboard grass-and-stone parking area.

Justus's wife, Vera, dabbled in gardening and landscaping, so she'd designed this parking area declaring it more welcoming than concrete. Every time his foot crushed the low-growing thyme in between the pavers, a sweet aroma filled the air. Leave it to Vera to deliver an unexpected gift to the person parking outside her home.

"Rick," Vera called out from the prayer garden she'd built behind the carriage-style garage. "Come see what I've found."

Rick could no more ignore the hint of pleasure in Vera's voice than he could turn out a hungry stray. Grains of happiness were few and far between for the woman Justus had brought to Cottonwood and made his bride over twenty years ago.

He rounded the corner and found her kneeling in a patch of withered canna lily stalks. He looked around at the garden they'd neglected during the holidays. "I guess I need to clear all this dead stuff away and put down another layer of mulch."

Vera looked up at him, her hair falling over her shoulders, brown eyes crinkled with a haunting smile. "I know, but look what I found."

He bent and pushed a hand through the matted pine straw. Small green stalks barely cleared the fertile loam. "Crocus?"

"Yes," she breathed, passing a bare hand over the tiny new growth rising in the grayness. "Ryan planted them when he was a child. Some years they don't come up. I don't know why, but this year they're making an appearance."

"A sign of good fortune, I bet. Better cover them well," he said, straightening and eyeing the low, dark clouds. "Those clouds carry rain and with temperatures dipping tonight, we might have a freeze."

She carefully covered the plants then stood. She

brushed her hands on her worn jeans and pulled her hair to the side. She looked much younger than her fifty years.

"Did you bring her back?"

Rick stiffened, dread uncoiling in his stomach. How did Vera know about Kate?

"He can't keep secrets from me, Rick," she said softly, tucking her hands into her back pockets and shivering. The wind had picked up and the jacket she wore afforded little protection against the air sweeping across the hilled pasture.

"Don't get involved in this, Vera."

She shrugged. "I know my husband. Knew what kind of man he was before I married him. A secret love child comes as no surprise to me."

Love child? Rick didn't think the term could be applied to Kate. Not the way Justus had talked about her mother. Rick didn't sense any tenderness where Susie Newman was concerned. She'd been just another woman who'd thought she could catch the mighty Justus Mitchell and failed.

Rick studied the woman who hadn't. Her face bore the tale of losing her only child and surviving her husband's declining health, yet, she was lovely. Touched by time and misfortune, Vera still held traces of that Alabama Southern belle she'd been. She was a woman who could serve up coffee and pound cake with the hands she'd just used to transplant a hydrangea or nurse a sick child. She'd been Rick's only friend for a while… aside from the gangly boy who'd dogged his heels when he'd first come to live at Cottonwood.

"You've talked to him about this girl?" he asked as he walked toward the rear of the house.

She followed, tossing her gardening gloves onto a

bench outside the mudroom. "Not exactly, no. But I always know what's going on, Rick."

"So you're just pretending not to?"

Vera smiled. "Of course. Justus will tell me when he's ready. He thinks I'm weak. That I have to be protected."

For good reason. Vera had been hovering on the edge of severe depression since Ryan's passing. Few things brought her joy.

They entered the kitchen where Rick's grandmother Rosa ruled. Rosa had been with Justus for over forty years. She ran Cottonwood, and she was the reason for every good thing in Rick's life.

"Hola," Rosa said, her accent still thick despite the years she'd spent in the United States. His grandmother stood at the stove stirring something in a pot. It seemed he could always find her there. The kitchen smelled like barbecue and made his stomach growl. "Mr. Justus said to go to his office. He just called down, upset you weren't here."

Rick shrugged. "He's going to get even more upset. Put antacid next to his plate tonight, *abuela*."

Vera disappeared before he could say goodbye.

Leaving Rick to tell Justus that Kate played by her own rules.

CHAPTER FIVE

KATE HADN'T GOTTEN MUCH SLEEP. Mostly because she'd stayed up late listening to Nellie lecture her. Eventually she'd fallen into a fitful, shadowy sleep. When she'd woken this morning, her head pounded and she could barely swallow. A suspicious substance dripped from her nose. The pine trees of East Texas had done their job. Her allergies were going haywire.

Even so, she'd staggered from Nellie's guest bedroom, managed a long shower, and pulled on a tight sweater-dress with black kick-ass Tory Burch boots. Of course, her slightly red nose didn't match the violet minidress, but at least it was in color range.

The kitchen was empty. Kate made herself at home, grabbing a cup of black coffee and a Pop-Tart. After three bites of the pastry, she remembered why she never bought them—they tasted like flavored cardboard. Her half-eaten breakfast hit the trash can just as the doorbell sounded.

Rick had not forgotten. Damn.

She took another sip of coffee with an unsteady hand. She'd once read an Emily Dickinson poem in college where Death had politely rung the doorbell. When answered, Death had taken the dude on a trip that ended at the cemetery. This felt a little like that.

The doorbell sounded again.

"I've got it," Kate called out, forcing herself to move.

She didn't want Nellie to answer. Almost always reserved, Nellie left the outlandishness to Kate, but if and when Nellie got her dander up, there was no subtlety about it. And last night, Nellie had been as mad as Kate had ever seen her. She wasn't sure if the fury was at her, Justus or Rick.

Kate threw the door open, and Rick jumped back before giving her a quasi grin. "Good morning, cupcake."

She snorted. "I've been called lots of names before, but never *cupcake*. Come in. I'll grab my purse and gun."

"Bring plenty of ammunition. His wheelchair is motorized and he's pretty fast in it."

"I have a whole box," she said as she turned toward the kitchen where she'd left her purse. Nellie hadn't appeared. Thank the Lord. She figured her friend didn't trust herself not to lash out at Rick for carrying out Justus's heinous mission. Kate hadn't been able to reason with her over this whole fiasco. And it was a fiasco, but Nellie didn't seem to understand Kate had asked for this when she'd written that damn letter. Nor did she understand why Kate hadn't come to her for the money.

Kate had thought Nellie would get why she hadn't made that call. Everyone in Oak Stand knew Kate and her grandmother had lived off donations and cast-off clothing, and everyone knew Kate was embarrassed by that fact. Kate had never asked Nellie for anything. Ever. No matter how desperate she felt, it was an unwritten code they never talked about. Another elephant in the room of Kate's life, one that had so many pachyderms in it, it was a wonder she had air left to breathe.

Kate wouldn't take charity. Not from a friend.

But she would take Justus's hush money.

She scooped up her purse and checked herself in the den mirror. She looked good for someone who had a raging sinus headache. She'd made up her eyes a little too heavily, but the blue streaks in her hair balanced the look. She'd finger-combed her hair into a straight edgy look and added dangly hoop earrings. The outfit was cutting-edge fashion. Overall, she looked like Justus's worst nightmare—something like Posh Spice meets Reno prostitute.

She sauntered to the foyer where Rick studied a collage of Mae. The whole damned house was Ode to Mae. Nellie must have taken a picture of the baby every single day of her fifteen months of life.

"She's a cute kid," Rick said as he turned to her. His gaze swept her length, lingering on the high points. Namely her small breasts. She hadn't worn a bra because she didn't really need one. She felt her nipples harden under his perusal. The friction of the sweater dress only served to incite the heat in the pit of her stomach.

Rick Mendez was a nice piece of work. He'd look good on her, no doubt.

"Yeah, she is," Kate said, crossing her arms over her chest. "But they could give the camera a rest. Jeez."

"Ready to go?" Rick stepped back to let her pass through the door he'd left open. The last day in January felt cool and rain-soaked.

"Yeah. You have the blindfold ready?" She shrugged into her coat and tugged the ties.

"Blindfold?"

"For the firing squad."

He narrowed his eyes. They were nice eyes. Chocolaty-brown, but forceful all the same. Like they'd seen and endured much.

She shot him a brave smile and trotted down the

steps toward the '66 convertible Mustang parked in the curved drive. The car was salsa-red with a white top. A muscle car to match the intensity of the man walking behind her.

"I carry the blindfolds in my glove box," Rick said, following her to the passenger door. He pushed a key into the lock, pulled the door open for her, then walked around to slip into the car beside her. His shoulder brushed hers as he pulled the modified seat belt over his chest and she got a whiff of him. He smelled clean. His short hair looked damp, as though he'd climbed from the shower only moments ago.

"So you *are* into kinky stuff. Nice."

For a moment, the air ignited. Heat came off Rick in waves. He wanted her. She knew that. But what would he do about it?

"Damn straight," he said, his accent low and danger-ous. Kate's stomach prickled. "But they're only for the really bad girls. You're not a bad girl, are you, Kate?"

Kate snorted. "I think you know the answer to that."

His response was to rev the engine. But he wore a smile.

COTTONWOOD LOOMED IN FRONT of them like the dream of a nine-year-old girl. Its stately columns and fanciful curved front steps ignited visions of hooped dresses and shiny carriages. Kate had stood outside the gates before, peering through the cold bars where an intricate M was carved. She'd dreamed of walking down those stairs, lifting the edge of her wedding gown and stepping into a limousine.

Once she'd imagined herself crossing the trimmed lawn to her smiling father. Imagined him lifting her veil and giving her a gentle kiss. It was a kid's dream. Utter make-believe.

She glanced at Rick as they approached the house. Even he seemed tense. His shoulders were bunched beneath the same jacket he'd worn yesterday and his jaw looked set. Rock hard. That image of Rick was both titillating and off-putting.

"Honey, I'm home." Her voice sounded on edge to her own ears.

Rick glanced at her.

She gave him a shaky smile. "Too soon to call it home?"

At this his lips twitched. Something in his smile gave her comfort. She wanted to thank him for that, for offering her some solace in this moment she faced. That comfort shouldn't have meant anything to her. Justus Mitchell had denied her once—it was entirely conceivable he'd do it again.

She had carried her hatred of him around with her because it had made her who she was. She didn't take crap from anybody and she lived by her own rules. That was what Justus had given her. That and nothing else. But now she wanted money from him. Money that was way past due.

Rick pulled onto an odd patterned parking area adjacent to the house and cut the engine. "I'll walk you in, then I'm running over to Phoenix. It's not far. My grandmother will call me when you're ready and I'll pick you up."

He was leaving her. For some reason, she didn't want him to. Even though he worked for Justus, he felt like the only guy on her team.

Which was stupid.

He touched her on the shoulder. "Hey."

She lifted her gaze to his, afraid he might see how much she wanted him to stay. He wasn't smiling. He looked as intense as the first time she'd met him, but there was a tinge of softness now.

"You're strong."

His words wrapped round her, doing as he intended, strengthening her, bolstering the courage she'd felt she'd lost for a moment as they'd driven up the lane.

Kate closed her eyes, then she leaned over and kissed him.

Not a peck, like she was thanking him.

But a full-fledged kiss.

At first he drew back, surprised her mouth was on his. But then he leaned in and allowed his lips to soften beneath hers. She opened slightly, tasting him. He tasted like spearmint gum and warm male, so she tilted her head and opened her mouth a bit more. He took advantage, deepening the kiss, sliding his hand to her jawline.

His hands were big and calloused. Something dangerous slithered inside Kate, a flash of desire.

She broke the kiss. "I *am* strong."

Then she threw open the door, grabbed her purse and climbed from the car. She didn't need Rick to walk her inside. She'd deal with whatever waited behind the back door. No sexy Hispanic crutch need apply.

As she lifted her hand to knock, she paused. The Mustang roared to life. She glanced over to where it idled. Rick watched her in the rearview mirror. She wondered what he thought about the kiss, but before she could search for his gaze again, the car pulled away.

She knocked on the door.

An older Hispanic woman answered. A smile curved her broad face, wrinkling the skin around her dark eyes as she said, "*Adelante*. You use the back door? My grandson leaves you here?"

"Oh, hello." Kate pulled her bag higher on her shoulder and tried to discern if the woman fussed at her or Rick. "Um, Rick went to Phoenix. He said you would call him when I'm ready to return to my friend's house."

The woman stood aside so Kate could enter, tsking all the while. "What manners he shows. Dropping you at the back door like a laborer. A man should walk a lady inside."

The phrase "I'm no lady" popped into Kate's mind, but she wisely held the snappy comeback inside. "No, it's fine. I'm a big girl."

"I fuss at him, but I am rude, too. I'm Rosa Mendez. And you are not such a big girl. A *chiquitita*. Very, very tiny. And so lovely."

Kate never blushed, but she felt heat suffuse her face. "Thank you, Rosa."

"It's true." Rosa bustled into the kitchen. Kate followed behind like a puppy on a leash, ogling the cavernous kitchen. Modern appliances gleamed and houseplants overgrew their planters. The smell of herbs and bread permeated the air. Spanish tiles flashed blue and russet upon the counters and a small television sat in the corner playing a Spanish soap opera.

Rosa picked up a handheld radio. "Mr. Justus, Miss Kate is here."

The radio crackled, but she heard his words. "Send her up."

Just like a job interview. *Yes, Ms. Mendez, please send the applicant up.*

Rosa smiled, showing a large gap between her teeth. "*Si,* Mr. Justus wants you to go up."

"I heard," Kate said, looking about the kitchen trying to buy some time.

Rosa wiped her hands on a dish towel. "Don't worry. I'll take you."

"Don't bother, Rosa. I'll do the honors."

The voice came from the opposite doorway.

Kate turned as an older woman—presumably Vera Mitchell—stepped into the room. For a moment, Kate felt as though she'd been dropped onto a remote island with no food or water. *Survivor.* Trust no one.

Vera looked like what she was—a rich Texan's wife with an expensive haircut, manicured nails and clothes from Neiman Marcus. Her expression was measured, as if she were prepared to serve tea to a bastard daughter and not even break a sweat. Kate watched her as she approached.

"I'm Vera Mitchell. Justus's wife. Welcome to Cottonwood." Kate took the extended hand. It was as cool as she'd expected.

"I'm Kate Newman. I have a—" what was it exactly? "—meeting with Mr. Mitchell."

The older woman released her hand. "Yes, I know. Follow me and I'll show you to his office."

Kate glanced at Rosa. Rick's grandmother stood watching, her mouth slightly agape. She assumed the woman hadn't expected Vera to greet the usurper to the throne. Of course, she wasn't really interested in anything from either of the Mitchells. Only a bit of money owed for all the times she'd eaten leftovers from the diner because her grandmother couldn't afford groceries.

She followed Vera to the foyer—noting the modern elevator sitting like an anachronism in the traditional elegance of the mansion. They climbed to the second floor and Kate scanned the massive oil paintings of barren

Texas landscapes, the impression of them as cold and imposing as the miles of marble they walked upon.

"Here we are." Vera swept her hand toward an ornately carved door.

"Thank you," Kate muttered, trying not to squirm under the other woman's scrutiny. She'd be damned if she felt remorse about what she was about to do.

"You're welcome," Vera said, catching Kate's gaze with her own. She held it for a moment before nodding. "Yes, you have his eyes."

Kate didn't know what to say. She waited, but Vera didn't say anything else. Instead, she melted away, leaving Kate standing there, feeling weird and out of place.

So Kate gave herself a mental pep talk. Vera didn't matter, Rick didn't matter, no one mattered. Justus Mitchell had denied her. This time, his chick had come home to roost. And this chick wasn't a scared little girl. This chick was a ballbuster.

She didn't bother with knocking—he didn't deserve the courtesy. She opened the door and walked inside as if she owned the place.

RICK MADE IT ALL THE WAY to Phoenix before turning the car around and heading back toward Cottonwood.

What had he been thinking, leaving Kate alone to deal with Justus by herself? He hadn't discussed anything regarding Kate with the old man, and Justus could be erratic. And, frankly, manipulative. He had come to Christ, but he was still a sinner as much as any man. Rick didn't trust him to not trick Kate.

And what about that kiss? The saucy little salon owner's taste still lingered on his lips.

He passed a hand over his face.

Damn, that kiss had felt good. Good in a scary way, because something had moved inside him again. Like when he'd watched her in Vegas, and again on the plane. What was she doing to him?

He didn't want to think about the compulsion that drove him to return to the ranch.

The Texas countryside passed him, dull and gray. This last day of January was grim, harsh and cool with little to no lacy snow to hide the hibernating earth. Yellowing grass and naked sweetgum trees mingled with the dusky green of the pines. The bright red of his hood was the only brilliance to meet the eye. The only gang-related color he allowed himself in his life.

It had been Ryan's car. The car they'd restored together, right before he'd died.

How they'd both loved the vibrant red paint—the original color, painstakingly researched and tracked down. It had gleamed beneath the many coats of wax they'd applied while nursing warm beers and listening to Santana's sweet licks. Sometimes it seemed like only yesterday they'd stood in the garage and joked about Ryan's girlfriends and the failure of the Cowboys to draft a good quarterback.

Tony Romo had proven them both wrong, but what had it mattered? His young friend would never watch another game with him.

And that haunted him more than any of his past mistakes. Rick should have believed Ryan. He should have known Ryan was telling the truth, but he'd refused to listen.

Rick rolled down the window and allowed the memories to be sucked out the car. The cold air hit his face. Reality had teeth.

Ryan was gone, but Kate was not.

He took the drive fast, kicking up crushed rock and causing dust to boil into the interior.

His grandmother met him at the door. "You shouldn't have dropped her off that way. Left her to face him alone—"

"I know," he interrupted as he beelined toward the door that led into the bowels of the house. "Did you take her to Justus?"

"No, Vera did."

"Shit," he muttered under his breath as he wound through the downstairs and took the stairs two at a time. Vera was nowhere to be seen. In fact, the house was eerily quiet. He stopped outside Justus's office and listened.

He didn't hear anything.

He eased the door open, not knowing what to expect. Then he stared in surprise.

Justus sat in his chair near the window, silent and solemn as Rick had ever seen him, and Kate stood about ten feet from him, hands propped on her hips. Her narrow shoulders were thrown back and her chin jutted high. She didn't see him enter the study. Neither did Justus.

"You're right, of course," Justus said. He did not pull his eyes from the window. He seemed to be looking out at Ryan's garden. No doubt Vera was rambling about. She went there daily to pray, to mourn and to celebrate the son she loved. Justus observed her grief from above.

"You're damned straight I'm right." Outrage laced her words. Only the slightest tremble of emotion in her voice gave any indication the conversation meant more to her than some random argument over a parking spot.

"Yes." Justus nodded before tearing his eyes from the scene below. His gaze met Rick's.

Kate spun around. "What are you doing here? This is a private conversation. I don't need your help."

Her violet-blue eyes flashed, much as Justus's did when he was irate. "Yes, I'm sure you don't. But Justus might."

A choking sound came from Justus. It sounded rusty and was seldom heard around Cottonwood, but was definitely a laugh. "True. She puts up a lot of fight, considering she's no bigger than a dust mite."

This seemed to bother Kate more than it should have. "Being small does not mean being without resource. I can handle myself fine. Now if you will just hand over my child support payment, I'll get out of your life."

A smile hovered on Justus's thinning lips. "Child support? I suppose one could call it that. But…"

A furrow popped up between Kate's eyes. Her brow lowered, like a dog smelling a trap. "But what?"

"I'm first and foremost a businessman, and I can see the apple doesn't fall far from the tree."

"What are you getting at?"

Rick remained silent and watched Kate. He knew Justus well enough to know he had a reason for summoning Kate to Cottonwood and it had nothing to do with money. It was something bigger.

"I have an offer to counter your illegal demand for money, Kate."

She advanced on Justus and stuck a finger in the middle of his chest. "Bullshit. Call it whatever you want, but you owe me."

The old man merely looked up at Kate. His wheelchair whirred as he moved it forward. His daughter stepped back. "If you want child support, I think it only fair to give me something."

"Wrong." Her word cut the air.

"No, hear me out. I'll give you child support, but I want my visitation."

Rick averted his eyes to the painting adjacent to where he stood. He couldn't look at Kate because he knew Justus had done what he always did. Pulled the rug out and left his victim gasping on the floor. It wouldn't be wise to get involved. She'd unleash on him, and Hurricane Kate could pack a punch.

Hell, what was he doing here, anyway? His head said, "run." But his gut said, "stay." Finally, he looked at Kate, whose mouth was open and he knew.

She needed him even though she didn't realize it. And for some reason beyond his understanding, he was going to help her.

CHAPTER SIX

KATE NEARLY CHOKED ON her rage. What the hell did the old man mean, *visitation?*

She put a hold on her anger long enough to glance over at Rick. His expression seemed composed. Had he expected to hear those words come from Justus's mouth? For the umpteenth time, she wondered what he was doing at Cottonwood. Why was he dancing to Justus's fiddle?

"What do you mean?" she asked, directing her attention to Justus. Her fingernails pressed into her palms hard enough to draw blood.

"I want to spend some time with you. Get to know you. It's simple, really. And makes this whole thing an agreement, rather than blackmail."

"No." Kate shook her head. He couldn't control her. Or change the rules. She'd come to Texas at his behest to settle what she'd started. Two days. That was all she was willing to give him.

"You want back payment on child support with no absolute proof that you are my daughter. I think it's only fair I get something in return." Justus's face was placid, calm. The man knew how to play a boardroom. He hadn't climbed to the top of a financial empire by showing his cards.

"*Fair?* You want to talk *fair?*" She couldn't stop her voice from rising, no matter how much she wanted to show indifference. For the second time in her life, she felt absolutely helpless to stop a wave of sheer anguish from crashing over her. She'd felt this way before…the first time she'd confronted Justus.

She'd been but nine years old, a feeble babe under the paw of a wolf. Yet that vulnerability had forged steel in her. She'd never forgotten.

She put aside that memory and concentrated on simply breathing. Why had she done this? Why had she sought out the only man who made her feel so worthless? "You cannot talk to me of fairness. You know what you did."

His face showed the first crack. He wasn't indifferent to her words. She saw this. Rick did, too.

"I'm not sure this conversation involves me. I just wanted to check on you, Kate. Make sure you were okay." His words were comforting. Someone cared, even if he wasn't supposed to.

"I—"

"I don't see why you can't stay, Enrique. I've never kept secrets from you." Justus's words interrupted her.

Rick stopped in his progress toward the door. His mouth turned down slightly. "I'd say that's not necessarily true."

For a moment silence hung over them, a wet blanket, cold, clingy, stifling.

"What do you mean by 'spending time' with me?" Her words brought both men's gazes to her.

Justus swung his one good hand toward the tray upon his wheelchair. He moved a piece of paper toward her. "Take this."

She didn't want to get that close to him again, but she made herself move forward and take the paper. It was a check.

A check for fifty thousand dollars.

"It's postdated two weeks from today. It's yours free and clear as long as you stay for that duration and allow me the chance to change your mind about me."

Kate looked at all those zeroes and swallowed.

This little piece of paper was her salvation.

But was it worth two weeks in Oak Stand? Two weeks with the man she swore she'd hate forever and a year? "Change my mind?"

"About having a relationship with me. Trying to repair the fences that have been broken. I am, after all, your father."

"That's not what you implied earlier," Rick pointed out. "You said she had no proof."

Justus gave a heavy sigh. "I employ you as my assistant for good reason. Nothing slips by you, boy."

"So, you're his assistant? I thought you were the director of that center." She pressed her hand against the throb in her head, trying like mad to figure out why Justus kept a Hispanic tough guy for a right-hand man while also planning on how to wrangle out of the old man's demands.

"I *was* his assistant. One with a vast job description."

Justus snorted, but it was humorless. She couldn't get a handle on their relationship. There were undercurrents, but then again, the room pulsed with undercurrents. She was a hapless traveler clinging to a tree branch in the middle of a raging river.

"I can't stay here," she said. "I have responsibilities in Vegas." She'd lose customers if she canceled any more appointments. Jeremy had already whined about having to be away from Victor so much. Of course, after she reminded him she was saving his ass, too, he shut up.

But she couldn't expect him to handle the salon and her customers while she sat at the feet of her long-lost dad so the man could tell her bedtime stories and buy her pretty ribbons for her hair.

Justus was delusional if he thought he'd win any smidgeon of respect or crumb of affection.

"It can be arranged," Justus said, with the assurance of a man who could make almost anything happen. Money and power cleared his path.

She shook her head. "No. You can keep the check. I only want the amount I originally asked for."

The man who sired her looked her straight in the eye. His eyes were a mirror image of her own, and it discomfited her. "No. You can have the amount on that check, but you have to give me the two weeks. That's the offer."

"I can get an attorney. We can do a paternity test, and then I can sue you for what you owe me. Owe my grandmother for raising me all those years." She lifted her chin, glared at him.

"Sure, you can hire an attorney. But there is the matter of the letter you sent." Her father pulled a paper from his shirt pocket and waved it. "I'm not sure a judge would look favorably on blackmail. Besides, a lawsuit will take years and there *is* always the chance I'm not your father. Presently, I'm not asking for proof. You can have the money and you wouldn't even have to be my real daughter. The odds are in your favor."

Kate felt the trap slam shut. He was right. She didn't have the time or money for a lawsuit. She needed the money now.

And Justus knew it.

She took her hands from her hips and crossed her arms across her chest. If she did what Justus wanted her to do, she'd be letting go of that tenuous branch and immersing herself in that raging river. She could only hope that there was dry ground ahead. And that she wouldn't get sucked beneath the surface and end up broken on the rocks below.

It was only two weeks of her life. She could handle anything for two weeks even if it would be a bitch to arrange…and endure.

She let go. "Fine."

Rick moved behind her. She could smell his cologne, feel his warmth. She wanted to lean against him. Or turn and bury her head in his chest. Which was dog-ass stupid. She didn't need anyone to take care of her. Certainly not a man she'd only known for seventy-two hours.

"Excellent," Justus said, moving his chair from the window toward the desk anchoring the room. "I'll have Rosa prepare a room for you."

"I can't stay here," Kate said, stepping back. Her back bumped Rick's chest. His hands slid to her elbows, bracing her.

"How will I get to know you if you aren't at Cottonwood?"

Kate panicked for a moment. He wanted her here alone in this house with him and his cold wife? The thought made her stomach twist into ropes. "If I stay here, you have to give me something to do. I can't just ramble around this house. I need a job. Cover. People talk about me enough in Oak Stand."

"A job?" Justus repeated. "I don't have a job for you."

"The center," Rick said. "We need to hire an administrative assistant to handle things like therapist appointments and grant paperwork. It's really piling up."

Justus frowned, but she felt a niggling sense of satisfaction. Rick had helped her. And there was a flash of something else. Something to do with spending her days with the sexy man. A sort of anticipation. "Good. I'll help at the center and then spend some, ah, time with you in the evenings. That's my deal. Take it or leave it."

Justus's eyes moved between the two of them. Several seconds passed before he muttered, "I suppose that will be acceptable."

Kate felt a string snap inside of her as relief flooded her body. She wasn't absolutely alone in this.

"Okay, I'll stay here with you." She swallowed the acid that had welled in the back of her throat. She could do this. Do it for her future. For the salon's future. "But first, I have to pick up my things. And I'll need to buy more clothes and toiletries. I only planned to stay a few days."

"Give her a credit card, Enrique," Justus said, without a single blink.

She lifted her chin. "I can pay for my own things." She glanced at Rick. "Although a ride into town would be nice."

"I'll be glad to take you into Longview after I stop at Phoenix. I've got a few things to do there."

"Well, then. I'll see myself out." She slipped from the room as quickly as she could manage. Though she still felt partially victorious for setting her own terms of surrender, she could feel a migraine headache starting. Little zigzaggy things were already shadowing her vision. When she got to the hallway, she pressed herself against the polished wainscoting and took several cleansing breaths.

Had she waved the white flag? Or was the battle only

beginning? She wasn't sure, but she was certain of two things. Something big loomed ahead of her, and her toes were sweating in her designer half boots.

"Do you think this is wise?" Rick asked as Justus maneuvered his wheelchair behind the colossal antique desk. "What about Vera?"

He shrugged, although it was a rather distorted shrug. "What about her? This doesn't concern her."

"The hell it doesn't." Rick walked to the window. Vera stood among the dead plantings, staring at the marble angel in the center of the circular garden. He could see her lips moving in silent prayer. "She's still hurting over Ryan. And bringing Kate—"

"Why do you care?" Justus's words were tinged with anger. "Vera's not your concern. She's mine. It's been three years. It's time she stopped wandering around this ranch like some shadow of a woman. She's like a Dickens character. All she needs is a moldering bridal gown and an old wedding cake. It's absurd."

Rick didn't know Dickens. He'd dropped out of school before the tenth grade, but he knew what Justus meant. Vera had spent long enough mourning, but Rick couldn't abandon the woman who'd first accepted him as something other than a thug. Besides he owed it to Ryan to look out for Vera.

"You're throwing Kate in her face."

"The hell I am." Justus used his good hand to slam a thick book of Irish folklore upon the desk. It caused the picture of a smiling Ryan clad in his graduation gown to fall forward. "I didn't go looking for Kate. She found me. For reprehensible purposes, true, but I've prayed for months for God to send me something, some answer, some way to bring us all back among the living. I think He sent me Kate."

Rick grew still. He'd never thought about the feisty Kate being someone destined to come to Cottonwood. And he certainly hadn't seen her as someone who could breathe life into a house that had folded into itself with grief. But maybe Justus was right.

Maybe Kate had a bigger purpose.

"Okay, I get what you're saying, but you have to promise to tread lightly." He walked toward the door.

"I don't have to promise you a thing," Justus said, staring at the fallen picture frame.

Rick paused with his hand on the knob. "That may be, but this time, I'm not going to allow you to pull all the strings. There are too many people with a stake in this for you to bulldoze over as if they were small saplings."

Justus's laugh was sharp. Biting. "Do you honestly think I'd let you scare me away from a girl who is my own flesh and blood?"

Rick knew Kate was Justus's daughter, but he used the old man's argument against him. "You said you didn't know if she were really your daughter."

"The girl's mine. I've known it for thirty years."

Rick flinched. The admission made his stomach turn. "Then why the hell didn't you acknowledge her?"

Justus's eyes met his. They were as frigid as an Alaskan lake. The way they'd been before Ryan died, before the stroke. The old Justus lurked inside the shell somewhere. "I've never had cause to."

"But now you do?"

"I do."

Anger welled in Rick. This man did what he did for his own selfish purposes. He did not have Kate's best interests in mind. But Rick would look out for her. Justus Mitchell mowed over many people, but Enrique Mendez was no damned sapling.

He masked his annoyance, nodded and left the room. There was nothing more to say.

He found Kate standing outside the office door, staring at an original Remington bronze of a Cherokee warrior. The piece was poised between two of the artist's original sketches. Justus loved the art of the Old West.

"Is that a real Remington?" Kate asked.

"I think so."

"My friend Billie would love to see it. She's a glass artist, but has a thing for cowboys and Indians." Kate's words sounded detached. She was trying to distance herself from her emotions. He understood.

"You ready to go?"

"Yeah. I couldn't remember how to get around this mausoleum, so I waited on you." Finally, her eyes met his. They were no longer distant. They were determined. "So let's go. I got myself into this, and there's only one direction I can head now."

Rick moved down the hallway toward the staircase, but then stopped. "You don't have to agree to his terms, Kate. I can get you a ticket back to Vegas. You can go home and forget about everything. It might be for the best."

He didn't want her to go, and that surprised him. But in her interest, she should head for Vegas.

She stopped in the middle of the hall. "You think he'll let me do that? I poked the hornets' nest, Rick. He's not going to let me slink away with my tail tucked. Plus, I don't work that way. He wants me around? Fine. I'll be around. But he can't control me. No one can. I play by my own rules, so that man back there may regret the hell out of wanting me here."

He couldn't help it. He smiled.

"What?" she asked.

He loved her eyes, which was weird, because they looked so much like Ryan's and Justus's. But they were different. He could get lost in hers. Sometimes he hated the romance in his soul. Lost in a woman's eyes? What a bunch of crap. "Nothing. I just...nothing."

She cocked her head, making her look like an inquisitive little mouse. But she didn't push it. She spread her small hands apart, palms up. "Okay, then. Let's go."

He led her down the stairs and out of the house, pausing only to shout a farewell to his grandmother who sat in front of the TV, immersed in a Mexican soap opera. Vera was nowhere in sight. He was glad. Justus needed to tell his wife about Kate coming to stay.

He stepped out into the blustery day, swamped with the need for separation from the Mitchells. He needed to cut the string that bound him to Justus. He watched Kate cross the drive and knew she'd taken hold of one of those invisible threads and pulled him in even closer.

And he'd gone willingly.

CHAPTER SEVEN

RICK DIDN'T SAY ANYTHING as they drove away. Kate was relieved because her emotions were tied into one giant knot that had parked itself in her stomach. It felt like a bowling ball. But she didn't want to acknowledge it. She wanted to pretend the scene in Justus's office meant nothing to her.

The window was open and the cool air tousled her short hair and caused goose bumps to rise on her arms. She pulled the three-quarter sleeves of her sweaterdress lower.

"Roll up the window," Rick said as he turned onto the county highway that would take them toward Phoenix and eventually Longview.

"No, it feels good. Kinda cleansing." She stared at the barren landscape, watching cows munching on clumps of clover that dotted the pastures. "Thanks for coming back."

Such simple words of gratitude were hard for her. She didn't like accepting the kindness of others, especially virtual strangers. But he deserved that much. He'd stood beside her as she faced her father for the first time in years, and he hadn't been obliged to do so. In fact, he shouldn't have. He'd picked the wrong side, considering his history with her father. But having him there had softened the trap that had closed around her.

Justus. She didn't miss the irony in his given name.

He was a man who meted his own brand of justice. Was being trapped with him for two weeks fair? Was this nature's joke on her for waking the monster of her past?

She sighed. Rick glanced at her before focusing on the highway. He left her alone with her thoughts.

Facing her father had been more difficult than she'd thought it would be. Seeing the man crippled, a shell of his former self, had been tough, had made her feel quite small for the act she was perpetuating against him. Like she was a bad person.

Then he'd turned the tables. Made her boiling mad. And she hadn't felt so very sorry for him after all. She'd felt absolutely warranted in demanding the money from him.

She pinched the bridge of her nose with her fingers. The roller coaster of emotions she'd just climbed from had sucked the wind from her sails and the shadow of the migraine lingered.

Rick chuckled. "You know, I didn't come back for you. I came back to protect the old man. You're fierce."

Kate allowed a smile to curve her lips. "I think he proved he didn't need you after all. He's got tricks in that bag of his that don't disappear with a stroke or some spiritual transformation. You can't change a leopard's spots."

"Yeah, but you can shoot the leopard and make a coat of him."

Kate summoned a laugh. "I've always wanted a leopard coat. It would look fabulous with my new Manolos."

"What are Manolos?"

And that made Kate laugh for real. "Shoes. But I'm kidding. I don't wear animal skins."

"Sure you do. You wear leather, don't you?"

Kate rolled her eyes. "I guess I should have said I don't wear furs harvested for the purpose of making women look haughty."

Rick looked over at her. "I don't wear furs, either."

"No full-length pimp-daddy coats in your closet?"

"Not anymore." His words sounded heavy, not teasingly light. Something dark tinged his words.

Change of subject needed. "So tell me about Phoenix. How did you come up with the idea for the place?"

The slight tension emanating from Rick vanished. "It's something I'd been thinking about for a long time. Actually, the idea came from Ryan."

"Ryan Mitchell?"

A new emotion touched Rick's face. Kate thought it was tenderness. "Yeah, he…well, we were friends of a sort. I started working for Justus eight years ago, when Ryan was a freshman in high school. When I first came to Cottonwood, I worked as a gardener. Justus gave me a job as a favor to my grandmother."

"Because of your past?" It seemed a touchy subject, but she asked it anyway.

"Si," he said, offering a smile, a mixed bag this time. Acceptance, regret, shame, pride—all rolled into one. "I think you've already guessed my past was something I'm not so proud of. I was in a gang, rolling with the Norteños, doing all sorts of things that still weigh on me when I have time to think. Phoenix is my penance, my salvation."

His expression turned sheepish, as if the poetics of his words embarrassed him. "What I mean is that the center is my way to pay it forward. Give others the chance I was given. Oddly enough, your father gave me the ability to do that. The center is his tribute to Ryan."

It explained a lot about why Rick had worked for Justus. Still, she sensed he had hidden issues with the man. It wasn't apparent at first, but she suspected there was a mire of complicated feelings between the two. "So Justus pulled you out of a gang?"

"Not exactly pulled me out. I didn't have much of a choice." He propped his elbow on the open window and leaned back into his seat, settling into his story. "I was in my early twenties and got picked up for possession of stolen property. I made bail and waited on my guys to pick me up. Instead, Rosa waited outside. With Justus. She'd actually shooed the gang members off the steps of the city jail."

Kate smiled at the thought of the diminutive Mexican grandmother taking a bunch of gang members to task.

"So I stepped out into the sunshine and she hit me with that look. I couldn't duplicate it if I tried. It was so disappointed and angry looking. When I walked up to her, she said, 'You've got one chance, *cholo.*' I didn't want to, but I climbed into Justus's truck."

His face seemed so worn. He'd seen and done things that had etched a mark on him.

"That was a pretty brave thing, walking away like that. I mean, it's hard getting out of a gang. Isn't it something like once in, always in?" Kate lightly touched his arm before withdrawing and tucking her hand into her lap. She had no right to touch him, even if her fingers itched to stroke the muscles beneath the cloth of his jacket. She'd seen the ink, peeking out of his T-shirt collar. Did it stretch across his chest? She wanted to know what lurked beneath.

"Yeah, it's hard when you go it alone. But I wasn't

alone. Rosa had convinced Justus to give me a way out. He pulled some strings and got me probation for the third time. Still don't know how he managed it, but if he hadn't, I'd be lost. I came to Cottonwood, and it was far enough away to give me a chance."

He paused for a moment, his mind obviously in the past. "So that's what Phoenix is about. It's about giving guys who want out of the life a way to get out. They come here, away from the streets, away from the temptation and the danger. That's going to make the difference."

"So by coming here, the gang can't get to them?"

"Well, sort of. Many gangs are ambivalent about centers like Phoenix. They don't like them, but some of the guys understand, like if they could give up the life, they would. I put the word out on the streets about the center at churches and community centers."

"In Dallas?"

He laughed. "Yeah. Oak Stand isn't exactly a hotbed of gang activity. Unless you count the Junior League. Those gals don't mess around."

"You're preaching to the choir," Kate mumbled.

"So, anyway, word is out there's a place you can go if you want out, want to get your GED or get a job. It's started some trouble. A few threatening messages, that kind of thing. But it's going to work."

"Hmm, so the gang leaders think Phoenix is going to steal their workers?"

Rick smiled. "Pretty much. They're a business like any other. There are leaders—shot callers—then there are the guys who carry out the mission. Basic business structure. But their business is drugs, fencing, even prostitution."

Rick turned the car onto a drive. Ahead she could

see a massive structure built to look like a lodge. The building was made of stacked stone and cedar planks with a long, low porch covered with rockers along the front. Pulling up to Phoenix felt like arriving at an old home place.

"It's fabulous," she breathed. "I mean, seriously, warm and welcoming. Awesome."

Rick took her hand and squeezed it. "Exactly what I was going for."

The pride in his voice was so evident it made her heart swell. And his hand on hers took on new meaning, new intimacy, and she rubbed her lips together as if trying to remember his taste. He'd tasted good when she kissed him. She wanted to do it again.

He looked at her and she met his eyes. They were a mysterious brown, dark and weighty. His broad cheekbones stretched above a chiseled jaw. This man was all hard edges, masculine and clean lines. His skin looked like aged honey, like she could run her fingers over it and feel the power beneath.

She leaned toward him, unable to stop herself from inhaling his scent. His cologne was woodsy, musky and reminded her she hadn't had sex in a long time.

He watched her, his lids lowered slightly. She could sense the hitch in his breath, feel the electricity uncork between them.

But suddenly he stiffened.

And pulled away.

"Let me show you the center and see what you think. You'll be working here, after all."

Kate blinked and watched him climb from the car. She felt a twinge of displeasure, as if he'd taken a toy from her and put it out of reach. She muttered a curse to the empty interior and climbed out.

The center sat on a hill, crushed granite surrounding the side and back parking area. Her boots slid in the loose rock as she scrambled after him. When she turned the corner, she found Rick, arms akimbo, staring at the back porch. A mangy looking dog sat on the sissel door mat next to an empty food bowl.

"Get out of here," he shouted at the dog, waving his hands in a shooing motion.

"I'm guessing that's not your dog?" she said, kneeling and motioning for the dog to come to her. It truly was a scrawny thing, with matted brown fur and rheumy eyes. Just pitiful. The dog wouldn't come to her. It looked at Rick.

"No, it's not my dog. It keeps hanging around here. The last thing I need is a stray crapping all over the yard and barking at every leaf that blows by."

"Then why are you feeding it?"

Rick tried to look disgusted. "Because it's hungry."

The dog yawned and looked bored. He turned a lazy circle and lay down.

"Hate to tell you this, but if you feed it, it's your dog." Kate walked up the back steps and knelt, extending her hand for the dog to sniff. The mutt lifted his head and licked her fingers. "What's his name?"

Rick stared at her and the stray. "I don't know. Banjo?"

Kate laughed, scaring the dog. The mutt ran straight to Rick and hid behind his splayed legs. "Yep, Banjo is your dog. An ugly dog at that."

Rick looked down at where the animal cowered at his knees. "I don't know. He's not that ugly. Maybe with a bath, he'd clean up okay."

Kate rose and looked around the area where she stood. Newly planted ornamental grasses flanked the back porch. A bird feeder sat at the back of the large bricked patio that extended off the porch. Adirondack chairs and matching benches scattered the patio and a fire pit sat in the center. Barren Texas countryside surrounded the building, presently desolate, but in the spring, it would be gorgeous.

Rick passed her, leaving the dog to sniff the bushes. He unlocked the center and stepped inside. She followed. The first thing she noticed was the smell. Fresh pine and cedar. The room was large and had a huge fireplace with a moose head over the mantel.

"Do they have moose in Texas?" Kate asked, as she took in the wagon wheel candelabras that hung by iron chains from the ceiling and the rustic leather sectionals. A cowhide rug centered the room. Whoever had come up with the vision for the rehabilitation center had done an excellent job. Kate felt as though she could wrap herself in a woolen throw, grab a hot chocolate and stare out at the countryside for hours.

"That's Winston. Grady Hart donated him. He killed him in Canada on a hunt with your father." Rick's words came from over her shoulder. He stood in the doorway of what was likely the kitchen. An enormous pine table sat in an area just past the large community room.

"It sounds weird for you to say *my father.* I don't really think of him like that," she commented as she moved around the room glancing at the framed photographs of Texas landmarks mounted on the wall.

"But he thinks of you as his."

"Well, I'm not one of his possessions."

Rick considered her. "No, you're not, are you."

Her exploration led her to one of the wide front windows. The Mustang sat forlorn in the drive. The dog had wandered around and now hiked his leg on the tires. She wouldn't tell Rick. Probably wouldn't sit well with him.

"Let me grab some things I have to take back to the office supply store. Might as well do the return while we're picking up things you need in Longview."

Kate nodded. "Don't worry about me. I'll poke around the center."

"Let me show you where everything is."

Kate could tell he enjoyed showing off the place, so she let him play tour guide, following him, past the moose head into a long hallway that stretched over fifty feet. Four rough pine doors sat on each side. Rick opened each, sticking his head inside for a quick survey. The rooms were each sparsely furnished with an iron bed, cheerful quilt and simple pine bureau beside a single window. The only other object inside was a small desk.

"These are the rooms for the clients. Our facility is different from other programs around the country. Some of those programs sit in the middle of the barrios and hoods. They provide therapy, job training, tattoo removals, things like that. There's a program in Los Angeles that even runs a restaurant. We want to give our clients the chance to remove themselves from the destructive environment before taking on the programs that will help them build new lives."

Kate watched him as he spoke. His face changed, took on a purposeful look. "That sounds like a good thing. It's got to be hard to enroll in a neighborhood program only to go home each night knowing the people you roll with are outside your window. Like too much temptation."

Rick's hand stilled on the doorknob. He faced her. "How did you know?"

"Know what?"

He set his hands on her shoulders, pulling her closer to him. "Have you faced addiction in your past or something?"

Kate didn't know why he'd asked her that. Strange question. "No. I just know there's a reason someone joins a gang. It's not to steal, run drugs or bang chicks. It's for companionship. For purpose. And if you are lying in your bed thinking about how you've got to rip yourself away from something like that, it has to be like a dieter sitting in front of a piece of cheesecake. Really hard to shove away."

Kate had just closed her mouth when his covered it. Warm, soft and as delicious as melted marshmallows on hot chocolate, the kiss curled her toes in those boots.

Rick's hands slid up from her shoulders to cup her head. It felt as though he drank from her, which really turned her on. She allowed him, pushed herself against him, encouraged him.

Her hands fluttered against his chest before sliding lower. The man had a serious six-pack. Nice. She curled her arms around his back and jerked him toward her.

She felt his smile against her lips.

"Bruja."

"Hmm?" Kate murmured, unwilling to tear her mouth from his for even a moment.

He drew back, his brown eyes glinting with a mixture of humor and passion. "You've bewitched me."

She smiled. Then lifted onto her tiptoes and jerked his head back to hers. "I don't want to talk about it."

This time she covered his mouth with hers. He reacted by hauling her against him. He felt so good. Hard.

All man. Kate allowed her hands to brush through his close-clipped hair as she opened her mouth to him.

"Well, ain't this the way I last saw you?"

Kate jumped, banging Rick in the nose, and looked over at the man lurking in the hallway.

"Bubba!" Kate shrieked, disentangling herself from Rick and throwing herself into the arms of the man laughing at her. The last time she'd seen Bubba Malone, he'd tripped over her and Brent Hamilton making out by the old dam out on Camp Lease Road. She'd been half-drunk on wine coolers and poor Bubba had been night fishing. He'd hit his head against a tree when he'd tripped and broken his best fishing pole.

"Didn't know you were in town, Katie. Do I need to lock down the liquor stores? Alert the Baptist church?"

She punched him on his beefy arm. "Whatever we need to do to protect folks around here."

Bubba laughed. It sounded like a donkey braying. "You're somethin' else, Katie. Ain't never seen anyone like you. Don't reckon I ever will, neither."

There was no way to describe Bubba other than Texas redneck. He stood about six foot four and wore the most god-awful clothing. Case in point, he was clad in a ratty long-sleeved T-shirt with a Carhartt vest. His jeans were splattered with red clay and his boots were untied with the laces frayed. His nose looked like a kid had shaped it out of modeling clay and stuck it to his face. But his bright blue eyes were friendly and his red beard reminiscent of Yukon Cornelius in the old children's holiday movies.

"Bubba." Rick nodded, drawing their attention to him. "Didn't know you were stopping by today."

Rick looked perturbed. Was he embarrassed to be

caught kissing her in the center? She assumed he was. She got the sense he wanted to portray himself as absolutely professional. Making out with the town rebel in the middle of the day was not professional. It was impulsive.

"I saw your car in the drive. I got that generator Jack said he'd give you. Thought I'd drop it by. I knocked but I guess you was busy." Bubba delivered a sly smile, then wiggled his eyebrows.

Rick ignored it, though she could have sworn a bit of color appeared on his cheeks. It was hard to tell on that smooth, golden skin. The yummy warmth emanating from him had disappeared. The interruption had reminded him of who he was and of what he had at stake. "I appreciate your bringing it by. We can put it in the storage building. I'll give you a hand."

Bubba pulled Kate into another hug. "Good to see you, Katie. Don't stay gone so long."

Kate gave him a squeeze before wriggling from beneath his heavy arm. "It's Kate, Bubba. And I don't have much reason to come back to Oak Stand. It can't compare to Vegas."

"You'll always be Katie to me. And just go watch the sun set over them hills out there. Vegas ain't got nothing on us."

Bubba disappeared and Rick followed, leaving Kate alone in the hallway, feeling a little small for being so defensive about her name and where she now lived. Everyone in Oak Stand knew her as Katie Newman and the people in this neck of the woods were proud of the quaint beauty of the little town, even if it did make them backwoods and small-minded. Kate was glad she didn't live here. And for the record, sunsets were spectacular against the Vegas skyline.

Who needed fresh air when there was excitement to replace it?

Rick's head appeared at the entrance to the hall. "You coming, Kate?"

"You bet your sweet ass."

And it was a sweet ass.

CHAPTER EIGHT

KATE SCANNED THE RACKS of clothes at the Longview
Target. Usually she loved to shop, even at a chain store,
but at present her head felt achy and her gut like an out-
board motor running at full throttle. Life had slammed
her upside her head.

And it was no one's fault but hers. She'd written that
letter. And, God, she wished she hadn't.

"I'm going to the book section. Meet me at the coffee
bar in thirty." Rick didn't bother waiting. He swerved
around a woman cajoling a toddler in a cart and disappeared. She didn't blame him. The kid was wailing
about wanting princess lip gloss and she had a set of
lungs.

"Chicken," Kate murmured as she pulled a knit sun-
dress from a rack. It was cute, but a season too early. She
needed jeans and sweaters. Texas weather was notori-
ously fickle. Heck, it could toss out a seventy-degree
day after one with light snow. But, for once in her life,
she had to be sensible about her clothing. She headed
to the clearance rack.

Just after she dumped two red-tag sweaters and a
cardigan into her basket, her phone erupted in a Ke$ha
tune. She pulled it from her bag. Jeremy.

"Hey, how's my favorite queen diva?"

"Fa-bu-lous!" Jeremy responded in a singsongy
voice.

Kate smiled. He always made her feel better. "Great. How's the salon?"

"I hate to tell you, darling, but it's fantabulous."

"That's the name of the place, dummy," she said, squinting at a pair of skinny jeans. They weren't True Religion, but they weren't bad. "Seriously, how's it going?"

"Seriously, it's going well. Mandy brought a couple of new clients along and not one peep out of your peeps. It's, like, totally working, doll."

"Well, that's a relief because I'm not coming back for a couple of weeks."

"Hello!" Jeremy cried, doing his impression of a gay Robin Williams. "What's with?"

Kate sighed. "Dear old Dad wants some baby girl time."

"You're joking," her friend said. "You mean he won't give you the money unless you stay in Texas?"

"Bingo. You're a smart puppy."

"I'm also a good puppy, and if you scratch me where I like it, I'll roll over for you." His tone was light. Maybe Victor felt better today. She didn't want to ask, though. When she'd called him yesterday, Jeremy had been in tears.

"You wish, gay boy," Kate said, studying the packaged panties on an end cap. They were assorted colors with little cherries on them. At least they weren't granny panties. And five pairs for under ten dollars. Cool. She snatched a package of bikini-style and tossed them in the basket.

"Don't worry, Kate the Great. I've got this covered. You do your thing and get that money. I'll focus on bringing in the clients. We'll be okay."

She eyed a black lace garter belt. It had hot pink

ribbons and a matching bra. She loved sexy undies as much as she loved comfy sweats and flip-flops. She plucked both from the display and held them aloft, eyeing them critically. Not her typical luxurious lingerie, but still…

"Wanna try it on for me?" Rick's voice came from over her shoulder.

Kate never blushed. Never. But she could feel heat creeping into her cheeks.

"Who's that?" Jeremy asked in her ear. "He sounds yummy."

She spun around. Rick stood, one arm extended above her so it stretched his gray T-shirt over his abs. He was close enough that she had to retreat from the heat he was putting off. The sexual static that had erupted between them earlier at the center buzzed again.

She cheekily rolled her eyes. "Jer, I gotta go. I'll call you tonight."

She punched End, even though she could hear her friend protesting.

Rick watched her with hawk eyes as she lowered the sexy bra and garter. She wanted to play with him. Taste him. Touch him. Indulge in him. She wanted him. That much was certain. But things right now were way bizarre and letting lust or whatever she felt with Rick swirl around within the confusion seemed pretty stupid. She had enough complication. Still, flirting with him made her feel like her old self. Like the Kate who could handle everything with a snappy comeback and the toss of her head.

She shrugged one shoulder. "Sorry, they won't let you in the dressing room."

With that she turned, scooped up the clothes she'd chosen—including the lingerie—and sauntered into the dressing room. She knew she shouldn't tease, but she couldn't resist the power she had. So before she disappeared into the depths, she leaned back and gave him a flirtatious smile.

"Let me know if you need any help," he called.

Her response was a wink.

RICK WATCHED KATE DISAPPEAR into the dressing room. What the hell was he doing? He needed to get his ass back to the book section. Standing in the middle of a grouping of thongs watching the sexiest little number he'd seen in ages strutting around waggling her tight ass in front of him was not the best idea at this juncture.

But she was the first woman who'd seriously tempted him in a long time. At Phoenix, he hadn't been able to resist the temptation to taste her again. And the whole way to Longview, he'd kept daydreaming about her skin sliding against his, her mouth opening to him, her hips clasped in his hands as he sank into her.

She made him want to put aside his vow of no more casual relationships, no more treating women like furniture. He'd retired that life when he'd turned over a new leaf. But Kate…Kate made him doubt himself.

And that should send him running, because he didn't need any more obstacles in his life. The center was opening in a matter of days. He had a lot to do. A list a mile long. And Kate Newman wasn't on the list.

But he felt powerless to stop himself.

He stood in the women's intimates section for several more minutes contemplating how wrong it was for him to want Kate before he noticed a few ladies giving him odd looks. Realizing he looked like a perv, he moved to where socks and scarves hung among purses.

Kate appeared at his elbow. "Okay, I gotta grab some toiletries and I'll be ready."

He started toward the other half of the store just as the kid crying over the lip gloss escaped from the shopping cart. He watched as the child tore away from her mother, shrieking about it "not being fair." He wanted to tell the little girl to get used to it, but that really wasn't his job. He knew nothing about wearing fluffy skirts and rubber boots. Little girls were alien.

Just like Kate was.

He watched the girl run toward him, her boots slapping the newly polished aisle. The mother, holding a pacifier between her teeth, shot a look at the shopping cart where a baby carrier sat before darting after her daughter. The little girl loped past Kate, collided with his knees, and wrapped her arms about his legs.

Rick looked at Kate in alarm. The little girl, who wore pigtails, turned her face up to him and in a most desperate voice said, "Will you please buy me princess lip gloss?"

Kate started laughing as the harried mother peeled her daughter from Rick's legs.

"Audrey! Tell the man you're sorry," the woman said, looking back at the cart she'd left a few yards away. "Now."

The girl poked out a lip. "I just wanted the princess—"

"Now," the mother said more firmly.

The girl's shoulders slumped. He figured she knew when she'd been beat. "Sorry."

He patted her on the head. It felt awkward. "That's okay."

"Wow," Kate said, watching the mother march

the child back to the cart. "You have girls throwing themselves at you."

"Yeah, but not really the kind I need."

Kate's eyes twinkled. "Oh, I don't know. Give her fifteen years. She's pretty cute."

"Look, I'll loan you some toothpaste," he said, eyeing another mother approaching from the opposite direction. Her cart held two squabbling kids. "I think I'm ready to get out of here."

"But you were good with Mae," she said, cocking her head in a questioning manner.

"She's a baby. She can't talk," he said, pushing her cart toward the front of the store.

"Oh, you just don't like your women to talk. Okay. I'll remember that. Let me just pay for these and we'll go before any more children tackle you and take you down." She swung the clothes in front of him. He didn't fail to notice she'd bought panties with cherries on them. Damn. Why had he noticed? Now all he'd be thinking about were those hot-pink cherries…and what lay beneath them.

Hell.

KATE STARED AT THE STRIPED walls surrounding the antique iron bed. They felt like bars. Prison bars.

Then again, she was doing time. At Cottonwood.

The room was elegantly furnished with a beautiful quilted coverlet in soft blues and greens. The hardwood beneath her feet was softened by a plush Oriental rug that complemented the ivory-and-periwinkle-striped walls. A fireplace anchored the room, bathing the cherry furniture in a soft glow. Dusk fell outside windows framed by tasteful drapes.

Kate couldn't help but think she'd rather be anywhere than facing dinner with her sperm-donor father and his deflated wife.

She spun and checked her image in the mirror. She'd pulled one of the cardigans she'd bought at Target over a white Hugo Boss shirt, pairing it with pants that looked painted on and a pair of soft blue leg warmers. She shoved her feet into a pair of snakeskin flats she'd bought on sale at Nordstrom's and hooked some Gerard Yosca glass stone earrings in her ears. Thank goodness she always overpacked. She hadn't had to spend too much at Target after all.

She took one last glance before blowing a kiss at her reflection and leaving the confines of her room.

Cottonwood was an enormous house and it took her a few wrong turns before she found the dining room.

Justus and Vera were already there, seated at a huge table gleaming with crystal glasses and shiny china. Weird. She felt as though she'd fallen into the TV and appeared on the set of *Dallas*. The theme song played in her head as she pulled a chair from the exact center of the table and sat.

"Evening," Vera murmured, her hand quaking as she lifted a glass of wine to her lips.

"Good evening, Miss Ellie," Kate said, pulling a snowy napkin from her right and placing it in her lap.

Justus frowned, but Vera actually laughed.

"It does seem like *Dallas*, doesn't it? I thought so myself when I first visited. Couldn't get that song out of my head for a good week."

Kate didn't expect Vera to catch on to her reference. It made her feel sorta petty. Time to play the guest. "Thank you for waiting on me. It took longer than expected to get back from Longview. There was an accident on the interstate, so Rick had to take a few side roads."

The whole situation was awkward. No way around it. She looked to her right at Justus. He stared at his empty plate like a grumpy bullfrog. She looked to her left at Vera, who smiled a brilliant fake smile. Kate didn't miss that Vera's hands still trembled as she cradled the goblet of wine. And when Kate looked to the center, she found Ryan Mitchell staring at her.

It was an enormous portrait of the half brother she'd never known. He had to have been around eighteen. His smile held hope, his eyes humor. Boyish charm oozed from the palette of muted paint. Unlike the other paintings scattered through the halls of Cottonwood, this painting had no windswept Texas background. No cowboys or grit. No horses or cows. Just a boy framed against a blue background, smiling as if he knew the answers to life.

As she noted they shared the same cheeky smile, a strange feeling washed over her. It could have been regret, or portent, or déjà vu. She wasn't sure, but it was something.

Before she could ask about the portrait, Rosa bustled in with several platters.

"Here I am. I made special dinner for Ms. Kate. *Chile verde con puerco*, and to start, *caldo de res*. And flan for dessert, Mr. Mitchell."

Justus visibly brightened as Rosa sat a steaming bowl of soup before him. "Well, now, it's been forever since you've gone to such trouble, Rosa. If I'd known all you needed was a guest, I would have brought someone sooner."

"Si," Rosa said. "We've had no one. When Mr. Ryan was here, we overflowed."

"I miss him so," Vera said, her eyes finding the monument to her son.

"No, no, Mrs. Vera. Ryan would say no," Rosa said, bustling toward Vera and setting down sweet corn cakes and fragrant corn tortillas. "You enjoy Miss Kate being here. Mr. Ryan brought her here."

Kate's hand hit her wineglass and knocked it over. Thankfully, she'd downed most of it. Still, burgundy spread like blood on the snowy cloth. "Sorry. I—"

"I get it, Miss Kate. You eat the corn cakes. They are made the way my grandmother made them. God rest her soul," Rosa said, crossing herself and pulling a towel from the pocket of her apron. She pressed the cloth to the spreading stain, soaking up the spill.

Kate glanced up at Vera. The woman's brow was furrowed and her expression perplexed. She wasn't going to let Rosa's comment slide. "Rosa, why would you say such a thing?"

The housekeeper looked up from her dabbing. Kate stiffened because she knew Rosa would say something about fate. Or God. Or some mystical Mexican superstition. Kate didn't make a habit of running from confrontation, but damned if she didn't want to flee the table.

"I saw your note to God. You asked him to heal you. To send you an angel like Mr. Ryan to make the hurt stop."

Vera flinched and Kate started a litany deep inside of "no, please, no," but Rosa charged ahead. "I found the paper when I was putting the hose back into the carriage house. Sitting right by the angel. And the next day, Miss Kate gets here. See, he answered your prayer."

Kate swallowed. Hard. Then she looked at Justus to

see if he might put a stop to Rosa's words, but he calmly slurped the soup before him, using his good hand. A trickle of the broth dripped from his chin. The bastard wasn't going to say a thing.

"You think Ryan sent her?" Vera's words were harsh. The woman pointed a slender finger at her. "Her? An angel?"

Rosa paused. Kate could feel the housekeeper's alarm. *"Si."*

Vera threw her napkin on the table. "This whole dinner is preposterous. Why don't you say something, Justus?"

He looked up. His blue eyes iced over. "Rosa is free to believe what she wishes."

Vera's mouth twisted. "You sit me at a table with your bastard and allow a crazy Mexican woman to spew garbage and say nothing. You have no respect for me. You don't care about me."

Vera started to rise.

"Sit down," Kate said.

The older woman paused. "What did you say to me?"

"Sit down." Kate pushed her chair back. "This is your table. I don't belong at it. I don't want to be here. The only thing that brought me here was justice. And I mean the word, not the man."

Rosa drew back. "But you are a guest."

"No, as Vera so accurately pointed out, I'm the bastard child. The one who has no place at this table. Let's stop pretending anything different."

"The hell you don't," Justus roared. He launched his spoon at the soup bowl. It clattered against the china and fell onto the tablecloth. "You are staying right there."

He used his good arm to point to the chair Kate had pushed forward.

"And you—" he pointed to Vera "—are going to be polite to my daughter."

Vera blanched but hesitated. "I don't march to your drum, Justus Mitchell. You may control everyone else. But not me."

He leveled her with his eyes. Kate watched as the woman visibly weakened under the duress of his stare. "Sit. Please."

Vera sank onto the upholstered chair.

Kate held on to the back of the chair. All she wanted to do was get out of here. She wondered if Rick would come get her. She didn't know where he was. Didn't have a number for him. Then she recognized where her thoughts were taking her. Did she really want a knight in red Mustang to swoop in and save her?

Hell, no.

She could handle it herself.

Vera spoke first. "Kate, please. I've forgotten my manners. Rosa has prepared a special meal. Surely we can put our feelings aside to enjoy something so generously wrought?"

Kate nodded. What else could she do? She hadn't eaten all day and had no way of leaving Cottonwood, save phoning Nellie. All she had to do was get through dinner. Besides, she didn't want to hurt Rosa's feelings.

Rick's grandmother pretended that Vera hadn't insulted her and handed Kate the napkin that had fallen to the floor and lifted her wineglass to refill it.

"No, thank you, Rosa." Kate rose. But not to leave. Instead she headed for the elegant sideboard holding assorted crystal decanters. She reached for a tumbler and a bottle of Scotch. She'd get through dinner with the help of Islay malt.

The first sip burned a path to her stomach. She nodded and returned to her seat. With a glint of approval in his eye, Justus lifted his own tumbler in her direction.

The approval made her wish she'd stuck with the cabernet.

Vera ignored him and placed her discarded napkin in her lap. She picked up the plate of corn cakes and passed them to Kate. "I'd love to hear about your salon. What is the name?"

Kate blinked. So they were going to pretend nothing had been said. Pretend she'd not just been called a bastard. She looked at Rosa as she lifted the stained towel from the table. The housekeeper shrugged. "Oh, um, it's called Fantabulous."

Vera passed her the container of tortillas. "Well, that's an unusual name. How did you come up with it?"

Kate took a tortilla and slathered it with verde sauce. "My partner came up with it. We didn't want a salon that played 'loons at daybreak.' We made it high energy. More Red Bull than green tea, if you know what I mean."

Even as Kate made polite conversation, she could feel the tension in the air. It was so thick that if an imaginary finger poked it, they'd all tumble to the side from the power of the explosion. But everyone ignored it. It was the strangest meal she'd ever had. And as she spooned the last bite of flan into her mouth, she looked at the portrait of her half brother.

If she'd been the slightest bit open to paranormal happenings, she would have sworn the boy winked at her.

But Kate didn't believe in divine intervention.

And she knew Ryan hadn't brought her to Cottonwood.

Money had. And that was something she could believe in.

CHAPTER NINE

KATE ARRIVED AT PHOENIX in a truck Justus had loaned her. Their conversation had been stilted at best, but her father had called his caretaker to bring the truck around. It was a huge Ford F-250 and ran like a tank. She'd had to slide the seat all the way forward and sit on a phone book, but she'd made it without wiping out any roadside bushes or boundary fences.

The first thing she saw as she drove up the lane was a huge lady climbing from a small car parked in front of the center. The woman's skirt rode up higher on one hip than the other and she visibly huffed as she balanced several boxes in her arms. She even carried a stapler under her chin.

Kate jumped from the truck, tucking the keys into the front pocket of her sweater. "Here. Let me help you with that."

"Oh, thank you, sugar." Puff. Puff. "I still gotta get that bag. Would you?"

Kate reached past the woman and scooped up a plastic bag full of office supplies. "I'm Kate, by the way."

"Trudy Cox," the woman huffed as she climbed the stairs. "I'm the GED instructor."

"Cool," she said as she followed the woman onto the wide porch and through the open front door. Again, the smell of cedar and pine tickled Kate's nose. It was a fresh scent, like a new car. She took in several deep breaths.

"Come on in here, sweet," Trudy said as she turned to the right and disappeared into the hallway. Kate followed her, entered a brand-new classroom that she hadn't seen the day before.

The room had pine walls covered with maps and grammar posters. A large whiteboard was mounted on one wall and the desktops shone like patent leather shoes on Easter Sunday. A potted plant draped itself over the massive desk where Trudy dumped the boxes she carried. "Whew. Those about killed me."

Kate set the plastic bag on one of the desk chairs. "Glad I only volunteered to bring the bag in. I haven't worked out in over a week. I can already feel the burn."

Trudy snorted as she began opening the boxes. "Girl, I could sit on you and nobody would find you for a week."

Kate laughed. "Nobody would come looking."

Trudy stopped and peered over her bifocals. Her black eyes pierced Kate. Maybe the woman had worked as an interrogator for the FBI or CIA. She looked as though she could smell bullshit from three counties over. "Huh. I haven't known you but a minute, yet somehow I didn't take you for a gal who'd feel sorry for herself."

The woman smiled in order to soften her words. All Kate could think was Trudy hadn't had dinner with Vera last night. Perhaps sitting at that table with a woman with an identity crisis and a biological father who annoyingly slurped his soup had given her license to throw herself a pity party, complete with streamers and a bad attitude.

"I'm over myself. Thanks for the reminder," she said,

lifting the bag from the chair. "I'm assisting Rick for the next couple of weeks. Anything I can do to help you while we're waiting on sleeping beauty?"

"Oh, he ain't sleeping, that's for sure. Probably out running or picking up this and that. He's always moving, that man," Trudy said, lifting several books from the box, squinting at the spines and setting them in two separate stacks. "But I guess I won't turn down any help. Would you mind alphabetizing these books on that bookshelf under the window?"

Kate took the first stack and headed to the bookshelf as Rick stepped inside the room. Uncanny how she felt him before he spoke.

"Morning, ladies." His words were like slipping on a favorite robe. Kate felt herself relax. This was even stranger than feeling him before seeing him. She never felt easy with a man. She felt angry, turned-on, interested, but never like she fit with him.

"You been out running in only that little bit of clothing? Are you crazy, boy? It's cold out."

Kate turned to look. Rick's nicely toned arms braced the door. He was wearing a sleeveless light blue workout shirt and dark blue running shorts. She could see some of his ink curving up his neck and scrolling down his arms. She wanted to know what his tats looked like. Wanted to trace them with her finger across his golden sweaty skin. The man made perspiration look sexy hot. Scratch that comfortable feeling. Replace with turned-on.

"Not that cold. You know I can't function without a run and a cup of coffee." His eyes swung from Trudy to Kate. "You're here early."

Kate tried to stop mentally undressing the man, but it was hard to stop imagining his flat stomach against hers, the way his thighs would nudge hers apart. She swallowed and diverted her thoughts from naughty to nice. "Thought I would make a good impression on my first day. And, like I wanted to stay any longer than I had to at the haunted mausoleum on the hill."

He tossed out a laugh. "So I'm guessing there were no family-fun pillow fights or board games at Cottonwood last night?"

Kate shot him a go-to-hell look. "Not exactly. More like *Jerry Springer.*"

Trudy kept pulling books from the boxes, but Kate could tell her ears were tuning in like a satellite dish.

So she looked at the woman pretending she wasn't soaking up the words between her and Rick. "Trudy, just so you know, I'm staying at Cottonwood with Justus and Vera Mitchell."

She didn't say she was staying because she was Justus's daughter. And no way her mouth even formed the word *blackmail.* She didn't know the GED instructor, but she knew Oak Stand. The town was talking about Katie Newman showing up and ensconcing herself in the mansion outside the city limits. No way in H-E-double hockey sticks the subject hadn't been discussed from the Dairy Barn to the hardware store. So she knew Trudy knew who she was. If she didn't, the woman had been in a hole for the past forty-eight hours.

"I'm Margo's cousin on her momma's side," Trudy said, as if that explained everything. And it did. That connection meant she knew all about Kate, Justus and every person in between.

"Heading to the shower. See you later."

Kate shifted her eyes from the overly wise ones of the GED instructor. She desperately tried not to imagine Rick standing naked beneath the stinging jets of the shower. She could just see him moving languidly as the water sheeted down his body, head tipped back as he lathered his hair.

"Kate?" Rick's voice interrupted.

"Hmm?"

"I asked if you'd had breakfast. Grandmother doesn't work on Wednesday mornings, so…"

"So?" Kate asked, rubbing her thumb along the creased spine of a thesaurus, still caught in the fantasy. "You asking me to—"

"Breakfast. That is if you want cinnamon rolls," he finished. She'd been hoping he'd say something more interesting, like scrubbing his back. Too bad. She'd rather have him than pastries. "Okay."

"I guess I just lost my helper, and don't think I didn't notice I didn't get an invitation to eat." Trudy said as she placed a stapler on her desk at a perfect ninety-degree angle from her tape dispenser.

Rick grinned. "I know Ernie got up and made you homemade biscuits this morning. I saw him at the gas station."

The older woman actually giggled. "You right, sugar. I got that man trained."

Kate rose, brushed off the new jeans she'd donned that morning, and gave Trudy a salute. "Don't worry, I eat fast. I'll be back to help you get set up. That is, if Rick doesn't need me for anything else."

She didn't intend her words to sound seductive, but they did.

Trudy raised her eyebrows then grinned as she plopped into her straight-backed wooden chair and started opening drawers. Rick simply vanished from the doorway.

She followed him down the hall and out the back

door. The wind had her snuggling into the fleece pullover she'd gotten on clearance for under twenty bucks. Rick should have been freezing, but he ignored the cold and jogged down the steps, hooking to the right toward a small cedar-and-stone bungalow that sat below the hill line.

"I never noticed this cottage yesterday," she called as she followed him. The house was a smaller version of the main building.

"Home sweet home," he called back over his shoulder. "Sorry I'm not waiting, but my pulse dropped and I'm cold."

She hopped across the stepping stones, glad she'd bought some inexpensive sneakers. Her flats would have been soaked by the cold morning dew.

Rick unlocked the door and ushered her inside.

A blast of warm air hit her, along with the smell of cinnamon.

"Holy cow," she breathed. His cottage was awesome. Modern mixed with Mission. Glass tabletops, streamlined aged wood and chrome lamps. It was Harley Davidson meets *This Old House*.

Rick shrugged. "I like it."

"Did you do this yourself? I mean, you're not gay are you?"

He shot her a look. "Are you serious?"

"Do you think I'm serious?"

He gave her a big, bad wolf smile. "I think you want me to show you."

She felt heat flood her body. It had nothing to do with the air blowing from the vents above her and everything to do with the Hispanic hunk who stood arm's length away. "I think you're a mind reader."

Kate didn't wait on him. She moved closer, allowing

her fingers to brush the Dri-FIT fabric of his shirt, to feel the power of the man beneath the clothes. She wanted to feel his bare flesh even if her stomach was gurgling over the prospect of cinnamon rolls.

But Rick didn't give her the opportunity. His mood shifted, and he caught her hands and gave them a shake. "Go pour yourself a cup of coffee while I grab a quick shower. Cinnamon rolls are in the warmer."

He gave each of her cold hands a brush of his lips before disappearing into the dark hallway behind her.

Well, hell. So much for scrubbing his back.

Or maybe…

But Kate nixed the idea. She wanted Rick, and any other time she'd do something about it, but she could see something held him back, so she resigned herself to eating.

The kitchen was galley-style, tucked beside a small breakfast nook. With light pine cabinets, black granite counters and stainless steel, upscale appliances, it was a masculine kitchen. But it was also well used. Rick liked to cook, if the complicated tools in the sink and the fluffy rolls were any indication.

She didn't drink coffee, so she opened the fridge to look for a soda. No soda. Lots of fruit, soy milk and organic eggs. The man was a health freak. She shivered and grabbed a carton of organic orange juice with extra pulp.

By the time she'd consumed almost two cinnamon rolls and a glass of orange juice, Rick appeared smelling clean and filling up the small kitchen.

"These cinnamon rolls are, like, really good," she managed to say around the last bite.

"Thanks. Rosa taught me."

He reached past her to open the fridge. She didn't

bother moving. Better chance of him rubbing up against her. She felt primed for him. What better way to forget the knots in her life than a hot session of sex with a fine specimen of manhood? For an hour—or if she were lucky, two—she could forget and simply feel.

He sidestepped her and grabbed a carton of soy milk.

"They say that stuff is full of estrogen. Sure you really want to drink that?"

He poured a glass and took a big gulp before smiling at her. "I'm not afraid to get in touch with my feminine side."

"I'll let you get in touch with my feminine side if you want to," Kate said, sliding against him like a cat.

He grabbed her arm. "Hey, about that. You know I find you hot—"

She froze. "I can hear a *but* in that sentence."

He set the glass on the counter. "Thing is, Kate, I feel not myself around you, and you make me want to toss out the promise I made to myself."

"Don't tell me you've made some sort of vow of chastity or something. Because that's so wasteful. And so passé."

His eyes shuttered. "It's not a vow of chastity. It's a promise to not engage in casual sex."

Kate cocked her head. She'd never heard of a guy actually wanting a relationship before hitting the sheets. Okay, she was sure there were guys like that. Sensitive guys. Guys who spent their Friday nights watching noir films and sipping espresso. Or guys who spent their weekends at self-help retreats. "Why?"

He gave a humorless bark of laughter. "Do you know how many women I slept with when I was rolling with my gang? I can't even count. When I wanted one, I took her. Didn't matter her name. Or her feelings. Or how wasted she was. I used her."

Kate swallowed. The juice felt sour on her stomach. "Oh."

"I'm not that man anymore. When I have sex, it will be with someone I care about. Someone I'm in a relationship with. Someone I have a future with. No more flings."

His words jabbed at her heart. For some reason, it hurt. So she crossed her arms over her chest as if that would protect her. She wanted to say something funny, saucy, but couldn't think for the life of her how to respond. He didn't want to have sex with her and he didn't care about her. Which one was worse?

He swallowed. "I shouldn't have invited you down here. It was a mixed signal. Things are hot between us. We don't need to stoke any embers."

Kate wrinkled her nose. "What? You think I have no self-control? You think I jump every guy I see and beg him to do me?"

"No. That's not what I—"

"'Cause I can resist you, buddy. I can." She moved away from him, toward the door.

He didn't say anything further. Just tore a roll from the pan and took a bite.

She cocked an eyebrow at him. "I'm surprised you eat that. From the looks of your fridge, I'd expect you to be eating tuna fish or coddled egg whites."

He smiled. It made him look as yummy as the sweet he crammed in his mouth, and it made Kate's stomach twist with regret. "Yeah, but some things are worth it, you know?"

She studied him framed against the sophisticated backdrop of the kitchen. He'd pulled on worn jeans and a tight long-sleeved Henley shirt. His chest was like a fullback's, his legs those of a runner. He was golden, dark and decadent. What a waste.

"Yeah, I know."

He smiled.

"Just so you know," she said, crossing her arms again. "I don't believe in love. And if I did, two weeks is not enough time to fall in love with you."

He choked on his soy milk. "Who said anything about love?"

"No one," she said, turning into the living room. "See you at the center. Thanks for breakfast."

She didn't wait for a response. She left. It was the only way she could uphold her promise not to jump his bones. Maybe cinnamon rolls made her horny. Or maybe it was simply Rick.

Kate stomped up the graded hill. She was a little pissed and she wasn't sure why. She thought it was because the man had hurt her feelings. Made her feel raunchy. Like trailer trash. Like the Katie Newman she could have been. Living hard and being easy. But she wasn't that person. She'd done better and she had standards. She didn't have to throw herself at a man to get laid. Usually, they came sniffing around her.

Morals and principles. Who needed them? Did anyone really pay attention to them in today's world? Please. Even the pious and righteous bent definitions to meet their needs. Kate believed in being honest. With herself and others. She wanted Rick. She liked the way he made her feel, even if it scared her a little. Okay, a lot. But she wasn't avoiding him or the feelings he stirred in her.

She was being true to herself.

She was being the Kate she'd chosen to be.

She had a full life. She had friends. She lived by her own rules and answered to no one. At least, she had until Justus had flipped the blackmail table on her.

"Katie Newman!" a voice shrieked from her left. "Holy heck! I haven't seen you since that Cowboy Mouth concert at Cooley's where we danced on the pool tables."

Kate watched as the former head cheerleader for the Oak Stand Rebels nearly tripped on a large iron ore rock beside the path. Tamara Beach was as clumsy as ever. How she'd managed to nab the prime spot on the squad was a mystery. Could have been because her mother was the PE teacher and had counted the votes, but that was only Kate's guess. Tamara still had the naturally wavy blond locks that fell past her shoulders, but the boobs that sat high on her slight frame were absolutely store-bought.

"Hey, Tam." Kate hugged her then stepped back. "You look amazing. I like the rack."

Her former going-out buddy laughed. "Thanks, they're almost paid for. And you don't look too bad yourself. I'm digging the streaks in your hair, Katie."

"Kate."

"Oh, yeah, I forgot." She cocked her head like a terrier sniffing out a rat. "Oh, my gosh, you know what?"

Kate suffered a flash of dread. Tamara always had something cooking. And whatever it was often got her into hot water. "What?"

"Crater Moon is playing at Cooley's tonight. You remember that drummer, right? He was so into you. You gotta come with me. Everybody will be there."

"Well, I—"

"You're staying for two weeks, right?" Tamara blushed, obviously realizing she'd admitted to knowing about Kate and the Mitchells. "What I mean is, I heard in town you were staying for a while. What's with that, anyway? You hate it here."

Kate felt Rick before she saw him. Again. He ascended the path to where she stood. "Umm…it's complicated. And kinda private."

Her friend averted her eyes and looked embarrassed. "Oh."

She hadn't really worked out what to say to people about why she was in Oak Stand. She thought that maybe she could get through the two weeks without having to venture out much. Not going to happen. She needed a cover story. Or maybe she would tell everyone to mind their own damned business.

"Well, what are you doing at Phoenix? Does it have to do with gang stuff or something?"

Kate shook her head. "No, I'm helping Rick with the center while I'm in town. Doing some…consulting."

"I thought someone said you owned a salon out in Vegas," Tamara said before catching Rick out of the corner of her eye. Kate prayed he wouldn't say anything that would call her bluff on the consulting thing.

He stopped beside her. She could feel his heat even in the cool breeze. "Hey, Tamara, did you bring the forms? I've got the planters ready to go."

"Silly man. All work and no play." She tapped him lightly on the arm and Kate could see her friend was into him. Of course she was—what warm-blooded single woman wouldn't be? "An awesome band is playing at Cooley's tonight and I'm trying to talk Katie, I mean Kate, into coming. You should come with us. It'll be cool."

He shook his head. "I got too much going on, but you girls go on ahead."

Tamara turned a full-wattage smile on him. "Oh, come on. This is your last chance. The guys arrive Thursday and you won't be able to get away. Dude, you never do anything but work."

Her pretty baby-blue eyes pleaded with Rick.

"Sorry, I can't," he said, sliding past them. "When you're done here we can look at those planters and see if they'll meet the green initiative. I want to keep that grant."

Tamara rolled her eyes as he turned his back to them and jogged up the path. "He's such a party pooper."

At that point, Kate had to wonder about Tamara's intentions toward Rick. Her former friend had always been open for fun with the right guy. She looked like she had her eye on Rick, and something about it made Kate feel a little sick. Tamara was a natural. Breezy manner, friendly smile and a string of broken hearts behind her, she partied, cajoled and danced her way through life. And had a lot of fun doing it. But he wasn't up for a casual relationship, was he?

Still, Tamara lived in Oak Stand. Kate didn't.

"So what's up with the grant and planters?" Kate asked, pulling the discussion away from Rick and going to Cooley's.

"Oh, I'm with the Farm Extension Bureau. I'm going to work with the clients at the center on nutrition and cultivation. We're doing outreach programs now, not just schools and stuff. We're actually going to help with a garden here as a sort of therapy. Rick was insistent on growing stuff."

"Oh," Kate said, trying to envision Tamara in overalls and work boots. Tam preferred less over more when it came to clothing. Case in point, she wore a thin long-sleeved T with a plunging neckline that hugged her generous curves.

"I always say, getting in touch with the earth is getting in touch with yourself." Tamara smiled as if she'd imparted the most sacred of insights, one that made Kate want to snort.

"Yeah," Kate said, stifling the need to make masturbation jokes. "I'm not sure about tonight."

Her taking off would likely make Justus hopping mad. Then again, the idea of a repeat of last night's dinner made her skin crawl. Besides, Rick had made her feel crappy about herself. As if wanting a man was a bad thing. She didn't have to sit around and moon over him like a lovesick calf. Nothing like hitting a bar to stroke her ego and take her mind off Rick, Justus and her flailing business.

"Come on, it'll be such a blast to hang with you. We used to have so much fun." Tamara's baby blues worked on Kate.

"Okay. Sure."

Tamara squealed and clapped her hands. "Yay."

"I don't have a car. Can you pick me up?"

Her friend nodded like one of those bobble-head dogs in the back of car windows. "I'll pick you up at 8:00."

Just enough time to have dinner with Justus and Vera. Damn. Another strained meal. Her stomach pinched. God, she wanted to go home to Vegas. Instead, she'd be hitting a honky-tonk.

"I'll be ready."

CHAPTER TEN

COOLEY'S STANK OF STALE cigarettes and spilled beer. In other words, it smelled like a honky-tonk and was oddly comforting to Kate. Country music ricocheted off a tinny ceiling accompanied by the crack of pool balls and the laughter of folks unwinding after a day's labor. For a weekday night, things were hopping.

"Hey, there's Brent. He's seen you," Tamara said, pointing one French-tipped nail toward the crowded bar.

Great. The first guy she'd gone all the way with. Horny and hot, Brent Hamilton acted like God's gift to Oak Stand's womankind. She'd say he was delusional, but he did fill out a pair of jeans nicely. "Well, don't point at him."

She had to yell into Tamara's ear. The place was loud and redneck rowdy. Just the reason why Kate felt safe here. This place, she could manage. Justus, Rick, Oak Stand? Not so much.

"Let's get a table near the band," Tamara yelled.

As they slithered through the crowd, Kate felt the eyes of the establishment upon her. She caught the eye of a girl who'd grown up in a trailer down from hers. The eye of a guy who'd spilled Kool-Aid on her lap in the second grade. The eyes of guys she'd never met. Girls she'd never pissed off. Everyone watched her as she swayed and bobbed her way toward an empty table.

They may have looked because she'd painted violet streaks in her hair. Or because she'd pulled on a yellow, satin halter top over skintight leggings. Or because her sweet Manolos made her look four inches taller. Thank God she'd squeezed them in her luggage at the last minute. They made her feel more powerful, like she could manage whatever came her way. She tossed her shoulders back.

"Hey, Tam. Who's your friend?"

Kate glanced over. "You know who I am."

Brent showed his polished veneers. "'Course I do. But it's been a while, Katie."

"Kate," she muttered under her breath as she sank onto a chair that had likely been used in a bar fight recently, if the torn seat and scratched legs were any indication.

"So what you drinkin', ladies?" Brent asked, spinning toward the equally brutalized bar. He waved old Bones Stewart over to fill his order.

"I'll take a Bud Light," Tamara called, raking her eyes up and down Brent like a prison guard about to do a cavity search. She lowered her voice. "Damn, but that's a fine piece of ass. Wasn't he your first?"

Kate sighed. "I don't want to talk about Brent."

Brent called over his shoulder. "Hey, Kate, pick your poison."

"Jack and Coke," Kate hollered before looking back at Tamara. "Have you two hooked up?"

Her friend shook her head. It caused her boobs to jiggle and three men standing at the bar nearly threw their backs out trying to get a second look. "Nah. He's my type, but it never worked out."

"Hmm. I thought he was like the DMV. You took a number and waited your turn."

Brent plopped a beer down in front of Tamara before pulling up a chair and plunking his tight buns on it. He slid a glass toward Kate. "Don't know why I asked. I know what you like."

His words carried extra meaning, but she chose to ignore him. Instead, she raised a toast. "When in Oak Stand."

The whiskey and soda tasted like a homecoming, especially with the Zac Brown Band blowing up the speakers and farm boys clad in tight Wranglers surrounding her. Kate Newman was finally home. Whether she wanted to be there or not.

"That's my girl." Brent didn't waste time. He was a man who always knew what he wanted. He liked whiskey, women and redneck honky-tonks. He was positively medieval. He might as well drag a heavy sword behind him. He'd look fine in a suit of armor.

Tamara edged forward, propping her cleavage on the table and twirling her platinum curls. "Brent, you wanna dance? I love this song."

He tore his gaze from assessing Kate and looked at Tamara. "I really—"

"Oh, come on, cowboy. I'll let you grab my butt." Tamara pulled Brent's hand from where it rested on the table and tugged hard with a won't-take-no-for-an-answer gleam in her eye. "Katie doesn't mind."

Brent's shoulders sank. She could see it in his eyes. He couldn't think up one good excuse not to dance. "Okay. Be back in a minute, Katie."

She watched as her friend pulled the former all-state quarterback to the crowded dance floor.

"Kate." She didn't have to mutter it this time. Rick had.

Her Latin fantasy took the chair Brent had vacated,

and it both aggravated and thrilled her to her toes. She'd never envisioned him in a backwater dive. Something about him seemed not necessarily above such a scene, but surely out of place just the same.

"I thought you were busy." She swirled the whiskey in the glass. Didn't seem to be much soda in it as she tossed the last of it down. She could feel the warmth of the liquor flooding her body, making her feel loose.

"Yeah," was all he said.

She couldn't sit there and look at forbidden fruit without misbehaving, so she set her empty glass on the table. "You wanna shoot pool?"

His dark eyes met hers. She couldn't read them. "Yeah, sure. But I'm warning you. I'm good."

God, she so wanted to know how good Rick Mendez was, but according to him, that wasn't going to happen. So she'd have to settle for kicking his ass at the table. "I've never backed down from a challenge."

He grunted, which wasn't sexy. But somehow this man made everything tempting.

She rose and moved toward where the pool tables sat in a section adjacent to the bar. Kate motioned Rick to get them a table while she collected another drink.

While waiting for her order she watched Brent dance with Tamara. Her friend practiced all the moves she'd seen in *Dirty Dancing* on the contractor. It would have been slightly pathetic if Brent didn't have a bit of a gleam in his eye. Tamara might get her hookup tonight, after all.

By the time Kate made it to the table where Rick stood twisting the chalk onto a battered cue stick, she'd nearly finished the whiskey sour she'd ordered.

"Here you go."

Rick took the drink. "Ginger ale? With a cherry?"

"I told Bones you like girly drinks."

He smiled and it slid down her body and curled around parts that were better left covered in public. "Ready to get your ass kicked?"

"That's my line." The rack was smudged from decades of use, but worked as well as the day Bones had bought it. She racked the balls and centered the faded cue ball on the mark.

"You wanna break?" she asked, finishing off the last of her drink.

His smile didn't curl anything this time—just made her wonder about the man sliding the stick between his fingers like he belonged on ESPN. "Are we playing for anything?"

She licked her lips, tasting the banana lip balm she'd applied before walking in the place. "You wanna play for…"

"A kiss."

"You think that's a good idea?"

He shook his head. "No, but it has to be something I want. You have to kiss me if I win."

"What if I—"

"You won't," he said, lowering his body toward the table. In one fluid motion, the balls spun to the corners in a dizzying explosion of color. Uh-oh. He hadn't lied when he'd said he was good. Suddenly she was happy. She rubbed her lips together again. She hoped he liked the tropics, because her kiss would take him there.

As RICK SANK SHOT AFTER SHOT, he silently beat himself up for coming to Cooley's and making such a stupid wager. He'd already stated his position earlier in the day, so why was he here?

Hours ago, he'd eaten his dinner and told himself

that what Kate Newman did at Cooley's was none of his damn business. He wasn't going to think about her sitting on a bar stool, chatting with some rough-and-ready cowboy. He wasn't going to imagine her in someone else's arms, spinning around the dance floor or shrugging out of a tight shirt and jeans. Kate didn't belong to him.

But regardless, thirty minutes later, he found himself pulling on his "going out" jeans and digging cologne from the back of his bathroom cabinet. He'd actually debated which colorless shirt made him look better. Hell.

What was it about Kate that was different from all the other women he'd encountered in Oak Stand? He'd resisted every woman who'd come to him looking for a hard man and a good time. Why couldn't he resist this one?

He slid the stick between his fingers and took his shot. He missed.

Kate beckoned a worn-out-looking waitress toward her. "I'll have another whiskey sour while I beat this guy. And tell Bones to give me the good stuff, not that crap he used last time."

The waitress rolled her eyes but nodded.

Kate moved toward him, brushing against him as she eyed her shot. "Did you miss that on purpose?"

"Of course not," he lied, enjoying her bottom brushing against the fly of his jeans. His hands literally shook as he forced himself to remain cool and ignore the flare-up igniting inside him.

Kate lined up the shot and sank her striped three ball in the side pocket. She was good, but not good enough to beat him.

So he let her win.

And that seemed to tick her off. Her eyes glittered as she sank the eight ball in the corner pocket and dropped her cue stick in the stand between the three tables. She walked a little wobbly in her heels. She'd had way too much to drink.

She placed a finger in the center of his chest. "Why did you let me win?"

He regarded her like a chocolate lover would a box of Godiva. Sweet temptation stirred his blood, swirled around in his pelvis and heated him. "Because if I kissed you, I might not stop. And I really want to respect myself, Kate."

Her mouth opened. Then shut. "Then why the hell did you come here?"

He wished he knew the answer to that one.

Kate's face softened. A seductive smile hovered on her lips. She pressed the accusing finger against his chest and allowed her hand to slide to his shoulder. "So what would you do if I kissed you anyway?"

He looked around the crowded bar. Every now and then, people blatantly stared at the ex–gang member shooting pool with the bad girl come home. No one had bothered them during their game, nor had Tamara or Brent appeared. Just him and Kate, in their own little world. He moved closer to her, smelled the spiciness of her breath, the subtlety of her perfume. "I might slide my hands down to your tight ass and pull you up against me. Then kiss my way down that pretty neck till I get to those   sweet little—"

She pressed a finger to his lips silencing him. "Or?"

He forced a bark of laughter. He wanted her so bad. Just a taste. Electricity thrummed between them, and everyone else in the bar faded away.

Kate didn't give him time to answer. She lifted onto her toes and kissed him.

He closed his eyes and savored the feel of her body against his. He felt like a man dying of thirst tasting water for the first time. He knotted his fists before reaching for her waist and stepped back. "Don't."

"I guess now I know what you'd do." The edge in her voice smacked him.

He flinched. He'd made it worse. Now she was hurt and a hurt Kate seemed a most dangerous thing.

He directed his gaze away to the writhing dance floor. It looked like a full-on line dance was in progress. "How about we forget pool and dance?"

She shrugged. "Whatever."

Kate spun a little too fast on her high heels, teetering before correcting herself and heading for the dance floor without looking back. He handed the cue stick to a bearded guy waiting his turn and followed her. As he stepped onto the scuffed oak floor, a slow country song started. He thought it was Keith Urban. Haunting and seductive.

Shit.

"You two-step, cowboy?" Kate asked. But she wasn't asking him. She'd asked Brent, who was heading toward the bar and a smiling Tamara.

"You know I do." Brent's nostrils actually flared as Kate crooked a finger at him.

Kate looked Rick right in the eye and said, "Then let's get it on, if you're man enough."

Brent feathered his brown hair with one hand and grinned. "And you know the answer to that one, too."

Rick's fist knotted again but this time for a different reason. He watched as Kate pressed her finger into the cleft of Brent's chin, then smiled the kind of smile that would get a girl in trouble. Brent didn't waste time gathering Kate into his arms and sliding smoothly across the dance floor.

Rick stood there for a full minute, feeling like a loser, watching them sway and twirl around the floor before turning toward a now unsmiling Tamara.

He sat on the empty stool next to her.

"Vintage Katie," Tamara muttered. "You wanna make her jealous? I'm good at the two-step and better at making girlfriends mad."

"She's not my anything," Rick lied, trying to pretend it didn't bother him seeing Kate's whiskey-bright eyes glitter beneath the Christmas lights strung among the beams above the dance floor. Her hands laced through Brent's hair, and that action made his blood boil.

Suddenly, she and Brent disappeared. His eyes scanned the crowd until he found them, in the process of getting tangled in each other's arms, pressed against an old pinball machine.

Oh, hell no. He moved toward them, jealousy pecking at him like a hen at seed. No way he was going to sit there and watch her wrap herself around another man. Especially since she was doing it out of anger at him.

He grabbed Kate's arm as Brent lowered his head toward her. "Let's go."

"Hey," Brent said, lifting his head and tightening his hold on Kate's waist. "Back off, dude. The lady can choose for herself."

"Yeah, I can choose for myself." Kate's words were slurred.

Rick looked at her. "You're drunk."

She twisted her arm from him while at the same time moving away from Brent. "The hell I am. I never get drunk."

Brent eyed her and nodded. "Yeah, she's drunk."

Kate crossed her arms. "I hate this damned place. I hate everybody in it, and I don't need you two assholes to tell me what to do. I'm not that stupid poor girl anymore. I say who and when. I make my own decisions."

Neither Rick nor Brent responded. Kate's gaze roved the honky-tonk wildly as if looking for a way out. She looked on the verge of coming unraveled. "I want to go home."

"Let me take you," Rick said, taking her by the arm and giving Brent a look that brooked no argument. He didn't want to fight the man, but he'd do it if he had to. Brent had a good three inches and thirty pounds on him, but Rick had grown up on the streets. He fought dirty.

But Brent nodded. "Go with him, Katie."

Kate looked at Rick, eyes burning. "He doesn't want me."

Her words ripped through him and he felt as though he'd been kicked in the gut.

He was saved from answering by Brent. The man stooped and planted a kiss on Kate's forehead. "Everybody wants you, Katie. Go home, sweetheart."

KATE COULDN'T EVEN MANAGE a wave to Tamara as they pulled away from Cooley's. "Why did I come here tonight?"

Rick shifted gears and ricocheted out of the gravel parking lot. "To get away from Justus. To get away from everything that makes you feel."

"Thank you, Dr. Phil," she said, slipping off her shoes. "I acted like an idiot."

"No one paid that much attention."

"Of course they did. Half that bar couldn't wait to watch me fall on my face. Or my ass."

Kate felt mooney. Light-headed. Of course, she *was* smashed. She could count on one hand the number of times she'd gotten drunk. Most of those times had been in college before she'd had the sense to know she needed to be in control. At all times.

"Don't you dare throw up in this car," Rick said.

"As if," she said, before hiccupping. God, was she drunk.

The moon played over the fallow fields, highlighting a random Angus cow or forlorn haystack. Trees flashed by in between fields and Kate felt miserable.

So she laid her head down in Rick's lap.

"What are you doing?" he asked. She felt his flinch.

"Resting."

He took one hand off the wheel and tugged at her shoulder. "Get up. You're going to hit the gear shift."

She looked up at him. His jaw was clenched. She liked the way it looked, so she reached up and traced the pulse throbbing there. "I won't hit it."

"It can't be comfortable lying over the console."

"I'm good." She slid her hand from his jaw to the collar of his tight T-shirt. It was gray and lifeless, like all the others he wore. But the pulse that beat beneath her fingers was very much alive. She smoothed the fabric over his chest. It was broad and hard, just like his stomach.

"God, Kate. Please."

She could feel his erection by her ear. She so wanted to touch him. Wrap her fingers around him. Her damned mouth watered at the thought. She slid her hand lower still.

His caught it. "Kate. Respect my decision."

She jerked from his lap and threw herself across the

car to the bucket seat. Her side hurt from where it had pressed against the console. "You're a tease."

His fingers clenched the steering wheel, knuckles white in the faint moonlight. "I'm not the one touching and kissing and—"

"Bull. You show up at the bar, looking like a present for me, brushing against me and teasing me with the chance of a kiss. Then you chastise me for wanting you. For doing what I know you want me to do. What kind of game are *you* playing?"

He glared at her. "I'm not playing games. That was you sliding your ass against me, licking your lips and slithering all over me. Then you went off with some other guy to punish me."

"Why did you come tonight? You said you had things to do."

She knew he'd come for her alone, and that made her blood simmer. If he wasn't going to do anything other than make her want him so bad she lost all reason, did things she'd never consider, like drown a fifth of whiskey and seduce Brent Hamilton, why bother?

"I wanted to do what Tamara suggested—go out while I still had the chance."

"Right. Whatever." She folded her arms across her breasts and watched the road's broken yellow lines rush toward them as they headed for Cottonwood. If he wanted to lie, let him lie.

"Okay, fine. You want the truth? Well, here it is. I can't stay away from you." He turned his head to look at her. She saw naked emotion in his eyes. Desire. Torment. "I couldn't stop myself from going tonight."

"Then why are you stopping this from happening? Why can't we have sex, please each other? Life is tough. You gotta take pleasure where you can."

"I stopped living that way." He paused before letting out a breath. She could see he was grappling with the right words. "I can't go back to the man I was."

"It's not using me if I want it as bad as you do."

He closed his eyes briefly before refocusing on the highway. "So *you* want to use *me?*"

At that, she fell silent. Did she want to use him because she felt something for him, or because he was forbidden? Or maybe both? But deep down in places she suppressed, she knew that Rick meant more than a standard affair. Normally, that would make her run from him instead of run toward him.

The alcohol had dulled her senses. She wouldn't allow herself to feel more than lust or friendship toward Rick. She couldn't. She wasn't wired like other girls. "No. Maybe. I don't know. All I know is that it could be good between us."

He nodded. "No doubt. But you use sex as a weapon, Kate. It shouldn't be a tool to control people."

Even through the haze of whiskey, she felt as though she'd been slapped. His words fell hard against her, stilling her, making her face the fact she did use sex as a way to maintain control. She always had. Sex made her feel powerful. Loved. What a sad notion.

Before she could give it more thought, Cottonwood appeared like an apparition in the night. Rick hooked a right through the gates.

Silence reigned as the car hurtled toward the huge white house. Kate was glad they were almost there. She needed to get out of the damn car. Get away from Rick and his accusations. Away from the guilt he made her feel. Away from the doubt he'd awakened in her. At that moment, she really wanted to hit him.

When Rick killed the engine, the back porch light went on.

Kate blinked at the brightness.

"What the—" She started as a man in a wheelchair emerged in the glow of the porch light. "You've got to be kidding me."

The Twilight Zone theme song played in her head. Her bio dad was waiting up for her like she was some fifteen-year-old home from her first date?

Her anger at Rick boiled over onto Justus. She felt as if ropes had been placed on her and they were slowly and surely strangling her. Once again, another man tried to control her, tried to tell her who she should be, tried to layer guilt on her.

She tasted bitterness in her mouth as she climbed from the car. The world rocked a bit, so she waited for it to steady. It didn't. She moved toward the man in the wheelchair, nearly tripping on the stupid herb stuff planted between the pavers. She righted herself, but still listed. She looked Justus straight in the eye and in her best smart-ass voice drawled, "What's up, Pops?"

CHAPTER ELEVEN

HER FATHER DIDN'T LOOK AT HER. He looked at Rick. "What the hell do you mean bringing her home at 2:00 in the morning in this condition?"

Kate didn't give Rick time to answer. "If I had my way, I wouldn't be home at all. I'd be in his bed. And, by the way, this is not my home."

She rocked a bit as the dark night swirled around her. Why the devil had she continued ordering whiskey? She stifled a belch as Rick shut the driver's door and came around to stand beside her.

Justus puffed up like a blowfish. "Right now, this is your home. And I am—"

"Not going to go there tonight," Rick finished, his voice soft but firm. He put a hand on the small of her back.

Before she could think better of it, she leaned into him, allowed him to support her, even though it made her angry he thought he had to intervene.

"Kate, come inside," Justus demanded, banging his good hand on the wheelchair tray.

"Don't tell me what to do," she said, aware she sounded more like a teenager confronting her dad after a night of necking at the drive-in than a grown woman. Her stomach lurched against her ribs.

"I'll damned well tell you what I want to. I'm your—"

A brittle laugh escaped her. "You want to play daddy now? Tonight? I'm nearly thirty-one years old, Justus. Too late, buddy. You had your chance and you didn't take it. Or have you forgotten that day? That would have been a good time to play daddy."

Her mind tumbled back to the day he'd rebuked her in front of all those people. Pain struck fast and fierce, boiling up inside her, banging against her heart. She couldn't stop the rage. "How could you do that? I was *nine*. Nine years old. Do you know what it did to me? You are cruel and the worst person I can even—"

"Kate," Rick said. "Stop. It's not the time."

"I hate you," she said, narrowing her eyes at the man who'd hurt her so many years ago. "I will never be your daughter, so you might as well save us the drama, give me the money and let me go back to Vegas."

Kate could feel the contents of her stomach rising, burning a path up her throat, through her nostrils. As the hurt and anger from long ago came forth, so did the whiskey. She broke away from them and ran for the garden behind the house.

She made it in time to vomit on Vera's emerging flowers.

She sank to her knees and let her body rid itself of the poison.

Then, for the first time in a very long time, Kate cried. She cried for the little girl she'd once been, a little girl who had stupid dreams of a family, of a room with a bed that didn't poke her with its broken springs, of a dinner not served on a TV tray. Dreams of shiny dolls and brand-new books. Thanksgiving dinners and Christmas Eve services. Good-night kisses and baby brothers with toothy grins. Then she cried for the woman she'd become. A woman who held so fast to the pain of the past that she couldn't see the present with a man. Any man.

And she wept because she didn't know what else to do.

Jeremy was wrong. Kate the Great couldn't fix what was broken this time.

RICK GLARED AT JUSTUS. The bastard didn't know when to quit. And neither did his daughter.

"I don't want her around you," Justus said, rolling forward. His thinning hair gleamed silver in the light of the moon. Shadows withdrew and emerged again in wicked patches of darkness as tree branches swayed with the stirring of wind.

"You're telling me to stay away from her? You sent me to get her, if you recall."

"I remember," the old man said, halting his chair directly in front of him, "but that doesn't mean I want you sniffing around her. Anyone with eyes can see what's going on between you. She's not—"

"The sort of girl to be with riffraff like me?" Rick couldn't stop himself from baring his teeth at Justus. He wasn't good enough for the daughter Justus had thrown away? The irony didn't skip past him.

"Come now, Enrique, don't play the poor servant boy with me."

"Don't treat me like one."

"Just because you feel subpar does not mean the world views you as such."

The man's words seared Rick. "Who said I view myself below any man?"

Justus shrugged. "It's evident in the way you react. If you paint yourself in that light, you should expect to be treated as less than what you are."

Anger boiled over. The old man was cruel sometimes, but there was an elemental truth to his words. Rick had been raised to accept he was of the servile class. His people were washerwomen, maids, gardeners and migrant workers. It did not matter that he was born an American citizen. In many people's eyes he was an intruder, unwelcome and unwanted like weeds in the cracks of a sidewalk.

Justus's mouth tilted in a parody of the Cheshire cat, his hand mimicking the animal's tail as he flicked it toward Rick. "I don't cotton to stereotypes. I respect the man you've become."

"Justus, I—"

"No, we won't speak any more of it."

Rick glanced away toward the swishing bush next to the Japanese maple, accepting the truth in Justus's words. He knew the old man had a healthy dose of fear and admiration for him. Rick had earned it many times over, doing what many would consider fearless. Or stupid. Depended on how one looked at it. But he'd helped Justus correct his past mistakes. All because the man had cared enough to save a stupid gangbanger and give him a second chance.

And Rick had returned that favor. One night, a little more than two years ago, Rick had taken the gun from Justus's hand. Broken and beaten, the old man had wanted to face death more than he'd wanted to face life. Rick had pulled him back to the world Ryan had wanted to save. He'd given Justus something to cling to—Ryan's legacy. Phoenix. Now the man wanted more. He wanted a daughter who was too wounded to live up to what he wished.

"Kate isn't the right woman for you."

Rick jerked his head up. "Why the hell not?"

"Both of you have strong personalities. It won't work. You need someone soft. Like Vera."

"I'll choose the woman for me, and I'll be damned if you tell me who I can or can't have a relationship with. If I want Kate, I'll take her."

Rick would never admit he was trying like hell to avoid tumbling into bed with Kate. He wouldn't give Justus the satisfaction of knowing he wasn't going to take his relationship with Kate any further.

Kate couldn't be the right woman for him, no matter how well she fit against him, no matter how right it felt every time she appeared like a lovely blossom on a deadened tree. She couldn't be the right woman for him because she was leaving in less than two weeks. And two weeks wasn't enough time to take a risk. Two weeks wasn't worth compromising all that he'd become. Not for a few nights of pleasure.

So he'd be content to play the upstanding good guy, Kate's guide, her protector through the minefield of living with Justus. The ties that bound him would be ones of honor.

Not of selfish impulse.

There was no future with Justus Mitchell's illegitimate daughter. That much was certain.

Justus interrupted his thoughts. "Hell, I've never tried to tell you what to do, boy."

At that statement, Rick lifted one eyebrow.

"Okay, maybe a time or two, but I think it's a bad idea to see Kate as part of your future." Justus curled his left hand into a fist and looked at Rick as if the Lord had spoken.

"Maybe I should say the same to you."

Justus's bushy eyebrows knitted into a furious frown.

"What do you mean? She's here, isn't she? She wants my money, doesn't she? Then she'll have to deal with me."

"Maybe so, but you're not mending any fences trying to control her the way you are."

"So what should I have done? Wired her the money with no questions asked? I wanted to have a chance to fix my past. Ever since I lost Ryan and found God, that's all I've wanted. Just to fix my past."

"Then why haven't you already fixed this with Kate? I ran all over Texas delivering checks to widows and selling land back to people you'd virtually stolen it from, but you don't bother to call your own daughter? What the hell did you do to her when she was a child, Justus?" Rick didn't understand this man, his motivations.

Justus's eyes shuttered. "That doesn't concern you. Let me fix this my way."

Rick knew it would do no good to continue arguing. "Fine, but remember this—Kate's like a dog that's been kicked, and you wore the boots. You can't expect her to come running to you and lick your hand like nothing happened. Your boot left a mark, old man."

Justus reversed his chair, settling it against the ramp leading to the back porch. "Not much I can do about the past."

"No, not much any of us can do about it. Just move forward. But you can't control Kate." Rick caught a glimpse of Vera slipping out the door and heading for the garden. He pulled his keys from his pocket and turned toward the car still sitting in the drive with the headlights on.

He needed space. He needed to think. He couldn't do that with Kate around. Vera would take care of her tonight. Tomorrow, he might have his resolve back in place where she was concerned. Stress on the *might* because deep down he knew Kate had already sucked him in and he was losing the will to fight her deadly combination of vulnerability and blatant sex appeal.

No matter what he told himself.

COOL HANDS PUSHED THE HAIR from her face as a damp washcloth appeared at Kate's elbow.

"Never as good coming up as it is going down." Vera's words held no judgment. For that, Kate was grateful.

"Tastes like I licked the bottom of someone's boot. Someone who works in a pasture." She took the cloth and wiped her face. Her stomach still rolled, but she felt enormously better.

"You can brush your teeth when you get inside."

"I don't want to go inside. I want to go back to Vegas and pretend none of this ever happened. This was a mistake." Kate couldn't believe she'd admitted to screwing up. Especially to the one woman who wished Kate would pack her bags and leave.

"I can't say I blame you. None of this has been easy, has it? Then again, once you start something, you can't leave it unfinished," Vera said. Kate immediately thought of Rick. If she left tomorrow, she'd leave things unfinished between them, too.

She turned to look at the woman who'd brought her small comfort. Vera wore cotton pajamas that likely cost too much to be worn kneeling on the dirty pavers of the garden. Her hair was loose about her shoulders, her face free of cosmetics, making her look both older and younger at the same time. Crow's-feet crinkled at the corners of brown eyes that were indecipherable in the faint light of the night.

"Must feel good to get it all out, though," Vera said, a soft sigh escaping her as she settled on her heels.

Kate wasn't sure whether she meant the liquor or the rage at her father. But either way, Vera was right. "Yes, it does."

Vera pointed to the crocus she'd baptized with Bone's cheap whiskey. "Ryan planted those when he was ten. Never know if they'll come up or not. Some years they don't."

Kate winced. She'd barfed on precious Ryan's flowers. "I'm sorry."

Vera shrugged. "Nothing the rain won't wash away. Organic, isn't it?"

Kate thought it rather weird they were talking about vomit being organic, but she went with it. "I guess. So, Ryan liked gardening? That's crazy for a guy."

Vera's lips twitched. "Well, he went through a phase one year. He'd attended a science camp and learned about botany. Growing things intrigued him. He went through the same phase again when Rick came to live with us—Rick worked as a gardener when he first came. That man took to the earth like no man I'd ever seen. It was odd, really. A gang member so angry with the world able to grow the most beautiful things you could imagine. Ryan tagged after Rick like a puppy. He loved that anger right out of him."

A lump appeared in Kate's throat at the thought of a boy loving Rick so much that he let go of the hate, that he began to dream about a future. "Ryan was special."

Vera nodded. Kate wondered if all Vera's thoughts wrapped around the past like a line anchoring a boat. "Yes, he was. More than anyone could ever know. You know, there are people who are born that way. Full of something so magical, so pure. He was like an angel. And I was lucky to be his momma."

Tears sprang to Kate's eyes. She could feel the sadness in Vera and something made her want to reach inside the woman and remove it. She touched Vera's hand, then wrapped her fingers around it so their hands curled together.

Vera flinched, but didn't withdraw. For the first time since Kate had stepped foot on Cottonwood, she felt something within herself shift. Click. A sort of rightness settled in her bones.

"I'd like to know more about—" she paused, the words getting clogged in her throat "—my brother."

Vera's eyes met hers. Honesty passed between. It was the first time Kate had admitted Ryan was indeed her brother. And Justus her father. No more pretense. Only truthfulness.

"You should know about him. It's a shame you never met him."

"I did. Sort of."

Like a puppy, Vera cocked her head. "How?"

"Shortly after my grandmother passed, I came to Oak Stand to settle some of her things, and he ran into me with his bicycle. Tore my new broom skirt." Kate frowned a little. She'd saved all her tips from the bar to buy that skirt from the boutique near campus. Sixty dollars had been a fortune back then.

Who was she kidding? It was a fortune now.

Vera smiled and clapped a hand over her mouth. "You were that mean girl?"

Kate laughed. "Well, I *was* mad. And the damn skirt looked like it had been shredded by a cat."

Vera laughed. The sound was soft against the night, and her face was framed against the fingernail moon.

"He said a mean girl screamed at him. I remember that day. He'd gone with a friend to get an ice-cream cone at the Dairy Barn. Justus hadn't wanted to let him go because he'd just gotten that mountain bike and couldn't handle it that well. But Ryan insisted he could ride it fine."

"Yeah, right into me," Kate muttered, before smiling. "He was a cute kid. Hated him on sight."

Vera drew back, but then realized Kate was joking. "He cried because he tore your skirt. He was like that. Felt everything too much. It worried him you were mad, and he didn't know who you were. Took all the quarters he'd been saving for the arcade and said he was going to buy you a new skirt."

Kate shook her head, as something new lodged in her gut. Something called shame. Remorse. Or whatever a person called the feeling of hating a golden-haired, blue-eyed boy because his father loved him, then finding out the boy was truly worth the love. "I left that afternoon. Only came to pack some stuff and dispose of the rest."

"He said he'd find you. You had eyes the same color as his. I never made the connection, though I should have. I'd heard the rumors, but I didn't want to face them."

Kate didn't want to talk any more about the past tonight. She didn't want to push it with Vera. Didn't want to undo the good that had been done. "Almost everybody knew, Vera. No one else wanted to face it, either." She gave Vera's hand one last squeeze.

Vera sat stock-still and watched as Kate rose to her feet. "Well, it's late, and you need to brush your teeth."

"And grab a shower." Kate reached down to offer assistance standing.

As Vera took her hand, a fleeting peace brushed Kate, gentle as the wings of the dragonflies that often buzzed lazily along the edges of the East Texas ponds. Vera accepted. Vera adapted. Vera would heal.

Kate didn't believe in divine intervention—she was far too pragmatic. But something had happened between the two women. Like stones being pulled from a wall of doubt, they had made progress in opening the boundary that separated them.

Silently, they walked the twisting path of the garden, emerging into the porch light where Justus sat like a worn gargoyle. Kate didn't acknowledge her father, just glided past him.

There was honesty between them, too. But it hurt too much to acknowledge or embrace it. Anger still licked at her insides like the aftertaste of the whiskey, only harder to wash away.

CHAPTER TWELVE

DAYS LATER, KATE SAT ON the back patio of Phoenix watching a clean and noticeably healthier Banjo chase doves in the brush. A cool breeze threatened the spiky locks she'd perfected around her face. She'd streaked her dark tresses with a deep red last night and liked how colorful it looked in the brightness of the day. She looked down at the planter at her feet. "Ugh! This soil keeps washing out of the pots. Why is it so light?"

Kate wiped her hands and frowned at the water spilling over the sides of the planter.

Random pots scattered the flagstone. Some were already filled, while others still awaited the tomato plants sitting in plastic cartons on the porch.

"Because we're using a moisture-binding potting soil. It'll help the plants stay succulent when summer gets here." Rick shoveled more soil into the pots. His tanned hands patted a hill in the center of one pot before cupping a hole in the center of the mound.

She and Rick hadn't spoken about the night at Cooley's even though she could feel the strings of tension tightening between them. She still wanted him with an intensity that surprised her, and he still fought against the magnetism between them, but they had other things to deal with. Rick's clients had arrived and Kate spent the past few nights making polite small talk with Vera and Justus at the dinner table. It was enough to set her on edge and make her grind her teeth as she slept. The only thing that got her through those evenings was the truce she and Vera had arrived at that night in the garden.

"My grandmother never planted anything until after Easter. It's already thundered in February, you know," she said, pulling a tender tomato plant from the plastic container.

"What does that mean, *bruja?*"

"Stop calling me witch," she grumbled, gently breaking apart the roots of the plant the way Rick had showed her earlier.

"You mean you don't know?" Georges, one of the clients, called from across the patio. "If it thunders in February, it will freeze in April, *cholo.*"

Kate smiled at Georges. He was the only guy who showed any openness toward the staff at Phoenix. The other four were eerily silent, almost sullen, as if they already regretted their choice to come here.

Carlos, Joe, Brandon, Georges and Manny had arrived by a church van, each hauling a makeshift suitcase and a scowl. Or at least that's what Rick had told her.

Only Georges had abandoned his serious demeanor for some lively teasing. He'd had Trudy pitching a fit when she'd found everything on her desk moved cock-eyed on the second day of GED classes. He'd also held an actual conversation with Rick, rather than merely grunting his replies.

"Well, that's why we're planting them in these containers. They'll be easy to move to the cover of the back patio if we get frost." Rick patted the soil around the plant Kate had set in the hole. He sat back and assessed the planting critically, narrowing his brown eyes as he studied his handiwork.

She watched as he rose and retrieved anther plant,

handing it to Manny without a word. The plump gang member wrinkled his nose at the container.

"So why we gotta plant these things, anyway? This seems stupid if you ask me," Manny said, setting the tiny plants beside the wooden pot and studying the other members sprawled about doing much the same.

"I didn't ask you," Rick said, returning to her side.

Georges snickered. "He already told you, dude. We're gonna grow our own vegetables. It ain't that bad. You ain't shoveling horseshit or nothin'."

"Shut the f—"

"Guys, you'd do well to note there is a lady present," Rick cautioned.

"What lady?" Kate joked, looking around. She hit Rick with a smart-ass grin.

He rolled his eyes. "Seriously, let's start watching the way we speak to others. Part of this program is learning to present yourself as a new person. We're letting go of who we once were to find a new path."

"Now *there's* your horseshit to shovel," Joe said, tossing a trowel onto the patio. It clanked against the rock before scuttling toward Manny.

Rick stiffened beside her. She placed one hand on his forearm in warning. There was going to be resistance. There was likely going to be out-and-out rebellion before Rick could make any true progress.

"The trowel will probably work, though I notice Georges puts out a lot of bullshit. Might need a shovel for his," Kate joked, squeezing Rick's arm. She could feel him take a deep breath, feel his forearm relax under her fingers. She liked the way he felt, warm from the sun, strong from the labor he performed. He was no milk-white accountant in a knockoff designer suit. He was full-on man, and even though they were far from being alone, Kate felt a familiar heat surge inside her body along with the buzz of aggravation that it would go unfulfilled.

Georges laughed, interrupting her wicked thoughts. "You know it, *muchachos*."

Manny pulled a face and slid the trowel toward Joe. "Just plant the damn tomatoes, man."

Joe looked at the garden instrument, then looked away, his jaw set. "Whatever. I'm out."

He rose from the patio, hitched up his sagging pants and headed for the center where Trudy stood at the side of the house, motioning a woman wearing a circus costume their way.

Rick sighed and pulled away from her. She felt the frustration coming off him in waves.

"Uh-oh," Kate said, watching as the woman in what was actually not a circus costume but a hideous Western skirt headed their way. "Betty Monk moving in at 12:00."

"Who's Betty Monk?" Georges asked, shielding his eyes against the rays bearing down on them.

"Yoo-hoo," she called, her brightly patterned skirt swishing around her red cowboy boots as she balanced a basket on one arm. "Hiya, boys!"

Betty Monk was the coproprietor of The Curlique Beauty Salon in Oak Stand, where Kate had worked each summer to earn extra money. All that was left of the bouffant Betty used to wear were faded wisps of rose-colored hair held in place with Aqua Net above her penciled-on eyebrows and road-mapped face. Bright red lipstick matched the boots she wore, curving into a Texas-size smile.

"Look what I brought you boys—muffins. Right from

the ovens of the Ladies Auxiliary," Betty said, shooing Banjo away as she maneuvered toward the patio.

No one said a word as Betty tousled Brandon's hair, which was as absent as her own since he wore a buzz. Brandon ducked his head and moved away, but it didn't deter Betty.

"Why, I'll be a monkey's uncle. If it isn't my favorite gal, Katie Newman. What in the blue blazes have you done to your hair, girl?" Betty handed Georges the basket. He immediately lifted the gingham cloth and peered within.

Kate brushed the dirt from her hands. "Hello, Mrs. Betty. The color is Fire two-oh-three, if you want me to do a little touch-up for you."

Kate gave the woman a brief hug, but the older woman wanted much more. She clasped Kate into a bear hug, which was remarkably easy for a woman who was descended from good Norwegian stock and stood five foot ten in her stocking feet. "The devil take me if I wear anything that bold, child. My color has been ravishing red for twenty-some-odd years, and that's what it'll stay."

Rick walked over and extended his hand. "Hello, Mrs. Monk. I appreciate your being so neighborly and bringing us some home cooking."

Betty took his hand and gave it a hearty shake. "Some folks didn't want me to do it, but I'll be hanged if I listen to a bunch of narrow-minded deacons' wives. That Sally Holtzclaw is plum hypocritical, and I've just about—"

"What kind did you make?" Kate interrupted before Betty could dredge up every wrong done her by her archrival and former best friend Sally. They'd been feuding for years, ever since Betty's design-challenged niece had reupholstered the Baptist church's choir chairs in teal satin, causing Sally to slip off the seat and show the whole congregation her girdle. One would think the two friends could have gotten past the bad feelings, but showing her undergarments to the township had stirred Sally to retribution. And so the battle had waged out of control for three years.

"Oh. I brought blueberry—Nellie's grandmother's recipe. Used the last of the frozen blueberries my grand-baby picked me over in Linden."

"Very kind of you," Rick muttered, looking a bit puzzled. It was a common reaction to Betty who name-dropped, subject-hopped and dredged the past with dizzying speed. Not many could follow her, let alone figure her out. Not even her dear departed Ed had tried. He'd always called her his Gordian knot. And he never claimed to be Hercules.

"Well, aren't you sweet." Betty beamed. "I've always liked you. You're a most handsome fellow, even with all those tattoos."

Rick looked at Kate before looking back at Betty. "Thanks, I think."

"No problem." Betty took Kate's elbow and moved her out of the hearing range of the guys cramming muffins in their mouths. "Now, Katie, Nellie told me you're staying with Justus Mitchell. I guess that not-so-secret secret is out front and center. If that's so, why the devil are you staying with a man who never bothered to claim you as his own? I'm a forgiving woman, but even I couldn't cotton to pardoning that sin."

Kate wanted to laugh. Betty could meddle with the best of them, and after putting up with temper tantrums and tears from the many who'd unloaded their problems in her salon chair, she didn't mince words. So Kate shot her straight. "Who said anything about forgiveness? I want his money."

Betty cackled like the old hen she was and clapped her hands together. "Damn right. No one messes with my Katie."

Rick's eyes widened. "Are y'all related?"

"Not by actual relation," Betty said. "Here's the way it is, handsome—this little girl thinks she belongs only to herself, but she belongs to Oak Stand. To all of us."

Kate shook her head. She'd never felt she belonged in Oak Stand. She'd always felt second-rate. Nothing like the way she felt in Vegas. There she had control. And no one knew her past. But Mrs. Betty had meant her remark as a kindness, and it struck Kate with its tenderness.

"Whoa, these muffins are good," Georges mumbled, his mouth half-full.

"Of course they are. I made them, didn't I?" Betty said, moving toward him. "Now, let me show you the right way to plant tomatoes. You've got to have a little bit of bonemeal."

Her words faded into the background as Kate fought the dampness gathering on her lashes. Rick noticed and moved toward her. He took her hand and brushed some dirt from it. "I like your hair. It suits you. And I didn't know Oak Stand owned you."

Kate loved the feel of his hands on her. Loved it too much. "No one owns me. Especially not this town."

She stepped away from him, sensing her words had jabbed him, hurt him in some way. But what did it matter? He'd made it abundantly clear several nights ago when she'd thrown herself at him.

He didn't want her.

Just like Justus hadn't.

Just like Oak Stand hadn't.

She didn't belong here. She belonged in Vegas, with Jeremy and her friends. She belonged to a city that didn't sleep, where no one called her Katie.

She belonged to herself and she needed to get out of the place that made her feel as though she didn't.

But, as Vera had said, some things you can't leave undone.

Kate grabbed the empty cartons and headed to the side of the house where the garbage cans sat. From the corner of her eye she saw Vera pull up in a Lexus sedan. The older woman stepped out of the car, looking quite pretty with her hair tied in a low ponytail with a scarf and wearing a lime-green jacket over her factory-worn designer jeans. She carried a large bowl and a bag from a fancy gourmet store that was definitely not located in Oak Stand.

"Kate," she called, stopping on the front pavers. "Will you give me a hand?"

"I'm filthy," Kate called back, but walking toward her anyway.

"Just grab the sacks from the trunk, if you don't mind. You can set them on the porch." She headed inside without waiting for Kate to agree.

"Fine," she said to no one in particular as she approached the car. The trunk was unlatched and she lifted the bags out and set them at her feet. Under the last bag lay a halter. She lifted it out. It was a strange item to be sitting in the middle of a perfectly clean trunk.

"That belonged to Ryan's horse."

Kate dropped it in the trunk, wondering if Vera had gotten the therapy she needed after Ryan's death. Carrying this kind of stuff was creepy. "Oh."

Vera's touch was a light caress on her back. "That was how he died. On his horse."

Kate had never thought to ask about how Ryan had died. Things had felt too heavy to think about much beyond the cold silence with Justus and the hot pandering for Rick. "He fell?"

Vera nodded. "Rick found pot in the ashtray of the Mustang. It wasn't Ryan's. Or at least he swore it wasn't, but Rick was hard on him. I guess because of his own mistakes. Ryan got angry because he didn't believe him and took off in a gallop on his quarter horse, Tolstoy. We don't know what happened really. Tolstoy came back and Ryan didn't. Rick found him crumpled in a ditch out by the ruins of the Spanish mission."

Sadness lurked in Vera's eyes, but she told the story in a matter-of-fact way. As if she'd told it the same way many times before.

"I'm sorry." It was all Kate could say.

Vera nodded, looking at the halter. "Justus shot that horse. Loaded the rifle, went out and killed him. It was Justus's way of dealing, as extreme as it was. But Rick…" She sighed. "Rick went crazy. He thought it was his fault."

"Why?"

Vera shrugged and shut the lid. "He kept saying 'I should have believed him' as if that would have prevented it. But it wouldn't have. It was a freak accident. I guess I knew. What's that saying? 'Only the good die young'?"

"I'll probably live to a ripe old age then."

At this the woman finally smiled. "Me, too."

Vera didn't say anything else. She headed up the walk with the remaining bags, leaving Kate wondering what kind of help she'd actually been. She hadn't done a thing other than pick up the halter.

She glanced at the porch as Rick appeared.

Is that why he stayed under Justus's thumb? Guilt? Perhaps he couldn't cut the ties that bound him to the Mitchells because he felt responsible for Ryan's death. Which was ludicrous, but the mind and heart worked in mysterious ways.

Rick rubbed a hand across his chest and looked out at the horizon. Kate could feel his angst. His trouble. If she had to guess the source, she'd say things at the center, work with the clients wasn't going as planned.

Yeah, welcome to the club, buddy.

CHAPTER THIRTEEN

"WE CAN'T HOLD A CAR WASH, stupid. It's February," Carlos said, leaning back in one of the chairs surrounding the dining table at Phoenix.

"But it's not cold outside when the sun's out," Georges said, spreading his hands. "You have a bad attitude, man."

Rick tried to be patient. The guys had only been here for four days and were still adjusting to one another. Two clients—Joe and Brandon—were from the Tango Blast organization, a relatively new albeit violent gang. They seemed the most dangerous of the group. The other three were Mexican Mafia, but from different barrios. They'd been low men in the gang and their personalities reflected their status. "We can disagree, but let's not name call."

Sullen eyes met his comment and worry settled in his gut. Nothing was working the way he'd envisioned it. He'd been a delusional fool to think the guys would accept him just because he'd been in their shoes at one time.

Not to mention he literally ached for Kate. He tried to stop himself from gravitating toward her, but time and time again, he found himself seeking her out, if only to soak her in as she teased the clients and did what he sought to do…bond with them.

Brandon spoke next. "Listen, not a car wash, man. That's, like, what the cheerleaders do in high school."

Joe grinned. "I took my mother's car for a wash every time. *Mochilas*. Tight asses and—"

"How about a detail place?" Brandon suggested. "We could wash, wax and buff that shit up."

Rick could see lightbulbs going off in their heads. He'd asked to meet with them right after their last GED class with the purpose of brainstorming ideas for raising money for the center.

The foundation had given the center enough money for the year, but the guys in the three-month program needed to earn their keep. Taking on responsibility was as much a part of their rehabilitation as therapy and education. Learning to work together to find solutions was key in getting them to accept a world where disagreements were met with honesty and compromise, not with guns and knives.

"That's whack, dude," Manny said, shaking his head.

Tension thickened.

Rick slammed his hands on the table, breaking through the testosterone flare-up in the room and drawing their attention to him. "Actually, there's nothing like that in Oak Stand, outside of a do-it-yourself place on the outskirts of town. I'm good with cars myself."

"Yeah," Joe said, glancing out the back window to where the Mustang sat in the drive. "That's a sweet ride."

Rick could feel their interest. For the first time. "I restored it. Me and a friend, that is. So I know my way around a vehicle."

The guys nodded.

"But we're too far out from town," Joe said. "Old ladies ain't gonna drive out here so this chunty can rag her car." He jerked his thumb toward Georges as he delivered the insult. Georges flipped Joe off.

Rick reminded them about using derogatory terms for the umpteenth time.

"Well, they damn sure ain't gonna let us drive their cars. They'll think we're stealin' them or something. We'll be laying the wax and hear sirens," said Joe.

Rick spent the next thirty minutes helping them iron out the particulars of the business. The guys were wary, but enthusiasm laced their words and several guys showed surprising entrepreneurial skills in their negotiations. Then he watched silently as they sketched out logos and talked about names for the business, one of which was Banjo's. Letting the dog stay had proven to be the right move. The guys loved the scrawny mutt. The dog was another piece in the puzzle for creating the right environment.

Rick drifted away from the table, leaving them to take ownership of the business idea. He'd follow up later and make a suggestion or two for drafting the plan, but he wanted to give them space. That seemed like the right move.

He entered the kitchen, set his mug in the sink and ran soapy water for the dishes stacked on the counter. Starting tonight, the clients would share in meal preparation and cleanup. Up until then, he'd borne the burden. For some reason, he hadn't thought much about feeding the guys. He'd spent much of his planning on the programs and supplies. Thank goodness, Vera and other townspeople had shown up with welcoming dishes. Another thing to tweak.

As he finished loading the dishwasher, Kate breezed in.

"Hey," she said, grabbing a kitchen towel and wiping the counters. "I finished organizing all of the paperwork into different files. When you have time, I'll show you how I set it up so it'll be easy to put your hands on what you need."

He watched her smooth strokes as she buffed the stove and knew exactly where he wanted to put his hands. And it damn sure wasn't on files. He looked at the half-eaten cinnamon roll sitting on a plate he'd missed on the far counter. It made him think of that morning several days ago. The morning he'd told Kate he'd made a vow. She'd teased him then about eating things that weren't good for him, and he'd replied that "some things were worth it."

He looked at the delicious woman bent over picking up a bread tie from the floor.

Wasn't Kate the same thing?

Decadent. Sweet. And absolutely worth it.

She turned and caught him watching her and the air crackled. "What?"

Laughter from the dining room jarred him from his wicked thoughts. It was getting harder and harder to drag himself from that place. And he knew his connection with Kate wasn't only physical. It was something more. "Nothing."

He took the towel from her and hung it up. "Actually, I do want to show you something."

She slid him a wicked smile. "Oh, really?"

He tried to ignore the stirring in his body and focus on where he wanted to take her. "Really."

He headed out the kitchen door past the guys at the table. Their discussion had grown pretty loud.

"That name is *chignon*. Beast," Brandon said. He leaned forward, forearms on the table in an aggressive manner.

Manny pulled his attention away from Brandon to look at Rick. "Yo, *chulo,* where you going with my *chica?*"

Rick shook his head. He was no player. Those days were long over. "Does she know she's yours?"

Kate rolled her eyes. "When will men ever learn? We ladies belong to ourselves."

"That's what we let you think," Joe said.

Rick told them they would return momentarily and the guys went back to arguing over a name.

He led Kate out the door and down the front steps. The wind announced another cold front moving in from the north, but the sun broke through the clouds to throw some much needed heat upon their shoulders. He headed down the sloping hill toward a small copse of woods that clung to the banks of a stream ribboning the property.

Kate didn't speak, just tilted her face up to the sun. He curled his hand and placed it in his pocket, so he wouldn't touch her, fall into her. His body was like a guitar string, tight and ready to be played by her.

But not now. There was something he wanted to show her, a secret place that he hoped would help her understand that someone had wanted her.

The pine trees didn't grow thick in the stand of woods. They towered above the dogwoods and redbuds, showing premature signs of awakening. Tangled graying vines curled around a small ramshackled fort built next to a huge pine tree.

"What's this?" she asked, approaching the weathered little building. She walked straight to the door hanging on rusted hinges.

"It's Ryan's fort," he said quietly, still feeling reverence for the secret place Ryan had hung out in.

She swung her head around. "Why would you bring me here? It's falling down."

He had good reason, but he wanted her to find out on her own, so he shrugged. Her brow furrowed as she turned and pulled the door open past withered dandelions blocking the threshold. The wood creaked and one board actually fell to the ground.

"Oops," she said, ducking her head to peer within.

"He built it himself with boards and scraps he found around Cottonwood. He'd started it before I came to live here. In fact, the day Justus pulled up with me sulking in the back of the truck, the roofers were accusing each other of misplacing boards and a box of nails. Turns out Ryan hauled the material almost two miles across the pasture on a four-wheeler they used on the ranch."

"I guess a lot of little boys want a fort," she said as she brushed a cobweb away and stepped inside. "I wonder why he built it so far away?"

"So nobody would find it."

She glanced out. "But you did."

"He showed it to me. You're the only other person who knows it's here."

Something flashed in Kate's eyes. He couldn't read it. She disappeared inside the fort, and he stood where he was. He wanted her to see something of her brother other than the portrait that hung over her as she shoveled peas into her mouth at dinner. He wanted her to feel like she had one tiny piece that neither Vera nor Justus held.

He wasn't sure why, but he knew that this would help Kate move toward a better place. He wished he'd

thought of it earlier, but he'd been so wrapped up in all
that had been going on that he'd forgotten Ryan's secret
fort and all that lay inside.

KATE WONDERED IF THE STRUCTURE was dangerous. A
young boy had built it, so it couldn't be too sound. Yet
it had weathered several years and still stood.

The tang of mold and decaying earth met her nostrils.
The floor of the fort had been covered in an old piece of
linoleum that curled at the edges. Faux wood. She and
her grandmother had had the same pattern in the used
trailer they'd rented in Happy Place Trailer Park—the
name was a total oxymoron. Nothing happy about a
run-down trailer park choked with weeds and soaked
in poverty.

The fort walls were held together by exposed rusting
nails. Large cracks allowed outside light to fall in bright
slashes across the dirty linoleum. Two large sheets of
plywood served as the roof and there was only one
window, which had Plexiglas covering it. The contents
consisted of one rickety TV tray, a camping chair and
several boxes. One lone, faded poster of Angelina Jolie
dressed as Lara Croft dated the fort as early 2000s.

Kate toed one of the boxes and a spider ran out.

She brought the heel of her sneaker down on it. One
down, dozens likely to go.

She cautiously lifted the water-stained flap of the
nearest box.

Baseball cards. Thousands of them. Most ruined by
the moisture. The Texas Rangers seemed to have been
his favorite.

The next box held rocks. Nothing spectacular about
them. Some were jagged with crystals, others were
smooth and perfect for skipping across a still pond. A

few marbles mixed within the depths. She decided to leave that box alone, for there was no telling what lurked beneath the stones.

A third box held a conglomeration of stuff: a yo-yo, a worn deck of cards with a casino logo on it, a watch that had stopped at 4:20, a bird whistle, an empty box of Hot Tamales candy and something that looked like a half-eaten Fruit Roll-Up. A couple of school papers littered the sides of the box. It appeared that at age nine or ten, Ryan had sucked at spelling but rocked fractions.

A large footlocker sat beneath the uneven window. It beckoned her like a topless dancer crooking her finger at a paunchy, bald guy.

Kate peeked out the door. Rick stood, arms akimbo, studying the writhing trees above his head. He was giving her time to get to know her deceased brother. To see the Ryan beyond the saint. But for what purpose?

She resigned herself to not knowing his motives and stepped toward the battered footlocker. She bent, flipped the unlocked latch and lifted the lid. The hinges creaked eerily. No spiders, but discolored paper hung from the inside of the lid. An address label affixed to the paper and scrawled in perfect penmanship declared the trunk to be that of Vera Horton.

Kate peered into its depths. A small stained bridle lay on top of a baseball jersey. Ryan had been number twenty-four for the Oak Stand Bears, no doubt his T-ball team if the size of the jersey was any indication. Beside that lay an elementary yearbook. She picked it up and leafed through it. Her brother had been in Mrs. Doyle's first grade class. One of his front teeth had been missing in the class picture, and it looked very similar to the one she'd taken at age six standing beside the same teacher.

She and her brother had shared the same homeroom teacher. Maybe Ryan had sat at the same desk she'd slumped in. Maybe he'd also hidden his pencil in the groove at the very back of the desk, hoping no one else would find it and take it.

She placed the yearbook back beside the jersey. Something pink caught her eye. An anomaly like something pink among baseball cards and disgusting boy stuff had to be explored. She tossed aside a baseball cap that matched the Bears jersey and froze.

She knew that backpack—it was hers. And it had been missing for so long she'd forgotten it.

She picked it up, brushing the cheerful face of Strawberry Shortcake.

It wasn't empty.

Hand trembling, she untied the frayed strings knitting the cloth opening together and tugged the backpack open. She pulled one item from the depths and cradled it in her hands. Carefully, she opened the journal to the first page.

Property of Katie Newman.

Beneath it, in childish handwriting were the words: *my sister.*

Kate traced the spidery words then wiped the tears that dripped on her forgotten journal. Obviously Ryan knew a lot more about that mean girl who'd chewed him out for tearing her skirt than he'd let on. That he'd claimed—even in this silent, private way—knocked Kate on her proverbial butt. Especially because he would have had to dig it out of whatever moldering pile of crap it had been languishing in—he'd only been a toddler that fateful day she abandoned her prize possessions.

Damn Rick for pulling her heartstrings. He knew exactly what he was doing.

Kate shoved the journal into the backpack and dug around until she found what she wanted. She stared at the picture of her parents laughing into the camera for a moment before slipping it into her pocket.

She didn't even know why she wanted to keep it.

CHAPTER FOURTEEN

AT JUSTUS'S REQUEST, Rick joined the Mitchells at Cottonwood for dinner that night. Upon his arrival, he'd dumped his frustration about the center on Kate. It seemed Sanford Stevens, the group therapy session leader, had requested that Rick not be present during his time with the clients. It had frustrated Rick to discover he wasn't needed at the center—he wasn't irate, but testy all the same.

After his vent, Kate and Rick had joined Vera and Justus in the formal living room for cocktails. Kate had actually been glad of Rick's presence because the tension between her and her father had grown epic. Neither of them could get past stilted formality with one another.

Kate was counting down the days to her return to Vegas while dreading them at the same time. Her reasons for feeling that way were murky at best, but she knew they had mostly to do with Rick and her burning desire to be with him. And not only in the biblical sense. She wanted to be around *him* all the time.

It was all very strange.

Vera remained cheerful through the first course, though she cast worried glances Rick's way when he began cutting his filet into tiny little pieces while staring off into space.

"How are things progressing at Phoenix, Rick?" Vera

asked, sipping her second glass of wine as she stared down at the dinner plate Rosa had set in front of her.

Rick muttered a terse "Fine."

"Well, are the boys nice?" Vera prodded.

"Yeah," Rick said, shuffling his green peas toward his mashed potatoes. Kate chalked his distraction up to his preoccupation with things not running the way he'd like them at the center.

"Well, that's nice. I hope they're adjusting to the quiet life. Is there anything more I can do to help?"

Rick shrugged.

"Why don't you answer her damned questions?" Justus exploded, throwing his fork onto the fine china of his plate. "I'm sick of this uncomfortable silence every damned night. The least you could do is carry the conversation, boy."

"Justus, watch your language, dear," Vera said, her hand trembling as she picked up her glass.

"I'll say what I want to at my table. And you stop drinking so much damn wine, Vera. That ain't gonna help one bit, woman. That boy—" he pointed his finger at the picture of Ryan, who looked quite amused at the whole situation "—is dead and he ain't coming back."

Vera burst into tears, Rick muttered a word that would make a nun blush, and Kate started laughing.

Justus turned his blue eyes on her. "What in the hell are you laughing about?"

"This is…this…is—" She snorted, before throwing a hand over her mouth. "It's the most dysfunctional family in the history of dysfunction."

Rick stared at her as if she'd licked acid tablets. "I'm not a member of this family."

Vera moaned and Justus cursed then asked for forgiveness with eyes cast upward.

"I mean, you guys are a bunch of loony tunes." Kate couldn't believe she'd lost control of her emotions. This afternoon had about broken her. Since she'd arrived at Cottonwood, she'd alternated between crying, cussing, laughing and throwing herself at a celibate guy—all indications that Kate Newman had lost her mind. Clearly she belonged at this table.

"I don't think feeling something means you're crazy." Vera sniffed as she shoved her half-filled glass of pinot grigio toward the Waterford saltshaker. "It means you're human."

"You're right, Vera," Rick said, his eyes connecting with Kate's. "Sometimes when you feel things, it's messy."

Kate felt his words. Knew he was talking to her, not Vera. But he need not have bothered. Didn't he know she knew things were messy? They were so messy she couldn't find a damn thing to hold on to.

"Thank you, Rick," Vera mumbled from the depths of her linen napkin.

"Oh, piss on it," Justus said, reversing his chair from the table. "I'm sick of holding my tongue."

He pointed a finger at Kate. "I don't know why I wanted you to stay here. You're more stubborn than any horse, mule or goat I've ever worked with. And that has been more than I care to remember. I thought I could make amends with you, but you won't even open your mouth and try. So I can't sit here another night and pretend." He rolled out the door.

"Justus, don't leave. We haven't had dessert," Vera called after him. He ignored her and kept rolling toward the elevator that would take him to his office.

Kate looked at Vera. Her misery was plainly evident

on her face and Kate felt like shit for upsetting her. "I'm sorry."

Vera waved a hand before looking at the portrait of her dead son. "It's not just you. Justus hasn't grieved for Ryan properly. And I've grieved too much. I wish I could stop, but the hurt won't go away."

Kate looked at the picture of the boy who'd kept her journal hidden in a damp footlocker. His smile seemed so knowing. So like her own. "At least you let yourself feel. That has to be healthier than holding it in."

"Maybe," Vera acknowledged, turning to Kate. "But I've gotten so lost in the grief that I've forgotten how to live. I'm tired of merely existing. Talking about Ryan has helped me realize he'd never want me to ramble about this house, spending hours in the garden wishing for something that can no longer be."

Rick silently watched them. His eyes looked very much the way they had when she'd emerged from the fort earlier that afternoon. Satisfied. Like a general whose battle strategies were going according to plan.

Kate cleared her throat, thinking someone should say something. Something to affirm what Vera had admitted. "From what you've told me, you're right. He'd be upset with you. But give yourself a break. You postponed your grief when Justus had his stroke, then you drowned in it. So now it's time to dry off and start living again."

Vera nodded, and reached over to grasp Kate's hand. Her touch was cool, but her eyes were finally warm. "Thank you, Kate. I know being here has been hard for you, but somehow, your presence has forced me to confront myself. You've unstuck me."

Kate gave the woman's hand a squeeze before withdrawing. The atmosphere felt too deep in the room.

Stifling, the way it had after Jeremy had told her the IRS news. She had to get out to process. To think about how to handle her father. "I—I think I'm going to skip the cheesecake and take a walk."

She scooted back her chair and rose. Rick did the same. "Pardon us both, Vera. I'll join Kate on that walk."

She had thought she'd rather be alone, but when Rick stood, relief flooded her. Having Rick beside her was becoming a habit.

Vera nodded. "That's fine. I'll eat the cheesecake for breakfast." She dropped her napkin beside her plate then followed Justus's path, heading toward where her husband had likely gone to sulk. Kate and Rick slipped through the kitchen, complimenting Rosa on the meal, before emerging into the moonlight.

The night was slightly cool, and the stars twinkled like a string of Christmas lights placed for the benefit of the two of them walking the garden path.

"I had to escape," Kate commented after they'd walked for several minutes with no words between them.

"I know."

They walked for several minutes more, stepping off the path and onto the land behind the house. A few Bradford pear trees showed off their snowy plumage against the dark velvet of the sky. Spring had arrived despite the cold front that had moved in a few days ago.

"You know, when I was rollin' with my gang, I tried like hell to be hard. That was living the gang life, to be hard." His words floated into the night, regret tinting them, making them sound prophetic. "That's why it's difficult to reach the guys at the center. Egos get in the way."

"Mmm," she said, enjoying his presence at her side. Had she ever taken a walk with a man beside her and felt comfortable?

"You know, I was never like that. Never hard."

Kate snickered.

"Ah, *bruja,* you know what I mean." There was a smile in his words. "I couldn't kick a puppy and laugh. I couldn't lift an old lady's purse when I knew it held her welfare check. I never got a kid to sell drugs for me with the promise of a pair of shoes. I tried to pretend I was a badass, but I wasn't."

She nodded even though he couldn't see her. And though she wore a sweater and jeans and wasn't cold, she moved closer to him.

"You are like me," he said, stopping and grabbing her hand. He brought it to his lips. His kiss was soft, and for a moment he became a Spanish courtier come to woo and win her. Kate was no romantic, but she couldn't seem to stop her heart from pounding, from wanting to feel his lips on hers beneath the fullness of the moon.

"How am I like you?"

"You got hurt early in life. Like me. So you build a shell. A tough, badass exterior. You try to be hard."

She shifted her eyes to his and he stopped beneath a redbud tree that had started pushing purple blooms forth. "You think you're going to crack me or something?"

She tried to make her words teasing, but they didn't come out the way she'd intended. Emotion trembled in those words, as if she were daring him, no, begging him, to find the real Kate beneath the razored hair and too-tight clothes.

His mouth descended, hovering over hers. "I already have," he whispered against her lips.

She lifted herself onto her tiptoes and pressed herself

to him as he claimed her mouth. She believed him. Maybe she'd been waiting forever for someone to find the real Kate.

The kiss was soft and sweet. And then it was not.

A rocket of passion exploded deep within her, filling her body with the sheer need to be claimed by Enrique Mendez. She wanted this man more than she'd ever wanted a man. And that wasn't romance, or lust, or anything other than the honest truth.

She opened her mouth to him and tasted him as she wound her hands round his broad shoulders. His mouth consumed her, hard, unrelenting.

Kate moaned, allowing desire to unwind within her, unfurl within every inch of her body. She reveled in wanting him. Loved the way he felt against her. So hard in all the right ways.

"I can't help it," he murmured against her lips, tilting his head so their foreheads met and their breaths mingled, frosty in the night air. "I've tried to resist you, but I can't. I want you, Kate, even if I'll have you only a little while."

She didn't answer. Merely pressed her lips against his once again. He lifted her against him, sliding her body along his so he could reach the pulse galloping out of control in her neck. Kate held on to him as he tugged at the neck of her sweater.

"Wait," she said, wiggling from his grasp. "You're serious?"

He dropped her to the ground. His chocolate eyes were dilated with desire and clouded with confusion. "Huh?"

Kate looked toward the house. Justus stewed inside. Vera could wander out to the garden for midnight prayer. Rick hadn't talked this through with Kate. This was bigger than mere sex. Kissing was one thing. Taking it to the next level was quite another.

"So you want me to leave?" he said, keeping his arms tight around her. His fingers played with the sensitive flesh beneath her sweater. The cool night air kissed her skin, but the cold didn't seem to reach her. Not with Rick touching her.

"Only if you take me with you," she said, half joking, half fearful he'd leave her standing here in the night wishing she'd kept her damn mouth shut.

His teeth flashed as he lowered his head to nuzzle her neck. "You're right. This is not the right place. I want to see you naked, watch you while I make love to you. I want to kiss every square inch of your body, love every hill, valley and plain."

Kate's insides turned to mush as her libido kicked into high gear.

Then he murmured next to her ear. "If I don't make love to you, I'll never get you out of my blood."

Kate stiffened. "Wait. You think having sex with me will cure you of this thing we have between us?"

He lifted his head. "Maybe. You make me crazy. I don't know how to make it better, but I know the vow I made years ago doesn't matter more to me than being with you."

Kate stepped back from him, ignoring her body as it protested the loss of warmth. She averted her eyes to the black horizon. "Look, I want you more than I've wanted any man. I'm being totally honest with you when I say that. I don't know if it's all this exploration of my past or if it's something more. All I know is that when I'm with you, it feels so…I can't even describe it."

She found his gaze in the darkness. She couldn't read his expression, but she could feel the desire still pulsing between them. "But even though I feel scared—not an emotion I ever admit to feeling to anyone—I want to respect the views you have on relationships. I'm not staying in Oak Stand. And I'm definitely not staying any longer than I have to at Cottonwood. I'm going back to Vegas. And everyone knows long-distance relationships don't work."

Rick's lips pressed into a thin line and it made Kate's heart ache. She couldn't allow him to give up something that made him who he was even though she reveled in how much he wanted her. She didn't want to be his mistake, the decision that would always haunt him.

"You amaze me, woman. So bold on the outside, but inside you're…tender," he murmured as he took her hand into his, cradling it much as he had on the plane. "When I was a boy, my grandmother gave me candies for being good in church. I loved them. They were hard on the outside, but sweet caramel on the inside. They were small, only a taste, but so very good."

He raised her hand and kissed it again, pausing to drop a kiss on the pad of each finger. The heat of his touch mixed with the seduction in his voice was kinky torture.

"Long-distance relationships start well, but don't end as well. That's true. I know you will leave, and I will stay here." He sighed as he imparted those words. "I can't leave this mission of mine. It is above me, and one commitment that I can't put aside."

Kate couldn't stop her shoulders from sinking. She understood. He was a man of honor. His principles trumped his passion.

"Still, I cannot ignore my body or my heart."

Her breath caught in her throat. "Your heart?"

"*Si*, my heart. I care for you, *bruja*. No matter what lies down the road, I will always care for you."

She didn't speak, only watched him. She didn't believe in love, but at that moment, she so wanted to think it could happen to her.

"You're like that candy, Kate. The memory of you will be as sweet."

The way he spoke told her he'd given the subject great thought. He'd weighed it in his mind. This was no rash decision. "I can promise you nothing but myself for the next six days."

"That's all I ask." He took her hand into his and brought her to him.

Kate kissed him, brushing her lips over his. Her heart swelled as she thought about how much he wanted her, how much he cared for her. She was humbled by this man. She turned her head and rested it upon his chest. "You are no longer the man you once were. There is nothing selfish about you, Rick. I've never met a man like you."

He lifted her face to him and placed his lips on hers once again, nibbling before demanding more. He broke the kiss and whispered against her lips. "Thank you."

Her answer was to brush her lips against his. He tasted good, like all things spicy and forbidden. His tongue darted out to trace her bottom lip ever so slowly, a dance of seduction that took her breath away.

Then sped it up.

He slid his hands down her sides then around her hips, clasping her bottom and tugging her against him. He fit her like a tailored suit. Every seam met where intended. Perfect length, perfect cut. Rick had been designed for loving her.

He groaned against her mouth and took their kiss

deeper. She could feel him losing control and thrilled in it. This man did not lose himself often. She would enjoy every minute of watching him surrender to desire.

"Let's go," he whispered, all the while letting his hands wander up her back then down again to her bottom.

She sighed against his mouth before trailing her lips down the side of his neck.

"Kate, we've got to get to my house. Fast."

"Yes, we do." She laughed huskily against his collarbone, before dotting teasing kisses along the hard ridge of his shoulder.

He lifted her up and tossed her over his shoulder.

"Rick!" she squealed.

He slapped her on the butt. "I don't like to be teased."

"Yes, you do."

"Okay, I do." His laughter floated on the crisp breeze. Her cheek bumped against the hardness of his back. She smiled. She felt so different, so not like herself. Three weeks ago she would have thought it uncool to have a guy tote her over his shoulder. So silly to giggle. To be happy. When had her world grown so narrow that she'd given up wanting to feel the way she did now?

And more important, what had changed?

She wasn't certain, but she knew at that moment she was the happiest she'd been in a long time. Rick was hers for a whole week. The possibilities seemed endless. Exciting.

"Hey, put me down." She slapped his bottom. "Though I must say, the view is nice."

"I'll put you down on my bed."

"Okay. That'll work."

CHAPTER FIFTEEN

RICK SET KATE ON THE PAVERS, not caring if anyone saw him toting her around Cottonwood. He felt damn good. The thought of indulging in Kate had his pulse racing. He'd spent every night of the past week thinking about her. How her essence would curl around him, soak into him, as he made love to her. He'd lain awake thinking of her skin beneath his lips and he'd woken in the morning wishing he'd been able to live his dreams of loving Kate.

And the daytime wasn't much better. His body craved her touch. He wanted her so badly he felt like an addict. He'd break out in spontaneous sweats and once his hands had actually trembled. He'd had to thrust them into his back pockets to keep from sweeping her into his arms and covering her in kisses.

He called her *bruja* as a joke, but it was no laughing matter. Kate had bewitched him body and soul.

And that had made him think. About his vow and why he still clung to it. Was he the same punk-ass banger he'd been when he'd made that decision? No. The vow had been fulfilled. He was not the man he used to be. In fact, he'd gotten so far away from that man that he couldn't relate to the guys at the center. No, Rick Mendez had been different for a long time.

So he made the conscious decision to let the vow go.

To take the days he had left with Kate and enjoy them rather than suppress every impulse he had to grab hold of her and make her his.

Kate took his hand and smiled at him. She was so damn pretty. So vibrant. So much a part of his life already.

They walked to where his car was parked.

"Rick!" The door flew open and Vera's voice cracked the night. "Rick!"

He dropped Kate's hand and broke into a run toward Vera. Her voice told the story. Something was wrong. Very wrong.

"Oh, Rick, help! Something's wrong with Justus. I can't wake him!"

Wicked thoughts vanished as fear struck him. Justus had been upset at dinner. His color had been off. Why hadn't Rick seen what was right before him? Of course, he knew the answer. He hadn't been thinking with his head. He'd been thinking with a part much lower.

Vera grabbed his arm as he reached the porch and pulled him inside. "Oh, God, Rick. I think it's another stroke. He's unresponsive. He won't talk to me."

He pushed past Vera, and before rounding the corner, he turned to Kate. "Call for help and stay with Vera."

He left both women and pounded up the stairs, wary of what he might find.

KATE REACHED THE PORCH in time to catch Vera before she collapsed with a sob. "Oh, no. No. I can't bear it."

Kate didn't know what to do. Her emotions had swung from happy to fearful, and Vera's crying didn't help. She dragged Vera to a kitchen bar stool and looked for Rosa, but Rick's grandmother had left for the night.

"Sit down and get hold of yourself, Vera."

The woman merely cried harder.

"Oh, for heaven's sake. You're a strong Southern woman. Start acting like it. Justus doesn't need you falling apart on him, so snap out of it, sister."

Kate slid her cell phone from her pocket and dialed 911. She gave the dispatcher as much information as she could before hanging up. She sat with Vera as the woman tried to reign in her emotions.

Finally, she wiped her eyes and straightened. "I'm strong."

"That a girl," Kate said, patting her stepmother's leg before jogging to the front door. It was a long jog. The house was too damned big. She yelled up the curved stairway, "I called 911. They'll be here soon."

Rick's head emerged. "Thanks. I'm bringing him down. Meet me at the elevator."

Kate glanced at the drive and saw the pulse of the ambulance lights in the distance. The low keen of the siren told her they were still on the county highway but getting closer.

The elevator car clanged into place, chiming as the doors slid open. Rick rolled the chair forward, carefully keeping one hand on Justus's shoulder as if he were comforting the man.

Her father looked horrible. His skin was pasty, making the partial paralysis of his face look more pronounced. A line of drool had formed a path from his mouth to the rigid collar of his pearl snap cowboy shirt. At that moment, pity and shame tumbled loose, smacking into her like a rock slide.

Had she been the cause of this?

Had her harsh words at the dinner table pushed him over the edge? The past week had been more than stressful. He'd gotten his wish—Kate had stayed at

Cottonwood—but she hadn't made the stay easy. She'd been stubborn and testy at every turn, and though she'd made progress with Vera and had gotten to know her late half brother, she'd turned her back on any opportunity to interact with the man who'd fathered her.

Guilt pooled in her stomach, rising up, threatening to choke her.

Shit. She shouldn't have been so darned hard on him.

"Okay, Justus. Hold tight. The ambulance just pulled into the drive. I can see the lights from here," Rick said, maneuvering the chair Justus usually operated with his left hand.

To prove his point, the doorbell sounded.

"I'll get it," Kate called, leaping into action and skidding toward the front door, nearly crashing into the Remington sculpture planted right in the middle of the foyer.

She threw the door open. "In here. Hurry."

The paramedics bustled inside toting a bright yellow gurney and several medical canvas bags no doubt full of lifesaving paraphernalia. She hung back as one paramedic whipped out a clipboard and started asking Rick questions. The other bent over Justus and started taking his vitals. Kate clung to the doorknob, glad she had something to hold on to.

Vera appeared at Justus's side. The woman had run a comb through her hair, swiped a dash of lipstick across her lips and pulled on a velour jacket. Her expression was determined as she nudged Rick back and took her place beside her husband. The dampness in her eyes had disappeared, replaced with the starch of a true Southern belle.

Kate watched the paramedics lift Justus onto the

gurney as carefully as if they balanced a serving tray of the finest crystal. After securing him, they rolled her way.

Kate caught Justus's eyes as he went past. Those eyes, so like her own, reflected sheer terror. He tried to say something as they lifted the gurney to clear the jamb. She stood stock-still, watching as they rolled the only blood relative she had from the mansion.

Justus struggled to speak again. "Ahhh…m…sah. Ahhhm sa…wee."

Kate pressed her hand to her mouth.

Dear God. Her heart squeezed so tight and hard that she could physically feel the intensity of it. She dropped her hand to her chest and tried not to cry.

Vera passed her, not looking her way at all. Did the woman blame her? Was she angry over Kate's reaction in the kitchen? Or was her mind wrapped around the fact that her husband might be dying?

Kate didn't know. Didn't have time enough to think about what needed to be said or done. Before she could move, the paramedics had loaded Justus into the ambulance and sped down the long drive.

I'm sorry.

Justus's words echoed and her head dropped forward as Rick's well-worn sneakers came into view.

"Kate?" His voice was soft, almost tentative. Not like him. But he seemed to know the emotion rollicking in her belly.

"What?"

"This isn't your fault." He placed his hands on her shoulders before sliding them down to cup her upper arms.

A single tear fell upon the mottled marble below. "I know."

He folded her into his arms. "No, you don't."

"I've screwed up, Rick. I messed this whole thing up. I so suck." She whispered this into the softness of his T-shirt. It was a muddy brown color and washed into softness. The front read Turkey Trot 2008. It was an absurd name for a five-k run. She didn't know why he wore it, other than it looked amazing stretched across his wide torso.

"You don't suck," he murmured against her curls, stroking her back. "This whole thing has gotten out of control. Justus, Vera, you and me."

Kate was silent, allowing Rick to shelter her in his arms. There was nothing left to say, no easy fix. "I should go to the hospital."

"Of course."

She looked at him. He seemed so grave. "I'm sorry about…you know…the other thing. About not going to your house."

He tried to smile. "Maybe it's best this way."

Pain zapped her right in the gut. She didn't want him to say they would have been a mistake, even if it were true. It hurt. She'd wanted to have that part of him, to gather together the memory of his taste, smell, touch— things to treasure in the empty days ahead of her. That was how she now saw her life in Vegas—empty. Nothing was supposed to change. This two-week pause had pivoted her into a new direction, one that had her looking hard at her old lifestyle and wondering what was so terrific about it.

How had everything changed in only days?

But she had changed, and part of her was angry as hell that coming to Oak Stand had caused it.

"Yes, you're right, of course." Her words were hollow. She didn't believe them.

"Okay, let's get to the hospital."

Kate nodded and pulled herself from the sanctuary of his arms. Life wasn't fair sometimes. And Kate was getting rather tired of coming out on the short end of the stick.

NELLIE MET THEM AT THE hospital in Longview, the nearest facility with emergency services. The place had a smell that could only be labeled as death. Despite the admirable efforts of disinfectant and urine, nothing could cover the scent.

"Oh, Kate," Nellie said, grabbing her and spinning her into a hug. Nellie had seven inches on her, so Kate had no choice in the matter. "Rick called me. How bad is it?"

"He's stable," Rick answered, something Kate didn't appreciate. She didn't need a man to speak for her or call her best friend, as if Kate couldn't handle herself. "but they're worried about further damage to his organs. Seems they don't always know the severity of the stroke until several hours pass. Right now his body is still engaging in small strokes, though they've given him medication to prevent that. He's having tests as we speak."

Kate looked at her friend. "Yeah, what he said."

Nellie's green eyes glinted. Even in such a grave situation, she knew Kate, and she knew Kate hated to be grandstanded by a man.

Rick issued a clipped "Sorry," before heading to triage where Vera had left her jacket. He obviously figured out that she was aggravated. He was intuitive that way.

Nellie and Kate stood alone.

"Are you okay?" Nellie asked, tugging her away from

the curtained bay where Vera sat waiting for the staff to bring Justus from the CAT scan.

"Yeah." Kate shrugged. "Sure. I'm dandy. The man I decide to blackmail just had a heart attack or stroke or something, and I'm fit as a filly."

"Come on, Kate," Nellie said, easing her friend into a plastic bucket chair. "You know this has nothing to do with you."

Kate shrugged. "God, Nell, everything is so screwed up. What am I doing?"

Her friend smiled. "I've asked myself that question about you for most of my life. Never could answer it."

Kate gave a harsh laugh. "I can't keep anything under control—my finances, my personal life, nothing. I can't even believe I'm admitting to being weak, but, shit, I am. Me. I'm falling apart. That's not supposed to happen."

"It happens to the best of us, Kate. You opened a can of worms when you wrote that letter demanding money. That gets icky."

She looked at Nellie. "No, shit."

"But the upside is that you're finally dealing with your past. You've needed to do that for a long time."

"Why?" Kate stomped her foot like a petulant child. "A month ago everything was good. I was an almost-successful business owner whose only sin was dressing too outlandishly, spending too much money and killing the occasional houseplant. My life was platinum. Now it's, like, crappy tin or something."

Nellie laughed but still shook her head. "Maybe, but you've been avoiding dealing with yourself for a long time. Coming home is about more than Justus. Or Rick."

Kate's head snapped up on its own volition. "Rick?"

"I'm no dummy. I have eyes. And this guy is different from any of the others. You're not keeping him at arm's length."

"He doesn't seem to let me. He's always there whether I need him or not," she groused, rubbing at a pull in her sweater. "And for some reason I don't want to keep him away."

Nellie smiled.

"Don't do that."

"Sorry, but you've always had a bad attitude about falling in love. Almost as bad as the attitude you have about Oak Stand," Nellie said. Her green eyes shot to Rick as he stepped into the bay where Vera sat waiting for word on Justus.

"Well, yeah. Every time I come back I'm reminded of who I am. Or more like who I'm not. I'm no founding father's great-great-granddaughter. I'm trailer trash, remember?"

"Oh, please. This again? Let me get out my hammer so I can hack away at that enormous chip on your shoulder. Screw that, I need a jackhammer."

"Easy for you to say, Nell. You weren't the resident charity case." Kate felt her ire grow. It was bad enough she sat in a cracked hospital chair wearing a cheap sweater while lusting after the only man who made her so crazy she'd thrown herself at him to no avail. It was bad enough she'd blackmailed her biological father into another stroke and made Vera cry so many tears she'd needed a hydration IV, but Nellie had to lump in her dissatisfaction with Oak Stand, too.

Give a girl a break.

"You weren't charity, Kate. The people in this town loved you. Why can't you see that?"

She blinked at Nellie. "Did you swipe pills from behind the nurses' desk? Are you hallucinating? People in this town don't think much of me. Get real."

"You are so full of crap, Kate Newman. This town loved you. Still loves you. Did you think people took care of you and your grandmother because they didn't care? Don't you think they knew your mother had left you to go off with some other man? And that the man who'd fathered you had turned his back on you?"

"Exactly. Charity."

Nellie shook her head, her disgust obvious. "You look at it from your point of view, not from the people who loved you. Listen. Do you really think the dress that fit you perfectly showed up in the thrift shop two weeks before prom by accident?"

"Huh?"

"Betty Monk ordered that for you based on the one you circled in that damn teen prom magazine. Think she did that because she didn't like you?"

Kate felt her heart tighten. "What?"

"And remember that trip we took with the church? The one where they suddenly had a spot open? You think that wasn't planned by the Ladies Auxiliary for months? And that time you got sick and had to go to the hospital? Dr. Grabel helped pay the bill. He gave you more than suckers, Kate. Left and right, the people of Oak Stand loved you, even when you acted like a bitch."

Nellie rose, pulling her purse onto her arm. "I swear, if I didn't love you so much and if you weren't in this mess, I'd kick your butt up between your shoulder blades."

"Nell—"

Her friend lifted a hand. "Don't. Just know this. Betty

Monk used to always say 'It takes a town to raise a child.' And she said that long before Hillary Clinton did. And she meant you."

Nellie didn't wait for Kate to reply, she stomped down the hall, never looking back.

At that moment, Kate hated Nellie. Hated her friend for being so damned brutally honest at a time she needed someone to lie to her. She needed someone to tell her everything was going to be okay.

The curtain to the bay opened and Rick stuck his head out. He was checking on her.

Kate bowed her head into her hands.

CHAPTER SIXTEEN

RICK WATCHED KATE WITH A feeling of trepidation. Kate's head was bowed and Nellie had left. His Kate looked so forlorn sitting by herself. When her gaze met his, he saw the raw emotion and despair. Things were starting to come unraveled, and there wasn't a damned thing he could do about it.

Destiny twined about Kate, wrapping her in its embrace, chipping away at the protection she'd built around herself.

He felt the same pull. He had known from the moment he'd first laid eyes on her in Vegas that it was inevitable he'd get tangled in Kate. Something had propelled him to her, and he'd been helpless to stop it.

Perhaps the incident with Justus had been part of destiny's plan, a nudge to remind Rick he was not in control. None of them were. Hadn't he seen that firsthand? His plans, promises and vows had twisted and turned upon themselves. He was no longer centered. The gang members resented him, Kate hovered out of his grasp and now Justus lay fighting for his life.

It made him want to hit someone. Equally strong was the longing to wrap his arms around her and love her for all she was worth.

Life was contradictory sometimes.

"You think he'll be okay, Rick?"

Vera's words cut through his distraction. He should be thinking of Justus. "I don't know."

Vera pressed her lips together and stared at a sign that demonstrated what to do if someone were choking. She looked as if she might need the procedure herself. But then she literally shook herself, and her eyes grew determined. "He will be okay. He has to."

He wondered if it might be better for Justus if he succumbed to the stroke this time. The man had been through so much. Rick didn't know how much more Justus's body could take. But the old man was a fighter. No way he'd leave this life easily. "You may be right. He's a tough old bird."

As he reached out to take Vera's hand, a nurse stuck her head through the curtain. "Mrs. Mitchell?"

"Yes?" There was a hint of misgiving in Vera's response.

"I have some forms for you to fill out. I know it's not the best time, but it will hasten the process in moving Mr. Mitchell to Dallas if need be. Do you mind coming with me for a moment?"

Vera cast a glance at Rick. He nodded. "I'll stay and wait. Go ahead."

She gathered her things and followed the nurse toward the admitting desk. Before she disappeared, she asked. "You have my cell number?"

He gave her a reassuring nod. "Of course."

Then he was alone with his thoughts. Not a good place to be. Not when the person who dominated so many of them sat just down the hallway. Alone. He should go to her, but knew she needed a moment to gather herself. His instincts about Kate came naturally. He got her in a way no one else did.

Man, he was screwed.

Because he knew he'd fallen hard for Kate. Ton-of-bricks hard. No way around it.

"Hey."

The object of his affection poked her head around the curtain. She looked as though she'd been kicked. Her hair stuck to her head in a couple of places, mascara was smudged beneath her hauntingly beautiful eyes and her normally stylish clothes were wrinkled.

"Hey, yourself," he said, sitting back and crossing his foot over his thigh. "No word yet."

"Oh," she said as she stepped inside the bay. "Where's Vera?"

"She went to fill out some paperwork. They may not admit him. They may transfer him to Dallas instead."

A different nurse appeared outside the curtain and looked at Kate. "Mrs. Mitchell?"

"No." She shook her head. "She's—"

"Down the hall," Rick finished for her, mentally kicking himself. He could tell it had bothered Kate when he'd answered for her with Nellie. He glanced her way. She didn't seem to care this time. The life seemed to have been sucked right out of her.

"Oh, well." The nurse hovered, hesitant.

"But I'm his daughter," Kate said. She bit her lower lip and he couldn't tell if she was nervous, or regretted admitting the fact for the first time in a very public way.

"Okay." The nurse smiled at Kate. "We're going to admit Mr. Mitchell for the night and make sure he's stable. They're taking him to intensive care as we speak. You can go up. Visiting hours will be over in fifteen minutes, but you might catch a moment with him."

"Go check on him, Kate. I'll get Vera," Rick said, rising.

Kate's brow furrowed. "Maybe I should find Vera and you can go up."

The nurse patted her shoulder. "Don't worry. He'll likely be sleeping. They've given him a sedative."

He couldn't tell what she was thinking. Maybe no one ever knew what she was thinking. Kate, the enigma.

She looked at him. "Come when you find Vera."

He nodded as the nurse disappeared.

They were alone. He moved toward her, brushing her hair from her forehead. "Are you sure you're okay?"

Her gaze moved from his. "Sure. I'm dandy."

He pressed her to him, tucking her head beneath his chin, wrapping her in his arms. She felt so good there. So right. "It will be okay, Kate."

She relaxed against him. "I don't think so."

He tilted her chin so she was forced to meet his gaze. Tears shimmered in their blue depths. "It will."

She blinked. "No, it's about as bad as it can get. My best friend is pissed at me. Vera's ignoring me. My father had a stroke because I acted like a shit. And, you, well, you make me confused and comforted and happy and scared all at the same time. Life is pretty much sucking right now."

He gathered her to him again. "It could be worse."

She nodded against his chest, wrapping her small arms about him and squeezing. "Yeah, I could be living in Oak Stand working at the Curlique for peanuts. Be fat and pregnant. Or on the Junior League board."

He sighed against hair that vaguely smelled like coconut. "Funny—what sounds good to me sounds like hell to you."

She snorted. "You obviously haven't met the Junior League."

"Oh, I've met them. Some of them have a secret desire to dabble with a tatted up bad boy. Not so different from you."

"I want to do more than dabble with you."

"Do you?"

Kate looked up at him. "I think so. But I can't, can I?"

She slid from his embrace, leaving him with questions and a small burgeoning of hope.

KATE WALKED THROUGH THE DOORS of the intensive care unit like someone walking her last few yards. She didn't want to face what was left of the man who'd sired her. But how could she not?

She couldn't tuck her tail and run. Not after she'd played a part in putting him here. So she pushed through the heavy doors that guarded the gravely ill and looked for a nurse.

"Excuse me." She noticed a flash of blue scrubs behind the curved nurses' desk. A petite woman with braided hair popped up from where she'd been digging in a drawer.

"Yes?"

"A nurse downstairs told me they'd brought, uh, my father here. Justus Mitchell."

The woman dropped the chart she had in her hand onto the cluttered counter. "You've only got—" she looked at her watch "—ten minutes." She swept her hand toward the row of small rooms adjacent to the nurses' desk. "He's in number five."

Kate hesitated.

"Well, come on." The nurse shook her beaded corn-rows. "You got to pick up your feet, child."

She followed the nurse to the room that beeped with equipment. The nurse shifted a tray out of the way. "Don't mind the machines. They beep all the time."

"Oh," was all Kate could manage. Her gaze was rooted to the man in the bed. He looked fragile. Small. Insignificant. So unlike any way she'd ever seen him.

"Ten minutes. That's all." Then the nurse left Kate alone with her father.

Kate didn't know what to do. A lone chair was in the corner. Perhaps she should sit and wait on Vera. She sat, but it didn't feel right. She was too far from the bed. Wasn't it good for the sick to know someone was close by?

She pulled the chair across the floor, wincing as it scraped against the shiny waxed tiles. She parked it in front of the blood pressure monitor and resumed her seat.

Justus stirred.

Tentatively, she reached out and patted his arm. It felt awkward, but she did it anyway. She was lame at giving comfort, but she owed it to him.

He opened his eyes and stared at her.

Kate drew back. She could tell he didn't recognize her.

He groaned, swiping at the oxygen tube over his nose. It registered with Kate as she swatted his hand that he could at least move that part of his body.

"Don't," she said. "Leave that. It's helping you."

He made one more attempt at removing the tube before dropping his hand onto his chest.

"Good. That's good," she said, using a voice she might use with little Mae.

"Katie?" he said, quite plainly.

"Oh," she responded, tucking his hand beneath the sheet and giving it a pat. "You recognize me."

He didn't say anything, just watched her as she settled into the chair. Sitting with a man she half hated as he lay helpless in the bed was uncomfortable, to stay the least.

Several seconds ticked off the clock on the wall before she could look back at him.

"Katie," he said again.

"What?"

"I—I—" Huge coughs racked his body. He pulled his arm from beneath the covers and grabbed her hand.

"Let me get you some water," she said, pulling her hand from his and searching for one of those little plastic pitchers they kept in hospital rooms. She didn't see even a cup. "Let me get the—"

"No," he barked between coughs. "I've got to—"

"Don't be stubborn. You're ill." Kate started for the open doorway. Surely that nurse could hear him.

The nurse met her at the door. She held a pitcher. She ignored Kate as she slid into the room.

"Awake, Mr. Mitchell?"

Kate wanted to tell her she was the queen of the obvious, but figured the nurse wasn't the kind to fancy a smart-ass.

"Katie," Justus said again, between gasps.

"Don't worry about the girl right now. She's over there. Take a little sip of this." The nurse placed a bendy straw between Justus's cracked lips. He sucked at the straw like a dying man. Then it struck Kate. What if he was dying? What if he didn't recover?

"There now. Not too much, Mr. Mitchell," the nurse said, removing the cup and placing it on the rolling table. She looked at Kate. "He can have another sip if he needs it, but let's not give him too much. I don't want him getting sick."

Kate nodded but said nothing as the nurse walked out.

Where the hell were Vera and Rick?

Justus blinked at her.

She had nothing better to do than sit down and wait, so she did. She tried not to focus on Justus, but she couldn't get away from him. She could hear him breathing, smell the Aramis cologne, feel his presence surround her even as silence descended upon her like a shroud.

"Katie."

She finally met his eyes. Fell into them. The pain there, the pleading.

"I need to tell you—"

She lifted a hand and patted the shoulder beneath the worn hospital gown. "You don't need to talk. You need to rest. Vera will be here in a moment."

He shook his head. Irritation evident in his eyes. Oddly, it made her feel better.

"No Vera. Need to talk to you." His words were labored, but he looked damned determined.

"I—" she started then snapped her mouth shut. She couldn't stop him. He'd say what he had to say. But part of her didn't want to hear it. Didn't want him to take away the anger, the part of her that made her Kate Newman. She didn't want to revert to being Katie. But this had been his intention all along. This was what her coming to Texas was about. Justus had regrets. About her.

He wanted forgiveness, and she wasn't sure she could give it to him. She thought about Nellie's words how the people of Oak Stand loved her. Kate had been wrong about them. Could she have been wrong about Justus?

She'd been a child. Had she seen only what she wanted to see?

"Okay. Tell me what you need to tell me."

It took several moments before Justus began to speak. "I'm sorry for—" he passed his good hand over his eyes "—that day."

Kate felt like she'd been thrown from a car with each one of his carefully articulated words. She hadn't expected him to pull no punches right out of the gate. "Oh."

"I was wrong." His words fell on her, heavy, sorrowful and Kate's memory tumbled back to *the day*.

It was the day she'd replayed in her mind for years. The day he'd taken away her childhood, balling it into a wad and tossing it into a corner like a broken toy. It was the day she'd started hating him.

And he'd deserved it.

CHAPTER SEVENTEEN

KATE WAS NINE YEARS OLD the afternoon her mother packed her bags. Not once as she'd tossed her cheap clothes and cheaper jewelry in an old suitcase had she bothered to look at Kate where she sat on the woven couch with the stained arms and missing buttons. Hadn't bothered to offer anything other than "I deserve better than this life." Hadn't bothered to admit she was being the most irresponsible of women, leaving her child with her mother, choosing a man over the little girl she'd given life to.

Kate had watched her mother throw her suitcase into the trunk of the slimy insurance agent's car, heading for a new job in Southern California. Her mother's promises of the beach and Disneyland rang in Kate's ears. She knew her mother lied. Kate would never spin in teacups or dip her toe in the Pacific—at least not with her mom. Her mother had driven out of the trailer park with a toot and a wave. Kate climbed onto her pink bike, the one with the cool water bottle Santa had brought her for Christmas, and pedaled toward Cottonwood.

If her mother didn't want her, her father would.

She was a good kid. She could do long division and climb trees all the way to the top. She didn't eat much and her long hair looked like an Indian princess's when she braided it. She could make her own bed, fold her own clothes and knew how to make grilled cheese sandwiches and peanut-butter cookies. He'd love having her in that big house, even if he was married to someone else.

She'd taken her time getting there. After all, she needed to study this new world she'd be entering. Cows stood around munching on grass. She didn't know much about cows, but she could learn. Her real father had lots of cows and lots of oil wells. She didn't know much about oil, either, except people used it to run their cars and lawn mowers.

By the time she'd reached the gates of Cottonwood, she'd drank all the water she'd put in her water bottle and had to go to the bathroom really bad. When she finally made it up the long drive, she saw a lot of cars in the yard adjacent to the huge white house. Cadillacs, Mercedes and Beemers—all the cars her mother drooled over in the TV ads. Around the back of the house was a white tent with big signs. She'd seen the signs all over town. They were for the governor's race.

Kate dropped her bike beneath a willow tree and pulled off her backpack. Her back was sweaty and her hair had come out of her braid on one side of her head. Grams had brought home leftover French fries from the diner for lunch and Kate had dropped ketchup on her shirt, but it didn't look too bad. Plus, her jeans were practically new and her knockoff Keds were clean and bright.

She smoothed her hair behind her ears and walked toward the people talking and holding glasses that sparkled in the light. They wore pretty clothes like the people on soap operas. She didn't see her father.

She knew what he looked like. He drove through town in his convertible sports car sometimes. He wasn't young, but he wasn't too old. He always wore a cowboy hat and his laugh was really loud. Her mother said he was a force to be reckoned with. Kate didn't know what that meant, but he had to love her. She was his kid.

She wove through the crowd, accidently stepping on one lady's high-heeled shoes. Some people looked at her funny, probably because there weren't any other kids here. She ducked under a man's arm and there he stood. Her father.

He wore dark pants and a light-colored cowboy shirt. A big straw hat perched atop his head. A broad forehead stretched above his brilliant blue eyes. Eyes just like hers. People gathered around him, smiling and nodding as he said something. Probably told a funny story. Kate smiled. He was handsome and rich. And he belonged to her now.

She threw back her shoulders and ran to him.

"Daddy," she called, her shoes slapping the temporary floor beneath the tent. "Momma's gone, so I have to live with you now."

He paused, the drink in his hand halfway to his mouth, and stared at her. His face looked the same way Grams did when a roach crawled across the floor in their cramped kitchen. Like he wanted to squash her.

She stopped about ten feet away from him.

All the people who were talking to him looked at her. It grew very quiet.

Her father set his glass on a nearby table. "Who let you in here?"

Kate could feel the butterflies in her tummy thrash around. Something was wrong. Didn't he know her? He'd sent her a bunny last Easter. Sent it home with her mom. Momma said he thought she was pretty. That he loved her. He was just too busy and important to mess with her.

"I—I— My mom left and went to California. I have to live with you now since you're my dad." Her voice trembled. She didn't want to cry. She had to go to the bathroom real bad and he was supposed to be happy his little girl had come to live with him.

"Who sent you here?"

"I— No one. I just came."

Everybody was watching her. One woman giggled behind her hand. Her fingernails were long and painted shimmery pink. Kate looked at all the adults. They seemed confused and embarrassed.

Her daddy looked mad. "Well, you can go back to where you came from. No one asked you to come here, girl."

Kate grabbed her stomach because it hurt, like the time Tommy Tidwell had kicked her during recess. "But—"

"Don't you argue with me, missy. Turn right around and leave. Right now."

Kate took a step backward. Then another. She couldn't believe it. He was mad at her. "Don't you want me?"

His eyes got all cold and icy looking. "I have a wife and son. You are not my child. I don't know who gave you the idea that you belonged to me, but you don't."

He pushed through the crowd. "Excuse me, Governor, while I deal with this, will you? I'll return in a moment."

His grip was steel on her arm. He dragged her through the crowd, avoiding their eyes but never loosening his grasp on her. She felt her sneakers slide a few times on the grass. Finally, they were beneath the willow tree where she'd left her backpack and bike.

He released her. "Get back on that bike and get off

my property. You have embarrassed me in front of the most powerful people in Texas, girl."

"But my momma told me—"

"I don't care what that woman told you. You don't belong to me."

His words felt like bullets whizzing through her body. They hurt and made her feel like she might sink down and die. Tears streamed down her cheeks, she couldn't stop them. They dripped from her chin as she picked up the handlebars of her bike.

She glanced once more at the man. His face was red like he'd been working in the sun. His eyes looked weird.

"You will never belong to me," he said.

Kate slid onto her bike and pedaled away as fast as she could down that hard-packed drive. She imagined that she was escaping from a bad man. A boogey monster. She pedaled until her legs burned, right out the gate, all the way down the county road until she couldn't see that big white house anymore. Then she jumped off her bike and ran. Ran till her lungs burned. Ran till she couldn't run anymore. At some point, she realized that she'd peed on herself. Her legs were wet and her new tennis shoes squished as she ran. But she didn't care. Nothing mattered anymore.

She finally collapsed near an old wooden fence that had been nearly eaten through with termites and lay beneath the brilliant blue sky.

She'd left her backpack. It had her opal ring and fairy journal in it. It also had the bunny he'd given her. And the picture of Justus and her mom at the state fair in Dallas, the one where her mother's hair looked like the girl from *I Dream of Jeannie*. All her good stuff had been in there. And now it was gone.

He'd probably throw it away like it was junk. Just like he'd thrown her away.

She hated him.

She'd always hate him.

The erratic beeping of the heart monitor pulled Kate from the memory into the present.

That same man lay before her, broken and weak.

She met his eyes once again. He'd killed part of her that April day. Taken away her innocence and made her hard. Made her rebellious. Determined. Guarded. Everything that constituted who she now was.

She'd lost her mother, her father and her dreams that day.

But she'd forged new ones. Ones that she still clung to. Dreams of Fantabulous. And independence. Dreams that felt cloudier by the day. Who was she if she didn't have her anger to protect her?

She looked away.

"I'm sorry," he said again. "I shouldn't have done what I did. I hurt you."

Anger boiled inside her. Even as he lay so vulnerable and sick, she wanted to hurt him. Make him pay for the act he'd perpetrated on a nine-year-old girl.

At the same time, as much as she longed to hold on to that kernel of hate, she wondered if perhaps it was time to let it go. To let the resentment slip into the past and take the hurt with it. Then, perhaps, she'd have room in her heart for better things. Things like faith, hope and charity.

Rick's image appeared.

And maybe she'd have room to fall in love.

"Yes, you did hurt me. I was young. I didn't realize the way the world worked." Kate sighed, finally glancing at him.

"I—I was a bastard. Mean. I hurt you out of pride. Damned pride." She could hear the disgust in his voice and wondered how long he'd felt that way.

Kate pressed her fingers into her eyes. She was tired of crying, but when she pulled her hands away, they were wet. "I shouldn't have gone to Cottonwood that day. I didn't know. I thought…" Hell, did it matter anymore? Was she any different than any other kid who'd been unwanted by a parent?

A choking noise came from Justus. She jumped up to fetch a cup of water, but his good hand caught her and pressed her into the chair. For someone who'd suffered another stroke, his grip was firm. Her eyes jerked from his hand to his face.

He was crying.

"I tried to forget about you. Tried to pretend you weren't my kid. But the wee hours of morning bring truth when they bring the sun. You can't hide from your mistakes at dawn." Tears slid down his weathered cheeks and dropped onto the sheet. He made no attempt to brush them away. His good hand was on her arm, gripping her the way he'd done the day he'd dragged her toward that pink bike beneath the weeping willow.

"I'm so very sorry, Katie. You were just a little girl. A little girl who wanted to be loved. I still see your face. See how hurt you were. It haunts me."

His words surrounded her, settling around her shoulders, pressing her down. And as the regret in his voice penetrated her heart, a flood of sadness, anger, need came gushing forth. "So why did you wait? Why did you ignore me all these years?"

His eyes shuttered. "I'm a fool. I didn't want to face you. I was about as ashamed as a man can be. And I was scared you wouldn't talk to me. When your letter came, I—" He paused. "I couldn't ignore what I needed to do."

She dropped her head. "It feels too late, Justus."

"No, don't say that. It's not too late for forgiveness. Even Jesus forgave while nailed to the cross. Please, Katie. I'm a foolish, unworthy man."

A sob rose in her throat, overpowering her. She let it loose. Let the storm that had gathered inside her for over twenty years come forth. Her body fell forward onto the bed as she shook with the emotion he'd unleashed within her.

And in that small room surrounded by the machines that monitored her father's vital statistics, Kate cried like she'd never cried…not since the day her father had denied her in front of a crowd of Texas's most influential. All the frustration, loneliness and hurt spilled out onto hospital sheets that smelled of bleach.

She cried until her nose ran and her head throbbed. At some point, she realized her father stroked her head soothingly.

"Shh, my Katie, shh," he said, his voice still heavy with the tears he'd cried.

But Kate couldn't stop. The emotion flooded her again and again until finally she stilled beneath his hand, exhausted and replete.

"It's okay, Katie," he said, patting her head in an awkward manner. "It's okay."

She lifted her head and looked at him square in the eye. "I forgive you."

And as she said the words, she meant them.

No more hanging on to the hurt of the past. No more hating Ryan because he'd had what she didn't. No more hating Vera because she'd stolen her mother's dream. No more hating her mother for being so weak. No more hating Oak Stand. Kate was just plain tired of being so angry about her past. It was time to let it all go.

Her father's hand slid to hers and he gave it a squeeze. She watched as his eyes closed and his face grew slack. His breathing rose slow and steady. He looked at peace.

And he was very much asleep.

Kate removed her hand from his and wiped her eyes. She turned toward the table for a tissue to mop her face, and that's when she saw them out of the corner of her eye.

Rick and Vera stood in the doorway.

Vera had tears streaming down her face, and the man who'd stood beside her over the past week had suspicious moisture glinting in his own brown eyes.

No words were said.

Vera simply held out her arms.

Kate didn't think twice. She rose, took three steps and fell into them. Vera wrapped her arms around her and held her, murmuring soothing endearments into her hair as she stroked her back.

Kate didn't bother to think about the fact that Vera was mad at her. Or the fact that visiting hours were over and the no-nonsense nurse had her arms crossed and foot tapping.

She let her father's wife hold her.

Because Kate thought that she might have finally found a family.

CHAPTER EIGHTEEN

RICK'S CAR ATE UP THE HIGHWAY as they traveled back
to Cottonwood. It was two o'clock in the morning. Kate
was utterly exhausted, yet, at the same, tingling from
the enormity of what had occurred.

She stifled a yawn and glanced in the little mirror
clipped to the sun visor. Yikes. She barely recognized
the person staring back. Her eyes were swollen from the
crying, her nose red as Rudolph's and her hair vaguely
resembled a dust mop. Outwardly, Kate was a mess.

But inside, she was as still as a pond in August.

It felt good to rid herself of the turbulent emotion that
had rocked so steadily inside her for so many years. She
looked over at Rick, at the way the light played on the
hollows and planes of his face, and her heart moved in
her chest.

And that was a first for her.

She'd always figured the heart that she'd protected
for so long had shrunk until it was a wizened little seed
like the ones they'd planted at the center. But now it had
awakened and throbbed within her. Aching and tenderly
new.

She didn't say anything. Just slid her hand beneath
the one Rick rested on the gearshift.

He looked at her.

The air crackled and the mood changed.

No sorrow or tears. Only potential.

"I've got to go by the center and check on things. I called the doc and he stayed for a while. Said he was making headway."

"Good. That's good." She studied his face again. What did he want? Where could they go from here?

"Do you want to go home with me?" His words were quietly spoken.

"So I won't be alone?"

A smile touched his lips. "Yeah, that, too, I guess."

Kate paused. Did she really want this? Her body did, had already reacted to his words, tightening and anticipating. But she didn't have the luxury of being impulsive with Rick. He was too important to her. "I thought we'd agreed it would be a mistake."

He nodded. "I know, but like everything with you, Kate, I can't fight myself. I can't let you slip through my fingers and not grab hold of some piece of you. That feeling hasn't changed."

He tore his eyes from the lonely road and looked at her. His dark eyes were almost mystical. "You'll go back to Vegas, but I want the memory of your skin on my lips. The memory of your smell, the sounds you make when you come, the feel of your hands on my body. I'll keep those memories."

"What if you hate me afterward?"

Another little smile. "I could never hate someone as incredible as you, Kate."

She worried her lip as she turned her head and looked out the window. He'd once said she used sex to gain control. Was she doing that again? Trying to recapture herself after pouring everything out in that hospital room? Reestablishing what she'd always been so that she didn't have to deal with the woman she'd become? A woman who could forgive and maybe love.

She wasn't sure.

She hadn't been sure about anything since she'd left Vegas…was it only a little over a week ago? Seemed impossible she'd experienced all she had in the course of such a short time. But there was one thing that was certain, and that, too, hadn't changed since Vegas. She wanted Rick. Body and soul. And that scared her so badly she didn't want to think about it.

"Rick?"

He tightened his grip on her hand. "Yeah, babe?"

Could there ever be a future for them? She couldn't believe she even batted around the thought of commitment. It had been her long-established belief that love was for other people. Not her. Was she contemplating letting herself go there? Long-distance relationships were hard for even the most stable of couples. *Stable* and *Kate* were never used in the same sentence. "Never mind."

His hand tightened on hers. "Stop overanalyzing. Tonight we won't think. We've done too much of it. No mulling, debating or talking ourselves out of it. Tonight we do. Even if in the light of day, it seems certifiable."

"No regrets?"

He shook his head. "I'm not a selfish boy anymore, remember? This is not about fulfilling a need, this is about being with you."

Her heart swelled and contracted. She nodded because tonight was different, almost magical, like destiny was at work again, binding them together.

His thumb stroked her hand in small circles. This time it did not soothe, it stirred.

Moments later, they entered the drive to Phoenix. The lights blazed in the house. There was life there now and it made Kate's heart glad to know the guys within were on the same path she'd walked. Letting go, nourishing their hearts with forgiveness, growing, becoming something they'd never thought possible.

"Wait here. Won't take but a moment."

So she did. And she didn't think about anything other than the way Rick would feel against her. His mouth. The inked breadth of his chest. His calloused hands clasping her hips. His eyes as he slid into her.

By the time he'd jogged back, she'd worked herself up to a fine level of anticipation. Anticipation for hot sex. No thinking. Only doing.

"Okay, everything's good." He slid behind the idling car's wheel and put the gear into Reverse before he even shut the door. Maybe he'd been thinking the same thoughts she had.

The short ride to his cottage was silent, each of them soaked in the thought of each other.

Rick shut off the car and reached for her.

She was ready and straddled the console to get to him. Her mouth met his as her hands sank into his short hair.

"Oh, yes," he breathed against her mouth before sliding his lips down her neck. His hands were just as busy, running up and down her back, cupping her ass before sliding up again.

With one hand she groped for the door handle. She had to get closer to him, feel him between her thighs, and she couldn't do that in the position they were in.

Rick dragged her over his body and out the door that fell open. He stepped out, breaking neither the hold he had on her ass nor the kiss he'd deepened so that she groaned with need. And then they fell onto the cold grass.

"Oh!" she said, landing on his body.

He laughed and rolled her over so he cradled her in his arms. Then he went back to consuming her with his mouth.

She sighed and ran her hands down the muscles of his back. He felt so damn good. So hot. Her body throbbed, pulsed, even, on the cold, slightly damp ground.

She didn't care if her butt grew numb from the cold. Not when one of his warm hands shoved the hem of her shirt upward then followed the path he cleared. All the way up to where her small breast waited beneath the lacy bra. The sweater was Target, but the lingerie was Parisian. And sexy. That's how she rolled.

His fingers plucked her nipple before his hand curved round the flesh that barely filled his palm.

"We've—" He groaned as her hand closed over the hardness lurking behind his fly. She stoked him through his jeans, enjoying the nice length straining against the denim. Very nice indeed. He ripped his lips from her collarbone. "We've got to get inside. Now."

She smiled. "Yes, we do. No free shows for your boys up there."

He lifted his head and smiled at her. In one motion, he leaped to his feet and held out a hand.

Kate took it then, as suddenly, she was in his arms, like Scarlett in Rhett's as he strode up the grand staircase. Except Kate wasn't fighting Rick, and she was no spoiled damsel. She was a willing participant, so she wiggled loose and swung her legs so they fell. Then she twisted and encircled his waist with them. "Better," she whispered against his lips as she rocked her hips so his hardness rubbed right where she needed it.

"Mmm…" He groaned against her mouth, grasping her hips and helping her with the delicious friction she was creating with her movement. "My keys…"

He pressed her against the door. The cold window-pane hit her back. She squealed.

"Sorry," he said, setting her on her feet. "I don't know where my keys went."

They both looked back at the red Mustang. The door was open, the interior light was on and the keys dangled in the ignition.

Kate pointed. "I found them."

"Hell," he muttered. He jogged to the car, grabbed the keys, pressed the lock down and shut the door with his foot. He returned and gathered her against him as he jabbed the key into the lock.

One twist and they tumbled into blessed warmth.

The house was dark, lit only by moonlight. And it felt appropriately intimate. Rick slammed the door, grabbed her hips and pulled her to him. "Do you know how much I want you, Kate?"

Her hand found him again beneath the zipper of his jeans. He was as hard as she'd left him. "I'm getting an idea."

She dropped little kisses along the stubble lining his jaw. "Remember that day you brought me here? When you took the shower?"

"Yeah?" he whispered, sliding his hands so they cupped her ass. He pulled her firm against him.

"I've been dreaming of you beneath the water. Imagining the water sliding over your chest."

"You want to take a shower?"

Her answer was to kick off her shoes and grab the hem of her sweater. One tug and it went over her head.

His laugh was throaty. "I'm taking that as a yes."

He, too, started shedding his clothing, tossing the Turkey Trot T on the floor, revealing to her for the first time the ink that marred the smoothness of his chest. He had no hair, just smooth brandied skin with whorls and images that didn't matter to her now. She'd have time to explore those later. He toed his tennis shoes off and unbuckled the belt at his waist.

Kate kept her eye on him as she shimmied out of her jeans and pulled the angora socks from her feet. He dropped his jeans to the floor and stepped from them, clad only in tented boxers with little hearts on them.

She paused, standing in her expensive lilac lace underwear.

Rick couldn't stop himself from growing even harder when he saw Kate framed in the seductive moonlight in the most amazingly delicate and sexy bra and panties. She was like a sea nymph risen from glittering depths.

Then she became a siren, reaching behind her back and unhooking her bra. She dropped it to the floor and tugged the matching panties down.

He couldn't even swallow. She was magnificent.

Lithe with hollows that rounded out to softness, Kate was all he'd ever imagined in a woman. She was perfectly proportioned with sweet upturned breasts, a sculpted stomach, trim thighs and graceful little feet. Even her bright red toenails were perfection.

"Well?" she said, and looked at his boxers. "Are you going to do the honors? Or shall I?"

He grinned. "Never afraid, are you."

She cocked her head and lifted her eyebrows. "Are you telling me you got something in there I should be afraid of? 'Cause that's getting my hopes up."

Rick slid his boxers off and tossed them over the sofa.

"Oh, yeah. I'm afraid," Kate said with a smile.

He couldn't wait any longer. He grabbed her hand and tugged her behind him toward the single bathroom in the house.

Luckily, the cottage was small and it only took a few steps. He turned on only the inset light above the shower so that they were bathed in a soft glow, reached in and started the water, then used his hands to check out the hills and valleys of Kate's body.

And she did some exploring of her own, sliding her hands across his body like a sculptor molding her subject. She knew how to tease, build anticipation, move him to greater need.

Soon steam curled around them as the tension reached new heights.

"In. Now." Kate pushed at his stomach before sliding her hand down to grasp the length of his erection.

"Mmm?" he murmured against the sweetness of her upturned breasts. The nipples were small and shell-pink. He sucked one into his mouth just as he swept the hand stroking her hip around her bottom, reaching through to stroke the slick heat between her thighs.

"Eek," she yelped, widening her legs before sighing.

He smiled against the sweetness of her breast before catching her nipple between his teeth again and tugging. He increased the rhythm of his fingers, teasing her, driving her crazy.

"No. Now." She pushed against him, more insistent this time. And he complied, mostly because he loved the idea of soaping her up and running his hands over her skin.

He opened the glass door and stepped inside the tumbled stone-tiled shower. It wasn't very big, but wrapped in each other's arms they didn't take up much space.

Kate's mouth met his as the warm water coursed down their bodies, washing away the uncertainty, melting away the questions, leaving only him and Kate and the magic that pulsed between them.

He couldn't get enough of her. Her hands were everywhere, frenzied and insistent.

"I can't wait," she groaned against his shoulder before nipping the skin there with her perfect little teeth. She lifted on her toes and hooked a leg around his waist.

"Kate, we can't have sex without a condom."

She dropped her leg and peered up at him with dazed eyes. "Huh?"

He ducked his head and allowed his mouth to explore the tenderness of her neck before working his way to her ear. "We need a condom."

She rubbed her hands down his back, stroking him as she rubbed her belly against the length of his erection. "Oh."

Rick grabbed the soap and spun her around, lathering up. He gently but quickly scrubbed her back, paying special attention to her delicious derriere. He finished the job on the rest of her body, giving her a sensual washing that left her nearly mewling. She slumped against the gray tile and watched as he made short work of washing himself. Her eyes were a caress and by the time he'd rinsed, he was as hard as a poker.

Kate reached out and grasped his erection. "You could put someone's eye out with that."

He laughed. "Oh, I'll put something out all right."

Her eyes glittered with humor and desire. "That doesn't even make sense."

"Yeah? You do that to me." He pulled the door open and stepped onto the gray mat, grabbing a fluffy towel.

Kate stepped out and he didn't give her time to dry off. He did it for her. A brief rubbing before capturing her lips again.

Man, she tasted good. Sweet, sweet, with a hint of spice.

She wrapped her arms about his damp shoulders and met the stroke of his tongue with her own. "Please, Rick. The bed. Now."

She didn't tease him this time. Simply flew by him as she ran toward the bed.

He laughed and padded to his room. He found her in the center of his bed, sprawled, digging through his nightstand. She pulled out a strip of condoms and waved them in the air. "I thought you weren't planning on having sex until you were committed."

He climbed onto the high mattress and crawled toward her. "I was never a Boy Scout, but that doesn't mean I don't follow their motto."

She fell back against his pillows, arching her back, thrusting her pink-tipped breasts into the air. "Watch out for bears?"

"You were a Boy Scout?" He tugged her knee so he could walk his fingers up her thigh toward the sweetest temptation he'd known in a while. She had a small tattoo of a butterfly on her hip. He tapped it with one finger.

Kate laughed, then sighed as his fingers found where she needed him most. "Nope. I just taught them real survival skills. Like how to get to second base or how to sneak bourbon from the family liquor cabinet."

"My wicked Kate," he whispered against her lips before tracing her bottom lip with his tongue. She widened her legs to give him better access. He didn't waste time accommodating her. Soon she was writhing, sighing and reaching out to touch him, stroke his shoulder, glance his jaw, tug his hair.

"Please, no more," she said, twisting away from him.

"I can't wait anyway." He grabbed the condoms from the hand she'd pressed to the quilt, ripped one open and quickly did the honors.

She raised on her elbows and watched as he sheathed himself with the condom. Her eyes were liquid pools, pulsing with desire. He knew he could get lost in them.

He rose onto his knees and moved toward her. She welcomed him, parting her thighs, and Rick knew it was a picture he would savor in the wee dark hours of the night when the taste of her skin had faded from his memory.

He entered her swiftly.

"Ahh." She threw her head back and clasped his shoulders. "Rick. So good."

He agreed, but couldn't find the words. She was so hot and tight and it had been so damn long for him. He established the rhythm, capturing her head between his hands, holding her so he could cover her mouth with his. His tongue met hers as he plunged into her again and again. Soon he was lost in the magic of making love.

To his beautiful, wild Kate.

She slid her arms from his shoulders to wrap around his neck. Jerking him toward her, she twined her legs about his waist, locking him in place, causing his chest to brush the tips of her breasts. He could feel her tightening around him, could feel his release building.

"Oh," she breathed against his mouth. Their bodies moved faster. He tilted her hips so she could take him deeper. He watched Kate as she caught her bottom lip between her teeth. Her eyes were closed, her face screwed up in concentration.

Her hands slid to his ass as she urged him to increase the tempo. He obliged, driving into her, moving her across the bed, bumping her head against the pine headboard.

He felt her tighten around him. Then her eyes flew open.

He caught her scream with his mouth as he tumbled over the edge to join her. Wave after wave of pleasure seized him, pounding into him. Until it finally subsided.

He fell to the side, pulling Kate on top of him.

She panted as if she'd run a race, and for a moment they lay utterly still.

"Wow," she breathed against his chest. "That was fantastic."

He chuckled as he smoothed her raven hair. "Yeah, pretty damned awesome."

She lifted her head. "I mean it was fantastic. Like something I'd never felt before."

He grinned. "You say that to all the fellows."

She shook her head and he could see she was serious. "No, what I meant is that has never happened before."

The realization smacked him in the head. "You mean you've never come before?"

Heat stole across her cheeks. His wild, cosmopolitan Kate had never had an orgasm? Something akin to self-satisfaction stole across him, swelled inside him.

"I've come before. Just not with a man." She sounded defensive. And embarrassed.

He dropped a kiss on her upturned nose before capturing her sweet little bee-stung mouth with his.

"Well, then. I'm assuming the other has been battery-operated?"

She smacked him on the arm before rolling off him. "Smug, aren't you?"

He smiled. "No, honored."

She ducked her head and rested it upon his outstretched arm.

"Hey," he said, tugging a dark blade of her hair. She looked up and the honesty in her blue eyes rocked him. This was Kate naked, literally and emotionally. "Guess what?"

"What?" she whispered.

He lifted himself upon one elbow and tugged her to him, nipping her silken shoulder. "My batteries don't ever run out."

She laughed. "That's an upside."

"Better believe it." And then he kissed her.

CHAPTER NINETEEN

RICK KEPT KISSING HER for the next five days. In the kitchen of Phoenix. On the back patio of Cottonwood. Below the statue of Rufus Tucker in the center of Oak Stand. And around the corner of the Longview Regional Hospital stroke center where her father was recovering.

No matter where they were, Rick didn't pass up the opportunity to pull her into his arms and let her know he wanted her. In fact, they made out like teenagers every chance they got. It would have been embarrassing if it hadn't felt so good.

For once in her life, Kate enjoyed being someone's—dare she say it?—girlfriend.

It was a title she'd never tolerated before. Oh, sure, she dated, even went out for second and third dates, but never had she wanted to feel like part of a couple with someone. Surprisingly, she liked it, so she indulged the little fantasy she'd created in her mind. The one where she was normal, like any other girl. The one where she didn't go back to Vegas. Where she expected a happy ending. Where she planned for weekend getaways, a princess-cut ring and a white lace veil.

The whole thing was a sham.

But she went with it anyway, mostly because she didn't want to think about this being a fling. She didn't want to think about her and Rick being over in less than twenty-four hours. She only wanted to savor the time she had left with the man who made her feel comfortable in her own skin.

With him, she didn't have to think. She simply was.

"Penny for your thoughts," he said, jarring her from her musings as they drove down Interstate 20 in his Mustang for yet another visit with Justus. It would probably be her last—her flight left tomorrow afternoon.

"Not even worth a plug nickel," she said. "What is a plug nickel, anyway?"

"Something people use to fool vending machines, I think."

They'd spent so much time on this stretch of highway that the landmarks were familiar. She'd miss sitting beside him while he took the twists and bends of the road. She'd miss a lot of things.

But she wasn't supposed to think about that.

"Nellie said she'd take me to the airport. I think it might be for the, um, best." The words rushed from her mouth. Damn. She didn't want to bring up leaving. Why had she?

"Why?" The word was spoken softly, shaded with hurt.

"I—I'm not sure I can—" She was afraid she'd say it—that she wouldn't be able to get on the plane. That she wanted to stay with him and pretend to be something she wasn't—a daughter, a sister, a girlfriend.

But she was none of those things. Not really. She was Kate Newman. And Kate Newman was a Vegas business owner. A hard-ass ballbuster with an attitude and towering stilettos. She was a good time party girl with no ties, no mortgage and no dependents on her tax form. She was an island and she didn't need anyone.

His eyes met hers. "That's fine. For the best."

Silence fell, hard and bitter.

A lump formed in Kate's throat, and she stared out the window at the scenery whizzing by. The past few days had been wonderful. Why had she ruined it by bringing up her flight tomorrow? She was a dumb-ass.

Just this morning she'd awakened to find him watching her sleep. She'd always thought that was something a character did in movies or words in a song by Aerosmith. Honestly, it had always seemed a bit hokey. But Rick's soft brown eyes had caressed her, reflecting the morning light and something she couldn't quite grasp. He'd given her a sheepish grin.

She'd stretched. "Are you watching me sleep?"

"Maybe."

"Why?" She'd curled her toes into his somewhat scratchy new sheets.

"It sounds lame, but you're always moving, always running that smart-assed mouth. It's nice to watch you curled up, like a little girl. You look almost innocent."

She smiled. "After last night, you know that's not true."

Rick wouldn't let the tender moment go. "I thought I'd take a mental picture."

Something sweet filled Kate at his words. And she'd taken a mental picture herself. Rick, bare-chested in a pair of striped pajama pants sitting in a rustic rocker framed against an awakening sky. His hair clipped short, his jaw whiskered with stubble, his feet crossed and propped on the end of the bed. The sun behind him cast shadows on his face, but she could see his eyes, see the way they moved over her and loved her.

She patted the still-warm spot next to her. "How about creating a mental video?"

He smiled and unwound his body, joining her. He pulled the quilt to their chins, tucking her close to him, spooning her. One hand curled round to rest securely on her ribs, and they lay together, each feeling the other's heart beat.

Her invitation had been for pleasure, and he gave her that by holding her in the still morning light.

She'd never savored such feeling before, simply being held in the arms of a man, and it surprised her how much she loved being secured in his warm embrace. Such ease. Such comfort.

The exact opposite of what she felt now as they approached Longview, caught in that horrible moment of regret. A moment she'd prayed wouldn't come.

"I didn't mean I didn't want you to take me. I just don't know if it would be a good idea. I don't think—"

He held up a hand. "Not a problem. I know the score, Kate."

He sounded hurt. That big guy who had sent shivers down her spine the first time she'd seen him in the post office. He'd been almost threatening, and she remembered how she'd hurried to her car, thinking him dangerous. And now here he sat, vulnerable, because of her.

"Rick, I have to go back. I don't have a future here." She touched his shoulder and felt him stiffen.

"That's nice. Remind me of why I should have said no to you. No future. Exactly."

"I don't mean with you, I mean here." She waved her hand at the outskirts of Longview. A feed store with gleaming orange tractors lined up like toys on a shelf. A run-down gas station. A fast loan place. A nail salon. It was a far cry from the glitz of Vegas. "I have a business, friends, a life somewhere else. I can't throw who I am away because I have a hunch."

He whipped his head around. His eyes sparked. "That's what we are? A hunch?"

Kate sighed. She wasn't going to win. She'd hurt him, and for that, she was sorry. But she wasn't staying in Oak Stand. She wouldn't go back to being Katie Newman. She wouldn't embrace a life she didn't want. "No, we are what we agreed to that night on the way home from Longview. We're a moment in time. I thought we said there would be no regrets."

He didn't say anything else. His face hardened as he stared at the traffic. Minutes later, the facade of Longview Regional peered gloomily at them as they entered the drive. Or maybe it wasn't the hospital that was depressing, it was the rotten mood in the car. Unspoken words. Fissures in the foundation of something fleeting.

"I'll drop you, then park," Rick said, swinging toward the entrance to the physical-therapy wing.

"No, just park. I'll walk with you," she said.

His foot hovered on the brake, slowing them, but then the car shot forward.

"Fine." He narrowly missed a pickup truck as he turned into the parking lot.

"Rick." She placed a hand on his arm.

He flinched. "What?"

"Let's not ruin it."

His dark eyes flashed as they met hers. He stopped the car in the middle of a row. "So we're gonna pretend that everything's okay? That you aren't leaving? That you aren't throwing us away?"

She drew back as if he'd slapped her. "What?"

"You know damn well what." He ground the words

out between gritted teeth. She could feel his anger burgeoning, crowding the interior of the vintage car.

A horn sounded behind them. Rick's car blocked the row.

"Shit," he said, stepping on the accelerator, jerking them forward. He rounded another row. There were no parking spots. Again, he spun the wheel and gave the car gas. It leaped to life, roaring down the next aisle.

"Please," she said. "Calm down."

"Ha. That's funny coming from you," he said in a not-so-friendly way.

So this is how it would end. Badly. Meanly. God, she hadn't wanted it to be this way, but had known it would be hard to pretend parting didn't hurt. That hearts hadn't gotten knocked around and bruised. "Insult me if it makes you feel better. Maybe you can learn to hate me so it won't be so bad."

He finally found a spot and swung the car into it, braking hard, jerking her forward. "Maybe so."

Kate pressed her hands over her face before dropping them in her lap. "Why are you doing this?"

He turned so his broad shoulders were squared with the door. They were wonderful shoulders, covered with looping ink, strong, capable of carrying burdens. How many times had Kate leaned on them over the past two weeks? How many times had she clung to them as he'd taken her to heights she'd never explored before? Now they tensed. "Because you are a coward."

She could feel the color leave her face. "Bullshit. I'm not a coward."

He shrugged. "I call 'em like I see 'em."

He pulled the keys from the ignition, climbed out and walked away.

Kate felt blindsided by his anger. She'd always been

straight with him. Never misled him. He knew she wasn't going to stay. No way in hell did she want to go back to what she'd been, even if she had a better understanding of exactly who that was. She couldn't take those steps backward, she'd worked too long and too hard. Fantabulous waited. Her clients waited. The IRS waited. It was time to return to the reality of her life.

How could he not understand?

She climbed from the car, wishing she could call Nellie and head to the airport right now. She even rooted around in her bag for her cell phone before realizing there was no way around saying goodbye to her father. No way of avoiding Rick's uncomfortable anger.

And no way of ignoring the twangs of hurt vibrating in her heart. These past two weeks had taken a chisel to the flinty emotions once cemented inside her, chipping them away in big chunks. The problem with a heart that had been emptied of bad stuff was the space made for good stuff. Really good stuff. Hopes and dreams had found their way in, filling her up, making her think of possibilities instead of doom.

She'd been foolish to fall in love with Rick.

And that's what she'd done. Allowed herself to fall head over heels. She'd never thought it possible. Almost didn't believe in the shifty emotion, even though she'd seen people immerse themselves in it completely. And not only had she opened her heart to Rick, but she'd made room for Vera, Justus and Oak Stand. She was consumed with lots of tender, new emotions. And she wasn't sure she could sort through them. Wasn't sure if they could be enough to pull her from her past life. From all things she'd wanted for so long.

The hospital doors swooshed open and she stepped

into the chilly interior. Hospitals always seemed to be cold and sterile, no matter how many prints of flowers lined their halls.

Rick wasn't waiting.

Kate gave a mental shrug and headed to the bank of elevators that would take her to the Stroke Center on the second floor, where her father would be cranky and weary in a bed outfitted for his rehab.

She made it to her father's room without seeing Rick. The door was half-open and she could hear Vera placating Justus.

She tapped on the door and pushed it open. The arguing stopped.

"Kate." Vera smiled. "I wondered when you would be by. Is Rick with you?"

She shrugged. "He's here somewhere. I don't know where he went."

Her father stilled and managed a lopsided smile. "Hello, Katie. Glad you came to see me before you left."

She still didn't feel exactly comfortable with the man she'd so recently forgiven, but she was trying to be nicer. More open. "Hello, Justus. How are you today?"

"Tired of them jerking me left and right, pulling me this way and that like I'm a piece of taffy."

"In other words, you're feeling normal?"

Vera laughed. "Didn't take you long to figure him out, did it?"

"Not really," Kate said, stepping into the room. Flowers covered every surface. She moved a planter from a guest chair and slid it next to Vera. "It looks like a flower shop in here."

"Yes, Justus has many associates." Vera looked around the room at the tulips, daisies, yellow roses and bluebonnets perfuming the air. Obviously, everyone thought the Texas state flower appropriate. "We should see if there are other patients who might be cheered by a few bouquets. Or a nursing home perhaps?"

"I'll check on it," Rick said, entering the room with a cardboard tray of coffees.

"There you are," Vera said, taking the coffee from him. "Kate said she didn't know where you were."

Rick didn't look at her. "She wouldn't."

His words were heavy with meaning. Vera's brow crinkled, but she didn't say anything, just shifted her gaze from Rick to Kate.

Kate tried to smile, but it felt pained. Shit.

Rick took a cup and positioned himself against the hospital wall.

"Thank you for the coffee," Vera said, moving the cardboard tray from Justus's reach. He'd inched his good hand toward the cup. "None for you, dear."

"I'm sick of juice. Feel like a toddler with all the grape juice they push my way," he grumbled, his blues eyes narrowing as he studied Kate and Rick. "What the devil is going on with you two?"

Kate stiffened and Rick shrugged.

"Nothing," Rick said. "Having some trouble at the center with one of the guys."

This was news to Kate. She echoed his response. "Nothing."

Her father opened his mouth to say something, then snapped it closed. He looked at his wife and Kate could see something pass between them. "What's the problem at the center? Thought things were going fine."

Rick stared out the window, meeting no one's gaze. "Nothing I can't handle. Just got my thoughts tied up."

Silence pressed down, interrupted only by the

chirping of one of the machines hooked to Justus. Seconds ticked by, but it seemed like hours.

Finally, Vera waded into the tension. "Justus should be released the day after tomorrow. His regular physical therapist has been briefed and the doctor says they can find no significant damage from the last stroke."

"That's good," Kate murmured.

"When will you come back?" Justus asked. She jerked her gaze to her father. His blue eyes pinned her against the striped wallpaper behind her.

"Well, I—" Kate paused.

"She's not coming back." Rick's harsh words echoed in the small room. He'd turned to glare at the Mitchells. "She did what you asked. Stayed two weeks. The money is hers."

Justus didn't react.

At that instant, Kate wished for a natural disaster to sweep through and save her from the sheer hell of the moment, but the sunshine beaming in from the window declared it impossible. So she closed her eyes and tried to propel herself through space to Vegas. Or the Bermuda Triangle. Or anywhere other than here.

"I never said I wouldn't come back." She opened her eyes. "But I need some time. A lot has happened, stuff I haven't even had time to process. I need a little space."

Vera nodded. "I understand, Kate. What I think Justus is trying to say—" she patted his shoulder "—in a rather abrupt manner, is that we hope you will choose to be part of our lives…even if it's in a small way."

Kate pressed her lips together and nodded. Rick had spun toward the window and no longer looked at any of them. His muscles were bunched beneath his long-sleeved T-shirt, and her hands itched to soothe them, to ply the muscles beneath her fingers, make him calm and at peace. But she couldn't. His anger at her would have to burn itself out. And that might take longer than a day. Or a week. Or a year. He might never get over his anger at her.

There would be no more tangled sheets with Rick. No more sweet kisses and wisecracks. What they'd shared was what she'd intended all along—something wonderful but temporary.

And it was time to go home to Vegas, to move forward.

She looked at her father. Her eyes softened. "I'll be back, Justus. But this time, I'll come on my own terms."

He nodded.

Rick walked out.

Kate looked from Vera to Justus, at a loss for what to say about Rick's behavior.

A nurse came in with a big bouquet of red roses. She nudged a box of tissues aside and set the vase on the bedside table. "There. Happy Valentine's Day!"

The lush roses were in full bloom, beautifully signifying the day for love.

Irony sucked.

CHAPTER TWENTY

KATE'S CONDO SMELLED like rotten Chinese takeout.

She'd forgotten to take the garbage out before she'd left Vegas, and so her homecoming was none too pleasant. Not that she'd expected it to be. But after the rollicking roller coaster of emotions she'd been on, a clean house would have been a small solace.

No balm for her heart.

And no more Chinese takeout for a while. Bluck.

Kate parked her rolling suitcase in the foyer and surveyed her domain.

White fluffy rug centered on slate floor. A Driade couch in fuschia, matching striped armchairs, funky George Kovac floor lamps and a glass sculpture made by her friend Billie filled the room. Very sleek, very modern, very designer.

And, oddly, not so welcoming.

Kate kicked off her flats and padded to the kitchen to remove the offending smell. Her answering machine blinked with messages, her one houseplant had died and she'd left a yogurt carton in the sink. Thank God she didn't have a pet.

After setting things right, she grabbed her purse and looked for her cell. The check for fifty thousand dollars stared at her from the gaping opening of her bag.

She pulled it out, studying the tight signature of her father, looking at the zeroes following the five.

She'd gotten what she'd set out for…and more.

So why didn't she feel victorious? Of course, she knew the answer. But she didn't want to think about him. Couldn't do that yet. Not when she felt so raw. And vulnerable.

She grabbed her phone, then stuck the check to her fridge with a magnet right beside the appointment for a dental cleaning she'd missed while in Texas. The check seemed to mock her, so she turned it over.

She punched out the numbers she'd dialed a million times. Jeremy answered on the second ring. "Let us make you Fantabulous."

"Too late. I'm already there," Kate said.

"Kate! You're back already? Why didn't you call? I would have picked you up, chickadee."

She smiled even though it was hard. Her face felt tight. She was a patched piece of plaster, praying the cracks didn't give way to crumbled dust. "I took a cab. Knew you were busy."

"Well, get down here, girlfriend. I've got something to show you." Jeremy sounded pretty cheerful, considering the last time she'd spoken with him Victor hadn't been doing well.

"I'm gonna take it easy this afternoon. I'm pretty tired—you know how flying makes me."

"How many pills did you pop? You've got your clothes on, don't you?"

Kate laughed. "The cabdriver wouldn't have picked me up if I hadn't."

"You'd be surprised," he said. Laughter sounded in the background and she could hear Jay-Z playing. Singing about concrete jungles. Places so different from gentle rolling hills and open patios where people grew tomatoes in old whiskey barrels. "Okay, sugar, tomorrow it is. You've got two on the books."

Kate frowned. Only two clients? Usually she was booked solid when she returned from a trip. But then again, business had been slow. She could sleep in, so it was all good. "See you then."

She hung up and faced her empty apartment…and her wounded heart. Her place looked lonely. Sad. Empty.

The phone vibrated in her hand as Sade erupted. Her friend Trish.

"Hey, lady," Kate said, tracing her finger over the dust on her glass table. She dropped into an acrylic chair shaped like a stiletto.

"Marshall's guest deejaying tonight at the Ghost Bar. Wanna?" Trish sounded like she always did. Smooth as Scotch. Totally unruffled. Marshall Wainwright, aka DJ Rain, was her current flavor of the month.

"I don't—" Maybe going with Trish would make her feel better. Get Kate back into her old vibe. She looked around the silent room. "Okay, sure."

"You want me to swing by and pick you up? I'm not going home with Marsh. I've got a deposition at 9:00."

Trish was an assistant district attorney for Carson County. She kicked serious butt in the courtroom, intimidating defendants like a hawk would a hapless mouse. She had an outstanding conviction record and was on the fast track to the top. She wouldn't jeopardize a case even for the wickedly sweet Marshall Wainwright, who played a thug DJ but was really from the wealthy suburbs of Chicago.

"Okay, um, sure." Kate glanced at the clock on her state-of-the-art stove she'd never used for anything other than boiling water for tea.

"You sound strange. What did they do to you down there in Texas?" Trish didn't miss a thing. Not the slightest hesitation or inflection.

"They put me in cowboy boots and made me do the two-step," she replied, trying to sound like her old self.

"Yeah. Whatever. I'll be there at 9:00," Trish said, sounding much more like she was saying, "I'll interrogate you at 9:00."

"Ciao," Kate said, but the line was already dead.

She rose with a sigh and retrieved her luggage. A hot shower would melt away the travel stress and a little nap would rid her of the vestiges of the Xanax she'd taken in Dallas. She had a new baby-doll dress to wear tonight, not to mention a pair of Stuart Weitzman strappy sandals that made her legs look longer. Sure. She'd be back to her old self in no time.

"Kate the Great is back in the house," Jeremy called out the next morning when she dragged herself in clutching a triple mocha latte and a bag full of clean towels she'd had at her condo for over three weeks.

"If you can call physically being here *back*," she muttered, heading toward their shared office and dumping the towels in a side chair.

She slipped off the dark glasses she wore to hide her swollen eyes and glanced in the mirror above her desk. Ouch. She looked like reheated oatmeal. Pasty, lumpy and unappetizing.

She couldn't go out into the salon looking the way she did.

She grabbed the tackle box she kept her lures in. No plastic worms or bright wooden fish with hooks. No, this tackle box contained a palette of lip glosses, concealers, mascaras, sparkling eye shadow and various liners and brushes. These were the real lures in life.

While she tried to hide the damage done from a late night—too many beers and a crying jag—she berated herself for going out with Trish.

It had been miserable. She'd sat on a stool in a corner, swilling beer and watching happy people get their groove on. The whole time, all she could think about was how this used to make her happy, and how it now seemed so stupid.

People pumped their hands in the air to the beat of the music, shot neon-colored liquor from test tubes and prattled about their Facebook status and how much they'd lost doing P90X. Thirty-something men wearing too much cologne roved in packs and behaved like a bunch of frat boys on spring break. Women her age, wearing cheap clothes that barely contained their store-bought boobs, tottered on heels that were too high and actually invited the wolf pack to sample the wares.

She'd spent the whole night drinking and wondering if her life had always been this way.

But she knew the answer deep down inside.

Vegas hadn't changed. The club scene hadn't changed. She had.

That hacked her off so much that she'd drunk too much. One Newcastle after another flew through her hands until she could see two Trish's when her friend finally came to tug her to the dance floor. But Kate wouldn't go.

And that pissed her off *even* more. She was supposed to get her groove back, put Rick behind her and move forward. Instead, she'd sat like a lonely sourpuss, warding off gelled-up dudes with a get-away-from-me death stare. She'd felt like a bitter, washed-up old maid. And in her beer-soaked mind, all she wanted was the man she'd left behind.

For this—thumping music, lukewarm beer and an empty bed.

She was a dumb-ass.

Jeremy stuck his head in the office, jarring her from her sad-sack memory. "Hey, you. What's going—"

He paused when she turned around. His waxed and perfectly tinted eyebrows crinkled. "Jeez, doll. Have you been crying?"

"No." Her response was too quick.

Jeremy moved inside the office and draped an arm over her shoulder. "They made you do line dances down there, didn't they? It's okay. We can get you some therapy."

Kate smiled. She had to. Jeremy was one of her best friends. "No. No line dances."

He dropped a kiss on her head. "Then why's my Katiebug so sad?"

Just him calling her *Katie* made tears spring into her eyes.

"Oh, God. Did they make you wear Wranglers? Because Wrangler butts drive me nuts, but not on women." He was trying to make her smile again. But this time she couldn't. She actually felt her chin wobble.

"I fell in love," she said.

Jeremy clutched his chest and fell into the chair holding the bag of towels. He yelped, hopped up, tossed the bag, then swooned again. Then he pulled her onto his lap and wrapped his arms around her. "That's great, Katiebug. Really great."

She laid her head on his shoulder. "No, it's not. It's impossible."

"Why?"

"Because my life is here. I have everything here. How can I be in a relationship that's a thousand miles away?" She wiped her cheeks so she wouldn't get Jeremy's Oxford shirt damp.

"Hey," he said, shifting her so he could look at her. "I want to show you something."

He patted her back, indicating she had to get off his lap. She stood and he walked to their none-too-tidy desk and pulled an envelope from under the blotter. He handed her the letter.

She read it and then looked up at him and repeated the same word she'd said to him over a similar letter a little over a month ago. "How?"

"My father gave me the money my grandmother had left me. Money he'd hidden. It was over seventy-five thousand dollars."

"Oh, my God!" Kate lowered the letter. Her mouth fell open as she looked at her friend. She was absolutely shocked. And he beamed at her, like a proud schoolboy. "Your father *talked* to you?"

"Better than that, knowing you were facing your past gave me the courage to face mine. I invited my father to lunch, and though he's no card-carrying member of PFLAG yet, he's offered to start therapy with me." He turned his hands over and shrugged. "It's a start."

She hurried around the desk and enveloped her friend in a hug. "I'm so happy for you. I can't believe it!"

He wrapped her in his thin arms. "I can't, either, but I'm happy about it. And the salon is okay. Better than okay."

Kate untangled herself from her friend and looked at the letter she'd dropped on the desk. No more bankruptcy. No more IRS threats. Fantabulous would stay fantabulous.

"I still can't believe it. I didn't even have to go to Texas after all." Her heart beat as though she'd ran a race. Why? She wasn't sure. She stared at a picture of her wearing a wig and sparkly dress. Jeremy had taken it on New Year's Eve before they'd gotten the first IRS letter. She looked happy.

The room fell silent for a moment.

She looked at her friend. He stared at her measuringly. "Maybe you did have to go, hon."

She sank into the chair they'd vacated moments before.

Jeremy fell into the desk chair and folded his hands on the desk like a high-school counselor. "Maybe all this was meant to be. A way for me to reconcile with my father. A way for you to face the past you've been running from all these years."

Kate stared at a dust bunny huddled in a corner. "Maybe."

"You said you fell in love, but you've changed more than that. I can see it in your eyes. The way you hold yourself. You seem vulnerable and, I don't know, deeper."

She shrugged. "I went through a lot of shit down there. A lot of stuff I needed to go through, I guess, but it changed me. I don't feel the same."

He nodded. "Let me tell you something, my dear friend. I'm learning that life is too damned short to waste time on things that don't matter. You know?"

Victor's cheerful face flashed into her mind. Jeremy likely didn't have much time left with his partner. No time to waste. "I get you, Jer, but I can't pursue something that's not right for me. My life is here. In Vegas. I can't throw everything I've worked so hard for out the window like it's nothing. It means something to me."

"Sure it does." He nodded, picking up her glass paperweight. The one Nellie had sent her. "But, you see, Victor is my life. I'd choose him over my career, my house, my car, anything. I'd throw everything aside if I could have him forever."

Kate lifted her head and met his eyes. She could see he meant what he said. What could she say to something like that?

He continued. "If I could go back in time, I'd toss out all those wasted years of clubbing, buying designer clothes, vacationing in St. Barts—all that stuff I thought was important—just to hurry up and get to the part where I had him in my life. He's made me so much more than I ever expected. And the thought of not having him with me makes me so ill that I can barely get out of bed in the morning. No way would I ever let anything stand between us."

She looked away because she didn't want to see his pain, didn't want to witness his grief. She was afraid she might find herself in his eyes. Knew she'd already found herself in his words. "I don't know. I don't know what to do. The salon—"

"Is a place. It's not a person, Kate."

"But it's mine. It's what I worked for. What I dreamed about."

He shrugged. "Then, darling, you've got to decide if it's enough."

He shoved the rolling chair back and rose. On his way out of the office, he gave her a sympathetic pat on the shoulder. But he didn't say anything other than, "By the way, Mandy wanted to know if she could buy into the business. She's brought in more new customers in the past two weeks than we've had in three months. Feels like destiny knocking, doesn't it?"

And he left.

Kate pressed her hands to her eyes and rubbed. God, she wished she could wipe away her thoughts. Her head pounded from her hangover, her thoughts whirled faster than the bike spokes at the Tour de France and her heart plain ached. Her throat clogged with unshed tears.

Damn. She hated herself for being weak. For not being the Kate she was a month ago. For not being able to pull out the emotions rolling inside her, shove them in a box and hide them underneath her bed.

She opened her eyes and looked around her office. At the mosaic tile mirror she and Jeremy had attempted to recreate from a *Design Star* episode. At the bookcase she'd found on the side of the road the one time she'd managed to drag her friend Billie to a garage sale. At the mug that read I Fix $8 Haircuts she'd been given by a stylist before she moved to Rhode Island with an accountant she'd met at Cirque du Soleil. At the ratty plant in the window, the stacks of catalogs on the desk and the framed picture of her, Nellie, Billie and Trish taken the night Nellie had met Jack at Agave Blue, his former nightclub.

Her world had seemed so full.

She looked at the bag she'd dropped beside the chair next to her favorite catalogs—Neiman's, Nordstrom's and Saks. An awesome pair of bright pink Christian Louboutins seduced from the front cover of the Neiman Marcus spring collection.

She sighed and pulled the check her father had given her from the depths of her purse. She'd stuck it inside that morning, intending to head to the bank. She studied all those zeroes and thought of what they could buy.

She had to decide where her future lay.

Should she stay in Vegas?

Or should she carve out a new future in the piney woods of East Texas with Rick?

One way seemed smooth and safe.

The other very uncertain.

She was in the city of second chances. A city of risk takers. Of rebels. Of the brokenhearted.

But could Kate really roll the dice on her life?

CHAPTER TWENTY-ONE

OVER TWO MONTHS LATER, Kate considered how silly her powder-blue VW bug looked parked next to the huge pickup in front of Phoenix. Especially with one of her George Kovac modern lamps looming in the backseat over a motley assortment of boxes and bags. Kate took a deep breath and pulled her canvas bag onto her shoulder. She hadn't had time to bring a covered dish for the postgraduation party. Hell, she couldn't cook anyway. She'd stopped and picked up brownies at Whole Foods before rolling into East Texas.

Her stomach felt fluttery, but she was resolved.

She'd made her decision. For better or worse.

She had no clue if Rick would have her. Or want to pursue anything other than friendship with her. He'd once said right before they'd made love that he would always be her friend. Always care about her. Well, she was about to test the truth of his words.

She approached the center, which was now awash in flowering Hawthorne bushes. Only one person stood on the porch—an older Hispanic man, who held a cigarette between his lips and nodded when she smiled at him. Heck. Even her smile felt nervous.

"They're in there. Already started," he said.

Kate nodded and opened the door.

The first sound she heard was her heart thumping against her ribs. Then she heard a woman singing a

Barbra Streisand song that she could never remember the name of but had to do with love being like an easy chair. And she realized it was Vera singing.

The vaulted main room of the center was filled with folding chairs placed in five even rows, on either side of a center aisle. Every chair was filled, and a few people stood at the back. Justus's wheelchair was parked at the end of the last row, and though she could only see the side of his face, she could tell he was enchanted with the way his wife sang the ballad. Everyone's attention was on Vera, who was the only person to see Kate slip inside.

Her stepmother's eyes widened only slightly, but she kept right on singing.

Kate eased into a spot at the back between a teenage boy with a tattoo of a skeleton on his forearm and a woman with curly black hair who smelled faintly of clean linen. The woman smiled at Kate. The teen looked at her then returned his attention to the moose head hanging above the mantel.

The center's graduates sat in the front row. They all wore white dress shirts and ties and, to Kate, seemed to hold themselves proudly. She scanned the crowd for Rick but didn't see him. She saw Nellie, Jack, Tamara, Betty Monk and even Sally Holtzclaw, but she didn't see the man she'd missed so much it had physically hurt. She'd been a mess, popping antacids for weeks, although the negotiations over Fantabulous, clearing out her life in Vegas and summoning up the courage to take this enormous leap of faith contributed to the acid churning.

She was midair and it was time to stick the landing. She just needed to find her spotter. And he wasn't anywhere to be seen.

Vera wrapped up the song with a soft, emotional note. The crowd clapped politely as she stepped from the platform that had been erected where the huge dining-room table usually sat. Outside the bay windows, Kate could see Banjo lying on the patio next to a barrel of tomatoes they'd planted nearly three months ago. Bright red plums perched among the spring green branches of the plants. All around the East Texas countryside, winter had melted into a cacophony of greens, each shade doing its best to one-up the other.

Vera patted her husband as she passed him, but she didn't stop. She came straight to Kate, slipping in between her and the teenager, earning a disdainful frown from the youth.

She took Kate's hand and squeezed it.

Justus swiveled his head to find his wife, but found Kate instead. The emotion that swept over his face wrung Kate's heart. She had vowed she wouldn't get overly emotional with her father. They both needed slow and steady. But they did have the start to a new relationship.

A microphone crackled then whined. The interference stopped when Rick stepped onto the stage and moved behind the podium.

Kate's heart paused. She grasped Vera's hand even harder, earning a smile from the older woman.

He looked amazing, if a few pounds lighter. His hair was still military short, his shoulders still broad beneath the navy sports jacket he wore over a light blue button-down and striped tie. He looked just about as good as any man Kate had ever seen.

"Thank you, Vera." His gaze sought the woman beside her, and just like Justus, he found Kate instead.

If lightning could have struck, it would have.

That's how powerful the moment felt. Like sheer electricity had zapped the air between them. Rick stopped and stared.

Many in the room swung around to follow his gaze.

"Kate," Rick said into the mic, still obviously stunned she was here.

Manny waved at her and she waved back, and the moment was shattered. Rick cleared his throat and recovered.

"Now I will read the names of those who are graduating from Phoenix today." His voice swelled with pride as he read each graduate's name and accomplishments. Every so often he'd look toward her and each time she could see his questions.

After the participants in the program received their certificates of completion, Justus rolled forward. Rick handed the microphone to her father and helped him steady it before he spoke.

"Today is a day of new beginnings, but it is also a day for remembering the past. What will be and what is no more. My son, Ryan Talton Mitchell, was the inspiration for this center. His belief that all people hold a piece of goodness, a desire to do right and a need for a second chance is the seed which grew into the fruit that is this center. He is no longer with us…"

Her father's words fell off for a moment.

"But his influence lives on in his words and his works. He believed in the power of love. And so do I. Today, I would like to present to Enrique Mendez, a man who is like a son to me, the deed to the land on which Phoenix stands. It is a gift from the Ryan Mitchell Love Foundation."

Applause sounded as her father handed a paper to

Rick. Rick bent to shake Justus's hand and someone snapped a picture.

Her father rolled away as Rick returned to the podium.

"Now, before we indulge in the cake and punch so graciously provided by the Oak Stand Ladies Auxiliary, I would like to invite anyone present who would like to say a few words to do so."

No one moved a muscle. Not even the graduates. The air was static once again.

Kate dropped Vera's hand. "I'd like to say something."

RICK WATCHED AS KATE MADE her way to the stage. She looked different. Her hair was longer, cut in a flattering fringe around her face. No flame-red or violet-blue streaked it. Just lovely raven locks framing a pert nose, lush lips and determined chin. And those eyes, man, they sparked, tugging new life into his blood, suturing the heart that had been gashed when she'd walked out of his life two months ago.

Her skirt swished around her trim ankles as she stepped onto the platform.

As he handed her the microphone, her hand brushed his. He felt a jolt to the center of his gut. Yep, he was a goner for Kate Newman. Stick-a-fork-in-him-done kind of goner.

She gave him a mysterious smile, then turned to face the audience.

"Hello, everyone. My name is Katie Newman. I'm Justus's daughter and Ryan's sister. I wanted to tell these guys how proud I am of them." She swept a hand over the area where Georges, Manny, Joe, Brandon and Carlos sat. "I know what they feel this day. I know this journey has been hard but worth it, mostly because I've taken a similar journey over the past couple of months, so if you all will indulge me for a moment."

"Go ahead, Kate," Georges called out with a grin.

"Okay." She sighed. "Facing your mistakes is hard. I was born here in Oak Stand and spent most of my life trying to get out. I was ashamed of who I was. And like these guys here, I resented many of the people who tried to help me, and I hated those who didn't. Over the years, I built up anger and fear inside me. I only took comfort in the material things of this world, and I tried to control my life by never being weak. Never opening myself up to anyone."

Rick watched her as she said those words. Her eyes shimmered under the recessed lighting. Her hands trembled only slightly.

"Over the years, I've hurt people who loved me." Kate looked at Nellie. Her friend was waving her hands in front of her eyes, as though trying to hold herself together. Jack wound an arm around his wife that she shrugged away, handing him a wiggling toddler.

"And, on this day of new beginnings, I want to say I'm sorry for not seeing the big picture earlier." She looked at the graduates. "Sometimes it's hard to ask for help. I'm glad you guys took that first step. And I'm glad I did, too."

She shifted her gaze to the crowd. "This town held me up, just like they are holding Phoenix up. I never saw that. Never noticed who I had become. I closed myself to love."

She stopped, pressed her lips together and glanced at Rick before continuing.

"Several months ago, I met myself. I came to terms with who I am. I discovered a brother I never knew, a stepmother I didn't like and a father I didn't think I could forgive. I was wrong. Just like I was wrong about this town. And for the very first time in my life, I fell in love."

Her words stunned Rick. Something rose and expanded in his chest. His wounded heart came to life and thumped against his ribs. He was certain everyone in the room could hear it, could see his emotions coming undone.

Tears fell from Kate's eyes, but she didn't stop to wipe them from her cheeks. They dripped off her chin onto the floor.

"My heart, which had been full of bad things, is now full of something I never thought I could feel."

A sob tore through her, but she pressed a hand to her chest and fought through it. "I went back to Vegas, but it wasn't the same. I wasn't the same because love had changed me. I don't know what my future holds, but I want it to play out here."

She finally wiped her face and smiled. "I can't believe I'm about to say these words, but, I've finally come home."

Nellie stood and whooped. Big Bubba Malone did the same. Betty Monk merely lifted her hands in a praise-Jesus gesture.

Jack shouted, "It's about time!"

Her father and Vera held hands and beamed as though life had finally found them again.

Kate looked at the graduates. "I didn't mean to steal your thunder because this day is about you and your journey. But I took that journey with you guys, whether you realized it or not. I'm proud of what we've become together—people who have risen from the ashes. We are new again."

The center erupted into applause, many of the audience standing.

Rick watched Kate as she turned to him.

"Rick?"

"What, baby?"

"I love you," she said right into the microphone.

Those words were the sweetest he'd ever heard. And Kate taking that chance on him was the most profound moment he'd ever experienced. There was nothing to do but welcome his Kate home with a kiss.

"I love you, too, baby," he whispered before he covered her lips with his. He picked her up and spun her around and around until the edges of the world blurred and there was only this incredibly brave woman in his arms and a future laid out in front of them like the sweetest gift.

Applause continued, stomping occurred and hands slapped him on the back. Banjo barked.

But nothing registered.

There was only Kate.

"Thank you," he whispered against her lips.

She smiled against his lips. "For what? Donating the fifty thousand dollars to Phoenix?"

He squeezed her tighter. "No. For coming home."

EPILOGUE

One year later

THE MUSIC SOUNDED AS KATE stood facing the French
doors leading out to the balcony. She pressed her
dress against her thighs and breathed a simple prayer,
"Please."

She wasn't exactly clear what she was praying for. It
might have been for the dress to stay put. The wind was
blowing pretty hard and the bodice was strategically
draped. Or it might have been for the grace she needed
to descend the stairs. She'd counted them. Twenty-six.

Nellie appeared at her elbow and handed her a clutch
of roses. "Don't fall. I'll be in front of you."

Kate rolled her eyes. "Oh, thanks for the concern for
the bride."

Her friend grinned. "Well, you're not always graceful.
Plus, I'm eating for two now."

Kate assessed her friend's expanding bump. Nellie
was five months along and the dress had had to be al-
tered. Could her friend stand the shock? "Yeah? Well,
so am I, sister."

"Holy shit!" Nellie screeched before clapping her
hand over her mouth and glancing out to the balcony.
"You're serious?"

Kate nodded and smiled. "But *I* still fit in my
dress."

"Oh, my goodness," Nellie breathed, jerking Kate into a hug. She sputtered against the flowers pinned in Kate's hair, and gave a suspicious sniffle. "Have you told Rick?"

"No. You're the first to know. And it really should have been him, but the devil inside me pops out sometimes." She pushed Nellie from her and wagged her finger at her. "Not a word."

Her best friend made the lock-and-key motion and picked up her bouquet. "Of course I won't tell."

Kate smiled at her friend before punching her on the arm. "So don't trip. I'll be right behind you and I'm eating for two."

"Whatever."

The music swelled louder and Billie squealed. "That's it. The cue!"

Trish appeared behind her, looking particularly regal in her seafoam-green bridesmaid's dress. Her coffee-colored skin looked lustrous, and Billie, newly married herself, looked fresh and innocent in her pleated dress of peach. But Kate knew firsthand her artisan friend was anything but innocent—Billie had thrown the bachelorette party, complete with a male stripper and penis-shaped cookies.

"Okay, let's rock this wedding," Kate said, giving Nellie a wink. The daffodil dress looked good against Nellie's tan skin and caramel-streaked hair. Her friend always looked radiant when she had a bun in the oven.

Trish opened the doors and the sound of the stringed orchestra floated inside. The sun broke through the clouds as she descended first, elegantly gliding down the curved stairs of Cottonwood like an African princess greeting her subjects. Billie followed, looking petrified and stiff. Nellie started out the doors behind Billie, but paused and caught Kate's arm.

"I love you, Katie."

"Love you, too," Kate said, trying not to mess up her makeup with the dampness misting her eyes. Then she pushed Nellie toward the doors. "Hurry up."

Jeremy emerged from around the corner. He'd been waiting outside, looking splendid in an Armani tuxedo. He'd tucked an outlandish peach handkerchief in his pocket. It perfectly matched the roses she held. "Let's go, doll."

And he offered his arm.

Kate took it and they emerged to a gorgeous spring day. The notes of the cello were plaintive on the breeze, but the violins livened up the traditional wedding march. Kate kept her eyes on Rick as she descended stairs that swept round the front of Cottonwood. From her vantage point, if she looked across the pristine lawn past the crowd of people sitting in white chairs, she could just glimpse the gates of the estate. The same gates she'd once sat outside of on a pink bike, picturing herself doing exactly what she did today.

Only her dress wasn't fluffy and she didn't wear a veil. Her gown was a gorgeous, tight Vera Wang. And her father wasn't escorting her.

But he would.

Justus waited at the foot of the steps. Jeremy handed her to him, and she tucked his hand into the crook of her right arm.

Vera had tied a white satin bow to the back of his motorized wheelchair. Together they faced the audience assembled. Kate watched as Vera, the stepmother of the bride, stood; a tender expression lit her face. The rest of the guests rose, and together, she and her father started up the white runner that led to Rick and her future. Her father's hand trembled on her arm and she tore her gaze from Rick to glance at him. He smiled, squeezing her arm and looking as proud as any father.

Finally, they reached Rick. He looked nervous, so she smiled. She didn't feel nervous at all. Certainty had made a home inside Kate Newman.

The pastor who'd dunked Kate beneath the eternal waters when she was eight began the service, talking about forgiveness, commitment and love. Three things Kate already knew about.

"Who gives this woman in marriage?"

"Her father," Justus said quite solemnly.

Then he put her hand into Rick's.

And gave Katie Newman the family she'd always wanted.

* * * * *

HARLEQUIN® *Super Romance®*

COMING NEXT MONTH

Available February 8, 2011

REQUEST YOUR FREE BOOKS!

2 FREE NOVELS PLUS 2 FREE GIFTS!

HARLEQUIN®

Super Romance®

Exciting, emotional, unexpected!

HSR10R

HARLEQUIN®

A Romance

FOR EVERY MOOD™

Spotlight on
Classic

Quintessential, modern love stories
that are romance at its finest.

See the next page
to enjoy a sneak peek from
the Harlequin® Romance series.

*Harlequin Romance author Donna Alward is loved
for her gorgeous rancher heroes.*

*Meet Wyatt as he's confronted by both a precious
little pink bundle left on his doorstep and his neighbor Elli
who's going to show him the ropes....*

Introducing
PROUD RANCHER, PRECIOUS BUNDLE

THE SQUAWKING QUIETED as Elli picked the baby up, and
Wyatt turned around, trying hard to ignore the feelings of
inadequacy as Darcy immediately stopped fussing.

"Maybe she's uncomfortable. What do you think, sweetheart?" Elli turned her conversation to the baby.

"What do you think is wrong?" Wyatt asked, putting the
coffee pot back on the burner.

A strange look passed over Elli's face, one that looked
like guilt and panic. But it was gone quickly. "I couldn't
say," she replied.

"But you were so good with her this afternoon." Wyatt
put his hands on his hips.

"Lucky, that's all. I just…remembered a few things."
The same strange look flitted over her features once more.

Wyatt took the coffee to the table. "You fooled me. You
looked like you knew exactly what you were doing." So
much so that Wyatt had felt completely inept. A feeling he
despised. He was used to being the one in control.

Elli and Darcy walked the length of the kitchen and
back. After a few moments, she admitted, "I haven't really
cared for a baby before. The things I thought of were simply
things I'd heard about. Not from experience, Mr. Black."

Her chin jutted up, closing the subject but making him

want to ask the questions now pulsing through his mind. But then he remembered the old saying—*Don't look a gift horse in the mouth.* He'd benefit from whatever insight she had and be glad of it.

"I don't really know what babies need," he said. "I fed her, patted her back like you did, walked her to sleep, but every time I put her down…"

Wyatt almost groaned. Of course. He'd forgotten one important thing. He'd been so focused on getting the formula the right temperature that he'd forgotten to check her diaper. Not that he had any clue what to do there either.

Pulling calves and shoveling out stalls was far less intimidating than one tiny newborn.

"She's probably due for a diaper change, isn't she." He tried to sound nonchalant. This was a perfect opportunity. Elli must know how to change a diaper. He could simply watch her so he'd know better for the next time.

Instead, Elli came around the corner of the counter and placed Darcy back in his arms. "Here you go, Uncle Wyatt," she said lightly. "You get diaper duty. I'll fix the coffee. Cream and sugar?"

Oh boy, Wyatt thought, looking down into Darcy's pursed face, his smug plan blown to smithereens. He was in for it now.

Will sparks fly between Elli and Wyatt?

Find out in
PROUD RANCHER, PRECIOUS BUNDLE
Available February 2011 from Harlequin Romance

Try these Healthy and Delicious Spring Rolls!

INGREDIENTS

2 packages rice-paper spring roll wrappers (20 wrappers)

1 cup grated carrot

¼ cup bean sprouts

1 cucumber, julienned

1 red bell pepper, without stem and seeds, julienned

4 green onions finely chopped— use only the green part

DIRECTIONS

1. Soak one rice-paper wrapper in a large bowl of hot water until softened.

2. Place a pinch each of carrots, sprouts, cucumber, bell pepper and green onion on the wrapper toward the bottom third of the rice paper.

3. Fold ends in and roll tightly to enclose filling.

4. Repeat with remaining wrappers. Chill before serving.

Find this and many more delectable recipes including the perfect dipping sauce in

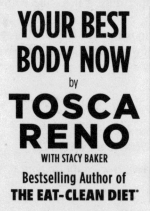

YOUR BEST BODY NOW
by
TOSCA RENO
WITH STACY BAKER

Bestselling Author of
THE EAT-CLEAN DIET

Available wherever books are sold!